BETH PAGE

The Midnight Coffee House

First edition

Editing by Susan Barnes
Cover art by Cormar Covers

This book was professionally typeset on Reedsy.
Find out more at reedsy.com

To Nana

*Hey, I did it. I promised you I
would publish a book one day and
here I am. Sorry for the smut.*

Foreword

This book is meant for 18+ with explicit sexual scenes, frequent swearing, and violence. These are sexy vampires on motorcycles, after all.

Content Warnings: non-consensual drug use, animal abuse, child SA, domestic violence/intimate partner violence, mentions of suicide.

Please take care of your mental health. You're important and valuable. I'm happy that you're here.

Suicide Hotline: 988 (call or text)
Crisis Text Hotline: text 'HOME' to 741741

One

Gage

A plume of dust sprung up as Gage plopped down on the beat-up couch that had found a home in the cave where he and his three boys always brought back their kills. They were not necessarily old vampires, but they were strong enough that they only had to do this morbid habit on a weekly basis.

Tonight they were dining on an older woman who had recently been released from prison after serving twenty-two years for burning her children to death in a house fire she'd set for insurance money.

It wasn't often he researched their kills, but he had seen her face on the news and wanted to know her backstory. When they'd come for her outside of a late-night convenience store, she hadn't put up a fight, which was not surprising since she had been high. She probably didn't even know what hit her.

He watched as Horatio bounced the decapitated head off the cave wall, admiring how he managed to keep the gore out of his hair. Horatio's twin, Matteo, was not as skilled and was sitting on the dirt covered floor untangling a tooth out of his short curls. Even though he had known the twins for years, he would never be able to tell them apart if Horatio didn't keep his hair longer and straighter than Matteo's.

Nikolas resembled them slightly too, so much so that no one would question if they said all three of them were brothers. The only one who stood out was himself, with his blonde hair and green eyes.

"I'm bored," Horatio groaned as the head began to grow mushy and much less entertaining. The body they had torn apart lay scattered around as they picked the woman's flesh from their teeth.

"Let's go check out that new coffee shop that opened up, the Coffee House Bunny." Matteo said. Horatio perked up at his brother's suggestion.

Nikolas's deep voice killed the eagerness in Horatio's eyes. "It's two in the morning, a coffee shop wouldn't be open."

Nikolas flipped his long braid over his shoulder and started to pick up the body parts as the brothers joined Gage on the couch. Gage knew this was Nikolas's favorite part. They had completely drained her blood, so cleanup should be quick even if they did not help. All he had to do was throw her parts into the ocean for the sea creatures to feast on. The tall Chippewa man found something enthralling about waiting for the dolphins to swim in, then feeding them the remains by hand. Gage assumed he found something similar in them that he also found in himself. They were both such gentle, curious creatures.

"Guess what dipshit? *This* coffee shop is open only at night." Matteo smirked and threw a detached finger at Nikolas.

Nikolas grabbed the flying appendage in midair, noticed it was a middle finger, and flipped Matteo off with it. "Why? Is it run by vampires?"

He shrugged. "I don't know. I don't think so, though. I didn't hear about any new vampires moving into our territory. Did your dad say anything to you, Gage?" He turned toward his leader.

"It's just a human running it, some chick that moved here from another state. I didn't care enough to ask any questions."

"Cool, let's check it out then." Nikolas rolled his shoulders like he was getting ready to throw a baseball and threw the body parts into a pile in the back of the cave. The dolphins could wait a while for their midnight snack.

The four boys slipped out of their cave and into the dark of the night to climb on their motorcycles. Due to the cave's isolated location and lack of streetlights, the sound of the bikes revving to life consumed the darkness. The four headlights illuminated the desolate and empty stretch of beach before turning to the unpaved road.

They made their way back into the city of Vista Maria that was full of lights, life, and traffic. The beachfront city near Daytona, Florida held a population of almost 100,000, most of whom apparently worked night shifts.

Matteo had been correct that the coffee shop was open at night, and made sure to gloat about it as the boys parked their bikes in the almost-full parking lot. The building was a former retro diner with a white and chrome exterior that was beginning to look worn from the salty air. Many of the customers were nurses or factory workers taking a break during their graveyard shifts, but scattered among them were a few drunks hoping to sober up.

"I guess this wasn't such a stupid concept after all," Gage muttered to himself.

He walked up to the counter and observed as Matteo and Horatio ordered their frilly coffee drinks with the confidence of people who knew what the hell a double shot venti macchiato was. Nikolas was a little more normal, ordering just a cup of black coffee, but asked about some house blend.

The girl behind the counter looked over to Gage with friendly hazel, bordering on green, eyes. She smiled in a way that made her whole face light up as he stared back at her.

"This is your first time in a coffee shop, isn't it?"

Gage was irritated by her taunting tone, but kept his cool to please his friends. "I prefer beer."

"Well I don't have my liquor license yet, so you'll have to try some coffee. Can I make you something special?"

He shrugged in response.

"Do you like sweet or bitter flavors? Any allergies? And do you prefer chocolate or caramel?"

"It doesn't matter. I won't drink it anyway."

Her smile finally faltered and the light disappeared from her eyes. "Okay, did you not want anything at all, then?"

"Just give him a black coffee. The darkest roast you have, to match his soul," Nikolas interrupted. He threw a twenty dollar bill on the counter and side-eyed Gage. The girl nodded and twirled around to begin making their drinks.

Gage watched as she conducted almost a dance, pressing buttons, pumping syrup, and stirring steamy liquids. He could tell she had been doing this for a while due to how easily and quickly she made the four drinks. He almost asked her how long she had been a barista, but decided against it. He wasn't interested in starting a conversation with random people he didn't care to know.

The barista made sure to tell them to have a good night, but purposefully did not look at Gage. The boys took up residence in a booth adjacent to the counter once their drinks were done. The nurses sitting at the booth behind them instantly got up and left the shop, knowing all too well who the boys were.

As much as they tried to blend in with society and not cause chaos, like how Hollywood portrayed vampires, some did not like the infamous foursome. The four made up the Vista Maria family, who owned more than half the city. Because of this, most people respected them yet kept their distance. There was a smaller portion, though, that completely loathed their existence as vampires.

Gage's phone vibrated in his leather jacket's pocket and he pulled it out to reveal a topless photo of a blonde woman. She was posed with her back curved, her perky breasts pointed upward, and her head tilted to expose her neck.

"I take it that's your plan for the rest of the night?" Matteo asked as he peered over Gage's shoulder to leer at the photo.

"I don't know if I'm going to go over to her place tonight. She's a good fuck, but clingy. She always wants to tell me about her latest shopping haul and what influencer she's been following. She hasn't learned yet that I don't care."

"Why don't you just use her for blood and nothing else then? She looks like she would taste good," Horatio stated as he joined his brother in peering over his shoulder.

"I haven't tried her yet but she has a weird smell, kind of like how those cheap plastic containers smell? I bet her blood tastes like that."

"Does she get a lot of Botox?" Nikolas remained where he was, not caring about the naked picture.

"Looks like she does. Those tits are definitely fake," Matteo answered.

Nikolas nodded. "I've noticed a difference between girls who are natural versus ones who get plastic surgery. There's some ingredient in Botox that spoils the blood."

Gage's phone went off again with a text from the girl, detailing everything she wanted to do with his dick. The twins' eyebrows shot up at what they read.

"Surprisingly, they're real. I got to go." Gage stated as he got up and left behind his untouched coffee. The girl behind the counter looked up and watched him leave without saying a word.

ɔɔɔɔ

Gage parked his motorcycle next to the trailer where the blonde lived. The trailer park itself was nice with well-kept yards, a crystal clear inground pool, and sidewalks that had been recently edged. Her trailer stood out, with dark brown siding that was turning a sickly shade of pink from the sun and a front window that was cracked from a drunken man falling into it during the last party she had thrown.

He had to think for a minute to remember that her name was Destiny. He stretched as he got off his bike and walked into the trailer without knocking. Destiny was sitting on her couch watching a reality TV show, and to Gage's disappointment, was completely clothed.

"I figured that would get you over here." She huffed but did not take her eyes off the TV.

Gage moved the random t-shirt balled up in the corner of the couch and flopped down next to her. He scooted some of the empty liquor bottles on the coffee table with his foot so he had somewhere to prop his feet before wrapping his arm around her shoulder.

"You call, I come." He smiled and nuzzled into her neck, gently nipping at her skin. She shoved him off with so much force it startled him, and he stared at her in confusion.

"Why is it you only come over when I promise sex? I made a cute dinner for you yesterday and you never showed up."

Gage wrinkled his brow as he tried to recall what he had done yesterday. He remembered her texting him, but he had never actually read the message. He'd skimmed it and sent a generic response. At the current moment, he couldn't even remember what he had texted back.

He had been busy helping remodel the manager's office at the marina his father owned. It was a huge, exhausting project, but he enjoyed building and creating things with his hands. He had found his flow with blasting some old-school rock and repairing all the cracks and dents in the drywall, so he had been in a slightly pre-occupied daze when he'd opened her text.

"Yeah, I was busy yesterday. Sorry. Do you want me to make it up to you?" He slinked back over to her and attempted to wrap his arm around her again. This time she stood up and leaned over him, sticking her finger in his face and breathing heavily.

"No! You can't just ignore this problem and try to get me to forget about it. I'm not interested in having sex with you right now. I want to talk about you making me feel ignored and insignificant. You always do this to me! Whenever I try to talk, you zone out or go on your phone. You never invite me to hang out with your friends or go anywhere with you. We've been dating for almost two months and I haven't even been to your place yet!"

Gage couldn't tell which was stronger: his anger at being yelled at by a woman he barely knew, or his annoyance at having to deal with this right now.

"First of all, get your finger out of my face. Second of all, when the hell did we start dating?"

Destiny dropped her hand the same time she dropped her mouth open. "What do you mean when did we start dating? The first time we had sex I considered us a couple! I don't go around sleeping with just anyone."

His anger flared and took over as the image of his ex-girlfriend unwillingly popped up. "Well, you considered wrong. I don't do girlfriends because I'm not the dating type. I thought I made that crystal clear by never referring to you as my girlfriend or taking you out on dates. Hell, I don't even consider us friends with benefits. Maybe there's a reason why I don't bring you over or invite you to hang out with my friends—you're just something to stick my dick into and nothing more."

There was a loud slapping noise and a sharp pain spread across his face. It took him a second to process the fact that she had just slapped him.

"What in the fuck was that?" He shouted.

"Fuck you! Get out of my house!"

"House? You live in a fucking trailer!"

"So what, you stupid bloodsucker?"

She seemed to instantly regret her insult as he stood up and towered over her. She ran toward her bathroom and he tried to follow her, but she was quicker and smarter than he anticipated. She flung over a bookcase behind her, causing him to trip and fall face-first onto the floor, which only caused his rage to grow more intense. He swore when she slammed the bathroom door and locked it behind her.

Gage sat up and contemplated how he wanted the night to go. He could let his anger take over and end things quickly, breaking down the door and ripping her throat out within seconds. He knew he would come to regret that, though, so he decided to have some fun instead.

He took a deep breath loud enough that Destiny would hear. "Okay, okay. Hold on. What the hell are we doing right now?" He stood up and walked over to the closed door, placing his forehead against the cool wood.

"Destiny, honey, can you please come out and we'll talk about this like rational adults? I didn't mean to scare you or for my anger to take over like that. I clearly have issues in that department and I need you to be patient. This is something I need to work on and I think you can help me. I've put my trust in the wrong woman before in the past, so relationships are a little scary for me. But I'm willing to try for you. Please baby? I'm sorry."

There was silence as she contemplated what he said. He held his breath, wondering if he sounded genuine enough with his switch of emotions. He wasn't one to plead for forgiveness, so this was all new territory for him.

"You promise you won't hurt me?" She replied weakly from the other side.

"Of course, how could I hurt someone as precious as you? I didn't mean what I said. You're more than just something to have sex with. You're a girl I want to get to know, a girl I want to love, a girl I would be proud to bring over and introduce to my friends. I was just so mad and I wanted to verbally hurt you, but I realized I was wrong. Please forgive me?"

He smiled when he heard the door unlock. She cracked it open slowly and peered at him through the gap. He noticed her eyes were dry and wide, like she was exhilarated by their interaction. She stuck her bottom lip out in a pout.

"Oh baby," he cooed. He reached out to tuck a strand of hair that had come loose behind her ear.

"Do you really mean that? That you want to love me?"

"Yes, I mean that with all my heart," he purred. "Will you let me in?"

She opened the door wider and he stepped in and embraced her, giving her small kisses all over her face. She started to giggle and kissed him back, wrapping her fingers into his shaggy blonde hair as she did so.

Her tongue explored his mouth as he unbuttoned her pants and slid them down her slender legs. She let out a little gasp as her thighs touched the cold porcelain when he lifted her up and placed her on the bathroom counter. He brushed his hands up her sides and lifted her shirt off, exposing the perky breasts that were photographed earlier. She leaned her head back against the mirror as he pinched her hard nipples and kissed the tender flesh on her neck.

She wrapped her legs around his waist and brought his face back to hers to continue kissing him with an intense passion. Her breath quickened, this time out of pleasure, as he slid his hands back down her sides and slipped one hand in between her legs, massaging her through her underwear. She closed her eyes, clearly enjoying the sensations he was stirring up inside of her. With his other hand, he gripped her hip tightly as she began to grind against his palm.

"I want you so bad," she broke the kiss to whisper into his ear. "Show me how much you want my forgiveness."

He smirked and looked her in the eyes. A quick sign of recognition flashed in them as she realized he had played her as prey. He quickly grabbed her head with both hands and sunk his teeth into the flesh of her neck.

"Gage! Stop!"

He released her and laughed through the blood seeping between his lips. "I don't want your forgiveness. Don't you know to never trust a vampire?"

Her small scream turned into a loud, guttural moan as he sank his teeth deeper into her neck. Blood dripped down her neck as she attempted to push him off, but it was useless. She gave in to the rush of sensation that came with his bite, and clung to him as she convulsed from the orgasm it gave her.

He drank more than he meant to, but his self-control returned in time before she passed out. He tore himself off her, took too many steps backward, and fell into the wall, causing the pictures hanging there to shake violently.

She looked at him with her hand over the rapidly closing holes in her neck and a stare mixed with confusion and fatigue. "W-what was that?"

"I shouldn't have done that. Fuck, I almost killed you." He cleared his throat and wiped the blood from the corner of his mouth with a shaking hand. "This is what I mean when I say I'm not the dating type. You don't want this, Destiny. Lose my number."

He left her stunned and silent on the counter as he made his way to his bike. Every night since Venice had left him, he'd felt himself turning more and more into a monster, and tonight he'd almost become what he despised the most. Killing innocents not only went against the rules his father set, but went against his own moral code.

If he lost that, he lost everything.

Two

Willow

"*H**ey mo stóirín, it's time to wake up! Wakey wakey, eggs and bakey!*"

An overly-cheerful voice stirred Willow from her deep sleep. As soon as she opened her eyes, the voice disappeared from her mind like a puff of smoke. Her chest felt heavy when she realized she had been dreaming about her mother's once-annoying wakeup call, which was now desperately missed.

She rolled out of bed and undid the bun that was falling apart into long brown tendrils around her face. She had been so tired last night after working an unexpected 13-hour shift at her coffee house that she had come home and flopped onto her bed without taking her hair down or changing her clothes. She still had her apron tied around her waist, though it was twisted and had crept up her back to almost resemble a cape.

She stripped off her clothes, redid her bun, started her shower, and watched as the water rained down from the showerhead, feeling like she was standing in a haze. The one downfall to owning her own business was that it consumed her life. She had her own apartment, but sometimes it felt like she lived in the coffee house. It didn't help that she had not hired anyone to work for her yet, but it was at the top of her list of things to do within the next few weeks. Or months. Or far in the future whenever she had time.

Once the water reached near-boiling, she got inside and let it run down her body, calming her nerves and untangling her sore muscles. She couldn't decide if she felt off because of her dream about her deceased mother, or the fact that she was overworking herself.

As of now, she worked from nine p.m. to seven a.m. every day except Sunday, her one day off. She made a mental note to change the hours her coffee house was open. Her current time was not working for her because she always had a line to the door right at closing time.

Last night had been especially brutal since the line did not end until ten a.m. People either did not see her "Hours of Operation" sign hung right in the middle of the front door at eye level, or they just didn't care. She didn't have the heart to turn away customers, either.

Tonight she would put her foot down and lock the doors at seven a.m., line or no line.

She told herself she wasn't complaining and loved the extra cash that came with the longer hours, but she could feel herself getting burned out. She couldn't even take a relaxing shower without thinking about work. Her apartment was a mess, she hadn't had the energy to wash her hair this week, and she was not eating due to all the stress. She had dropped down to one meal a day, and it was usually fast food.

She sighed and mumbled a not-so-encouraging pep talk to herself. "Just a few more days and I get a break."

She toweled herself off and looked in the foggy mirror. Her eyes were sunken and her hair a greasy bird's nest, but her body looked better than it ever had. She might be on the edge of a mental breakdown, but she'd lost the extra fat around her waist and her arms were toning up from putting away the truck orders by herself. It surprised her how heavy one box of paper cups could be, especially when she had to chuck it on a top shelf.

Once she was done in the bathroom, she grabbed some orange juice and groaned. It was already 8:15 p.m., which gave her just a few more minutes of free time before she had to leave to open her café.

The idea of a midnight coffee house had been in the back of her mind for a while. She had always wanted to be a female business owner and had been saving money for that dream since she was in high school. She came up with the business plan when her ex-boyfriend had worked the midnight shift at a factory and complained about never having anywhere to go during his lunch break. She tried to share it with him once, but was instantly shut down by his criticisms.

When she moved to Florida, she decided since she was starting a new life, she would also start her dream. And so she opened her midnight coffee house and named it The Coffee House Bunny in dedication to her pet rabbit, Snickers. She'd even shelled out the extra money to get a custom logo of him made for the sign.

Willow walked around her kitchen twice before finally deciding to spend her fifteen minutes of freedom washing the dishes that were piling up in her sink. She let out a startled scream when a small army of fruit flies sprung up from a mug. She glared at the buzzing cloud as they dispersed through her kitchen, thinking about how she'd left her past behind to live a life of being overworked to the point her home had become a breeding ground for insects.

Even with burnout on the horizon, she was glad she had made the move and felt like she was restarting her life. There were 1,188 miles between Detroit, Michigan and Vista Maria, Florida. 1,188 miles between her past and her new life.

She tried to push away the unpleasant thoughts of her ex-boyfriend and focused on the dishes before her. When that didn't work, she thoroughly washed the serrated knife, imagining it was covered in his blood and she was on an episode of *20/20*.

She smiled at her violent little thought.

Before she knew it, she was back at The Coffee House Bunny turning on the lights and starting the first brew of the night. She fell into her usual rhythm and her night began like any other. Standing on her tiptoes, she restocked the espresso beans in her espresso machine. Dumping the long, silver bag into the containers that were perched on top released the relaxing scent of coffee, which would forever bring her a sense of peace. Before flipping on her open sign, she did one last sweep of the café so that it was presentable to her customers. With the flip of a few switches, she was ready to start her night.

"Hey Willow!" A boy with short brown hair, thick framed glasses, and a lanky build walked in and sat at the counter connected to the register. His friend who looked similar, but with darker hair, trailed quietly behind him. They were both wearing their usual blue WebRX polos and black slacks.

"Hey guys, busy night tonight at work?" She smiled at them and prepared their usual drinks. John liked his plain cappuccino and Ryan enjoyed his flat white.

"Actually, it's been pretty slow. Once we finished that website rebuild from last week, we just had a normal workload. We've mostly been dealing with customers from Australia calling in with minor problems. I feel more like an IT consultant than a web developer." John took his drink and paid her, making sure to leave his typical two-dollar tip.

The tip was small, but he made sure to come every night, and it added up. Willow preferred his company over his money, anyway. Most of her business consisted of regular customers, some more friendly than others. John was the friendliest, with Ryan hardly ever saying a word or barely making eye contact. She'd once accidentally touched

Ryan's hand while handing him his drink, and he'd almost passed out. John pulled her aside and explained that Ryan had never been given positive affection by a woman before, and not to take it personally.

"Maybe I'm in the wrong field. I should have started a techy business instead of a coffee house. I would kill for a slow night." As soon as those words were out of her mouth, three more customers walked through her door.

It wasn't long before her business filled up with nurses and factory workers laughing and chatting while on their breaks. Once she was caught up with all the orders, she looked around. Her counter resided in the back center of the store, so she had full view of her shop.

When she'd first rented the building, it had been ready to go thanks to her landlord, Clay. He had been more than helpful with getting her set up, and had allowed her to make minor changes to make the retro diner more modern.

She kept the purple and white vinyl booths and tables, because she wanted to go with a lighter color scheme, the opposite of the typical dark browns of most coffee houses. Her customers were already tired from being up all night and hardly ever got to see the sun, so she'd wanted to provide them a bright place to relax.

She watched as a factory worker covered in grease stains tried to put the moves on a tired-looking nurse who smiled and seemed revived by the compliments. In the corner booth, she saw a drunk couple coddling their coffees, occasionally looking at each other and giggling about the mischief they had been up to that night. From the corner of her eye, she caught another couple in a booth holding hands under the table. Love was in the air, and it was starting to smother her.

She was tired of being alone, but alone was how she felt the safest. She had opened her life up once for a man she thought she could trust, only to find out he was worse than a monster.

She pushed back more intrusive thoughts of her ex-boyfriend as the four men from the other night walked in and came up to the counter. The two tallest ones of the group looked like twins, with their dark hair and olive tone skin. They were decked out in matching black leather jackets and grey ripped jeans. The only thing telling them apart was that one had shorter hair and freckles sprinkled across his nose—or possibly it was dirt, she couldn't really tell. The other one had straight hair past his shoulders and was wearing a single earring. It took her a second to notice that the silver cross hanging from his left earlobe was upside down.

"Hey gorgeous, we came back because your coffee is so good." The possibly freckled, possibly just dirty one smiled and leaned against the counter. "I'll take a double shot venti macchiato with just a hint of caramel."

"And I'll do the same, without the caramel," the other one said.

"I feel like these are going to become your usual drinks. And if you're going to become regular customers, I need your names."

His earring dangled as he leaned against the counter. "My name's Horatio, and this is my idiot brother Matteo. The cool cat over there is Nikolas, and Mr. Grumpy Pants is Gage."

She noticed that Gage was staring daggers into the back of Horatio's head, but ignored him and turned her smile to Nikolas. He looked like a man who didn't have a care in the world. Everything about him seemed relaxed, from the long hair loosely braided down his back, to the black button-down shirt that was left unbuttoned to reveal a white undershirt with a turquoise necklace resting above it. He was the shortest of the group, thicker around the waist, and had the kindest brown eyes she had ever seen. There was a sense of quiet confidence wafting off him.

"And what are you having?"

"The same as yesterday too. Your house blend was the best I've ever had," he said with a half-smile that made her heart skip a beat.

"Well thank you." She smiled back at him before turning her attention to the last man.

He looked like a surfer, minus a golden tan, and his windblown hair gave her the hint that he'd rode in on a motorcycle. He had broad shoulders and rough hands that looked like he built things for a living. She felt like a man as she tried not to stare at how his tight black shirt accentuated his muscular chest and arms. He was the only White one out of all of them, with shaggy blonde hair and green eyes that looked annoyed. She wasn't sure if it was that expression or his attractive looks that made her nervous.

"Still no liquor license, do you want anything? I can give you an empty cup so you don't feel left out from your friends."

"The black coffee was fine."

She slapped her hand on her chest in mock surprise. "Wow, I thought you didn't drink it. I swore I threw away a full cup of coffee after you left."

"I didn't, but it was nice having something to toy with while we were talking. Your thick mud of a coffee was fun to poke at."

Her nervousness was starting to drain away, replaced by annoyance when she realized he was a douche. She wasn't surprised, though—most attractive guys were.

"Well maybe my mud would taste better if you let me turn it into a latte and add some flavor."

"I don't feel like getting diabetes tonight, and actually I can't stay anyway, so skip the drink."

"You don't want one for the road?"

"I'm not a dork, I don't have a cup holder on my bike." He rolled his eyes before walking out the door.

As she turned to start their drinks, she noticed Matteo frown. "There's nothing wrong with a cup holder, how else would I hold my whiskey?"

"In a flask in your pocket like a real man," Horatio teased.

Willow smiled and wished she had a sibling to banter with, but she was an only child. She wasn't raised with a big family, and now that both her parents were deceased, she had none. Maybe in the future she could build her own family, but for now she was content with her café and her customers.

To her surprise, the boys took their drinks to go. She peered out the window and watched as they got on their motorcycles, which were perfectly parked in a row by the front door. She let out a breathy chuckle as she watched all three of them place their drinks in their cup holders before revving their engines and taking off.

"Ugh, they give me the heebie jeebies," John laughed awkwardly from the other end of the counter. "I know you have to be nice to them because they're customers, but be careful, okay? We've got to get back to work. Goodnight, Willow."

Willow scrunched her brow, but John and Ryan were already headed toward the door before she could ask what he meant.

She was still thinking about his odd warning when Clay walked in an hour later. He looked around with a smile that crinkled the corner of his eyes. She still couldn't pinpoint his age, he appeared to be late twenties or early thirties, but his personality and knowledge made him seem much, much older.

He was the first person she had met when she moved to Vista Maria, and he had taken it upon himself to give her the rundown of the city. He'd told her which restaurants were the best, what neighborhoods were the safest, and had even helped her find her apartment. He had been nervous when she told him she wanted to open a midnight coffee house, but she'd assured him that she wasn't new to the nightlife. She used to work nights at a gas station in Detroit. If she could handle the crackheads and drunks there, Vista Maria would be no different.

"I was driving past and thought I would stop in and see how you're doing." He stuck his hands in the front pockets of his dress pants when he arrived at the counter. She had only ever seen him dressed in a suit with suspenders and wire rimmed glasses that gave him an 80's Wall Street vibe.

"Thanks for checking, I've been busy, but busy is good. Can I get you anything to drink? It's on the house."

"I'll take an Americano."

"I can make that decaf if you like, I know it's getting late." She looked at the clock and noticed it was even later than she thought. How odd that he would still be up and dressed at this hour.

"I need all the caffeine I can get, I have a long night ahead of me. We're short staffed at the casino, so I'll be stuck there all night."

"Oh! I didn't know you worked at the casino. I haven't had a chance to go there yet, but I've been having the urge to play some slots."

He laughed and not-so-subtly slipped a twenty into her tip box. "I don't work there, I own it. It was one of my first big businesses I started with my brother way back when. But tonight I'll be working, since I can't seem to hire staff that want to stay."

"Well I hope your night goes fast for you, I can't imagine it would be that busy on a weekday night."

"This is Florida, and a prime vacation place right by the ocean. Trust me, this city never sleeps and loves to gamble."

"You got a point. Thanks again for checking in on me, I really do appreciate it."

"No problem. If you ever need anything, feel free to reach out to me. Take care, kiddo."

A warm feeling spread through her stomach and up her chest as she waved goodbye. When she'd first met him, she had been taken aback by his caring kindness. Now, she cherished it. He seemed to want nothing from her but to have her be successful in this city. She'd never known what it felt like to have a father, since hers had passed when she was a baby, but she assumed it felt something similar to talking with Clay.

Three

Gage

"So you did end up eating her?" Horatio asked Gage as they walked into the coffee house.

It wasn't Gage's first choice to hang out here tonight, but it was three against one when the others requested another visit. He didn't mind, though, because he was in a much better mood after his meal from earlier.

"Yeah, she pissed me off enough that I didn't even mind the plastic taste." He smiled a cocky smile as he leaned against the counter, and thought about the woman he and Nikolas had found trying to sell heroin to a teenager. Nikolas had been right—Botox did change the flavor of blood.

He had still been full from the unplanned meal he had made out of Destiny. Usually, they only killed when they needed to, but watching the haggard woman entice the pimply-faced teenager down a path of self-destruction made him relax on his rules. He knew if he was going to become a strong leader like his father used to be, he would have to practice better self-control and set firmer rules, but lately that had been difficult. So he'd pulled her aside and sank his teeth into her jugular.

He watched the hazel-eyed barista take their orders. He noticed her eyes looked browner than the previous night, with dark circles under them as she avoided his gaze and coyly tucked a loose curl behind her ear. Her voice was also less enthusiastic as she asked what they were having.

Matteo was the first to order. "Same thing as yesterday. A double—"

"A double shot venti caramel macchiato." She finished his sentence and grinned at the impressed look that crossed Matteo's face.

"I have a pretty decent memory." She pointed to Horatio and Nikolas. "You had the same but without the caramel, you had a large black house coffee, and you—" she paused and lowered her finger "—you prefer beer."

"And did you get that liquor license yet?" Gage asked.

She pursed her lips. "No. Now are you willing to try something new, or would you prefer a cup of black coffee to stare at all night?"

"Just give him the black coffee." Nikolas responded, looking like he clearly did not want to deal with Gage's rude attitude.

Between feeling energized from his latest snack—probably due to the methamphetamines she had been on—and feeling bad for the girl who looked so sleep deprived, he decided to do something rash. "Hold on, I'm in a good mood tonight, so fuck it. Surprise me with something different."

The girl's eyes grew big, like she had discovered an answer to the mystery of the universe. "Do I have complete freedom, or do you have any requirements?"

"I literally do not care what you make. You can go crazy."

The girl clapped her hands in excitement and twirled around to begin creating her concoction, completely forgetting to take the money Nikolas had been holding out. Gage frowned at her excessive reaction and sat down in a booth, leaving his friend to pay. Like clockwork, the group of nurses that were sitting in the next booth got up and left. Nikolas joined him, but Horatio and Matteo stayed up at the counter to talk to the girl as she prepared their orders.

"Did Clay's bid get accepted on that plot of land?" Nikolas asked.

"No, he got outbid. He was pissed about it and went on a rampage remodeling the office at the marina. I got sucked into helping him somehow."

"That's what he does when he's mad? Hell, if I piss him off do you think he would remodel my room?"

"Nah, if you piss him off he'll just throw you off a cliff. He got so mad this time because he jumped the gun. He wanted that land to turn it into a campground and already had the layout all planned out, along with contacting some companies to build the office and restrooms. I told him that was a stupid idea, there's already too many campgrounds around here. It's fricken Florida, vacation central." Gage gave an exasperated sigh and ran his hand through his thick hair.

His father was an excellent businessman and investor, but sometimes he tried to take on too much. He would grow tired of whatever his recent purchase was, then pawn it off on Gage to find a new investor. The only consistent businesses he kept were the casino, the marina, a handful of apartment buildings, and the old video store-turned-smoke-shop on the boardwalk. The only perk to his dad's career in investment was that Gage never had to get a job. His dad would always keep him busy as a maintenance man for the properties, and paid him well.

"Yeah, but all the current campgrounds are booked for the whole year already. People love camping, and it's an easy business to manage. Not much maintenance besides the lawn and bathhouses, plus if a camper gets too rowdy and destructive you can just kill him and blame it on an alligator. It's a perfect business, really." Nikolas shrugged his shoulders like it was the most obvious thing in the world.

Gage sighed and rubbed his forehead. "My dad already has too many businesses, though. He doesn't need a campground on top of it all. It's one more responsibility he will expect me to help with. It's like he forgets that I'm trying to rebuild this family and start my own motorcycle shop. I want something that's my own and not part of my dad's empire, but how am I supposed to start it when he makes me help manage all his properties?"

"Wasn't he supposed to buy you a shop for that?"

"Yeah, I'm still waiting for that. That's part of the deal with me helping him, he was supposed to find me a good location for a shop. Every time I try to find one myself, he says it's not good enough or there is too much wrong with the building and it would need too many repairs, so he never puts a bid down."

"What if you start running it out of the garage? It's big enough to fix up and store a couple bikes, plus I live there so I'll always be available to help."

"With what time? This week alone I have to finish up the marina's office, help plan and set up a tent for the casino at that music festival on the beach, and it's nearing the end of the month which means I have to help collect rent. That's not even including all the maintenance orders we have from our renters."

"Sounds like your dad needs to hire another manager."

"He's going to have to someday, because I'm not doing this forever."

"Scoot over, asswipe." Horatio interrupted the two and shoved Nikolas over, placing a coffee cup in front of him. "One black coffee for you."

"And one mystery liquid for you, Prince of Asswipes." Matteo copied his brother, pushing Gage over and placing a cup in front of him. "I couldn't see what she put in it, but it smells good."

Gage eyed the frothy cream on top of his coffee and poked it with his finger. Part of it stuck and he licked it off, intrigued at how sweet it was.

"What did you two talk to the coffee girl about?" Nikolas asked the brothers once they were settled in the booth.

"First of all, her name is Willow, not coffee girl. She was named that because she was born under a willow tree," Horatio said.

Gage squinted his eyes in confusion. "She was born under a tree and not in a hospital?"

Horatio shrugged, "Her parents were Irish Travellers born and raised in Ireland, so I'm guessing they were a little different."

"She seems a little different herself," Gage mumbled under his breath.

Matteo picked up in a long-winded rush where his brother left off. "Don't be rude, you don't even know her. Her parents came over to America before she was born and she was raised traveling around in an RV, but lived her last few years in Detroit, Michigan. Both her parents died and she has no one, so she moved to Florida to start fresh. And she is still single, in case you were wondering."

Gage's ears perked up at the last sentence, but he brushed it off. It didn't matter to him if she was single or not, his father would kill him if he got involved with someone that rented from him. Especially since he almost killed the last girl he was seeing. One of his biggest rules was to never mix business with pleasure.

"Does she know about vampires? I know some humans don't pay attention to our kind and live in obliviousness," Nikolas asked.

The twins shrugged.

"So you two asked her a million questions about her personal life, but not about that. If she doesn't know about us, don't you think that's kind of important, since vampires are going to make up half of her customer base?"

"I'm assuming she knows, and if she doesn't, then I don't *want* her to know. I like that she treats us like normal people," Horatio answered.

"I want to become her favorite regular. She's so pretty," Matteo gushed as he looked over to her.

Gage rolled his eyes. "Please mop up the drool dripping down your chin. It's unattractive and grossing me out."

He looked over to Willow to see what enthralled Matteo so much. She looked like a pale version of Esmerelda from *The Hunchback of Notre Dame*, complete with large golden hoops dangling from her ears and bracelets jingling as she stirred a new customer's drink. He had to admit that even with her eyes dull and tired and her face plain with no makeup, she still had a certain quality about her that made her pretty. Perhaps it was the thick, dark lashes that gave the illusion that her eyes were lined in charcoal. Or the thick halo of long, brown hair that hung down her back in a ponytail.

He turned his attention back to the table, but shifted in his seat so he could keep her in the corner of his eye. He took a sip of his coffee as the boys discussed the lineup at the upcoming music festival. Most of the time he helped set up the tent advertising the casino and then was able to attend the festival as a normal patron. This year, due to being short staffed, Clay had requested Gage's help in running the tent throughout the night. It would be the biggest tent at the festival, and they needed all hands on deck to make sure it was successful.

Horatio scoffed at Matteo's suggestion that they start the night off with an 80's hair metal band. "Dude, I don't want to waste time listening to some shitty old metal band when we could be listening to a dozen other artists that don't suck."

Matteo scoffed back. "Excuse me? W.A.S.P. is iconic and the members will probably be dead soon, so we need to see them while they're still alive. And who are you to judge me for who I like while you're over there listening to country music?"

"Country music is America's music and tells relatable stories through song."

"Dude, we're two Cuban stoners born and raised in a giant beach side city. How is anything about bonfires, beer, trucks, and women in cowboy boots even slightly relatable?"

Gage interrupted them before the brothers could start arguing over their music tastes. "How about instead of watching bands you come help me out at the tent? I'll pay you guys well and none of us have to be stuck there all night. We can take turns watching it."

Nikolas and Matteo confirmed they would, but Horatio hesitated. He looked like he was nervous as he said, "I actually kind of won't be able to. I, uh, have plans."

"He's got a hot date with a girl he doesn't want to eat." Matteo winked at his brother.

"Well, I'd eat *something* on her," Horatio smirked back. "But yeah, her name's Sammy and I've been taking her more seriously than just for a blood supply. This is our first official date, so I want it to go well."

"Where did you meet her?" Nikolas asked.

"She works at the marina. Clay asked me to repair one of the docks and she came up to me while I was cussing up a storm after I'd nailed my finger into a board. I kind of owe her a nice date because I may have accidentally caused her to fall into the water. She's a little bit of a spitfire." His grin turned into a large, dopey one. "I like them sassy. Plus, she knows I'm a vampire and is cool with it. Clay likes her and wouldn't mind making her part of the family if she ever wants to turn."

Gage was dumbfounded. "Jesus dude, fall in love much? You haven't even been on a date with her yet and you're already talking about adding her to our family. You know she has to get *my* approval first before she's turned."

"I've been visiting her at the marina for a while, I just haven't talked about her. I didn't want to piss you off. You've always been weird about girls ever since Venice left."

Gage felt his rage beginning to creep in and his good mood disappeared. "I don't care if you're dating, but I did tell you to never mention that whore's name again."

"See what I mean? You're getting all weird."

"I'm only getting weird because you said that name."

"Guys, chill. Willow's coming over," Nikolas cut in.

Gage looked up and made eye contact with Willow, whose face was full of anticipation. The eagerness in her eyes was almost childlike and he was able to get a handle on his rage, even though it still simmered in the back of his mind.

"So? How did you like it?" She bit back a smile and waited for his answer.

He looked down at the sweet drink that tasted of chocolate and hazelnut with a hint of vanilla. It was delicious and could easily become one of his new favorite drinks if he was planning on continuing to come here.

"It's alright."

Her face fell, and an unusual pain tightened in his chest. He didn't want to give her the satisfaction of making something he actually liked, but he also felt bad for destroying that glowing smile and causing that tired, dull look to return to her eyes.

He grunted and surprised himself by continuing, "Actually, it's pretty good. But I'm not a coffee drinker so I don't know if that means much."

Her face lit up again. "I'm glad you liked it! I was worried you would be a hard one to impress. I felt like even if I made it with coffee beans I'd harvested myself and served it in a cup made of pure gold, you still wouldn't be amazed."

"You're right, I wouldn't be. Also, I didn't say I was impressed, just that it was good."

"Good is better than mud." She gave him a smug smile like she had won some battle. "Don't forget I'm closed tomorrow night, but I'm sure I'll see you guys Monday."

"You'll for sure be seeing me." Matteo smiled at her. She patted him on the shoulder before heading back behind the counter to serve two new customers that had appeared.

Gage realized that the prickling sensation of rage had completely dissolved. The boys went back to their discussion of the music festival, but he zoned out, caught up in his thoughts.

As much as he wanted nothing to do with Willow, he couldn't stop himself from complimenting her drink and returning that glow to her face. Even the color of her eyes shifted from a muted brown to a piercing greenish brown. There was something addictive about knowing he'd caused that change.

He used to feel that way about Venice.

The rage started to return again, so he pushed Matteo out of the way and exited the booth, leaving the half-drunk coffee on the table.

"Where are you going?" Nikolas asked.

"I need a ride before I work a long night," Gage called over his shoulder. As he left, he noticed Willow's reflection in the glass door watching him with a curious expression.

Once outside, he started his bike and swung a leg over. He dared a glance back toward the coffee house, but by now Willow's attention was turned to another customer. He drove out of the parking lot and hit the throttle, speeding off into the night.

Four

Gage

Gage did not end up going back to the coffee house over the next week, but the others made sure to stop in. There was something about the calm, accepting atmosphere that kept them coming back.

Willow made sure to keep the lighting so that it was not too bright that people were blinded, but not so dim they were sleepy. The music was soft enough that it provided a quiet murmur customers could talk over and the A/C was at the perfect temperature. For the boys, it was a perfect oasis away from the typical nights of hunting or hard labor they were used to.

Gage kept himself busy renewing leases, fixing leaking roofs and broken dishwashers, and collecting rent for his father, along with preparing the casino tent for the music festival. The casino's manager was a new hire and was not great at helping with the planning, so most of that was left to him. They also had a limited crew to work with, so physically setting up the tent and slot machines would also be left to him.

All of this gave him very little time to do anything fun. He barely had time to hunt down dinner. He did end up coming across a sex worker who offered to sell some of her blood. He normally would have been ashamed for having to stoop so low as to buy blood, his looks and relation to Clay usually made it easy to find women willing to give up a pint, but being numb helped cure that shame. Plus, hiring someone was so much more time-efficient and didn't require any emotions to be involved. Tonight involved a quick exchange of cash, a bite in his truck, then she left without so much as a glance back at him so he could continue on his way to the marina.

"Hey Pops," Gage said as he brought in a roll of carpeting on his shoulder and flung it to the ground with ease.

Clay nodded at his son as he finished taking measurements of the marina's office space for the new trim. Tonight he was wearing a colorful polo shirt tucked into his khakis with his dirty-blond hair still perfectly slicked back. Even with his dorky exterior, he was still intimidating to people, and held an air of confidence that made others know he was the man in charge. Even though Gage had taken over leadership of the family after the tragedy that had happened, he still found himself going back to his father for advice.

Gage was obviously his son, with his matching angular face, green eyes, and confidence that seeped out of every pore. Gage was just a little bit rougher around the edges with his unkempt, shoulder length hair and monochrome outfits. What they had in common was the rosary tattoo on their chests in remembrance of Gage's mother, who had passed. It was a simple design of black beads wrapping around the base of their necks, with the red and black cross resting on their left pectoral muscles.

"It's about time you showed up. I was beginning to think you'd bailed on me." Clay frowned at his son.

"Nah, I just had to make a quick pit stop." Gage held up the coffee cup with a green mermaid printed on the outside.

Clay sniffed the air and wrinkled his nose at the sickeningly sweet scent emanating from the cup. "Are you sure that's coffee? Or dessert?"

"It's a little bit of both. Your new tenant can make surprisingly good coffee and got me to like this stupid latte shit."

"Why didn't you stop at her café, then?"

Gage shrugged, not fully sure himself why he avoided The Coffee House Bunny. "I didn't want to be seen carrying around a cup with a rabbit logo on it."

"But a mermaid is better?"

"Yeah, it makes me feel like a pirate." He placed the cup on a windowsill and grabbed a broom to clean up the sand they had dragged in on their shoes. As he swept, his thoughts kept going back to the café with the pretty barista.

His desire to know more about her caused him to break the silence. "Hey, where did you find her anyway?"

"Who?"

"Willow."

Clay had been crouched on the floor retaking a measurement, but he didn't move. Instead, he peered at his son from the corner of his eye. "She found me. She inquired about the building since it was so close to the hospital. I liked her idea of having an all-night coffee shop, and she had an amazing credit score, so I rented her the place. It looks like it's doing well. Every time I go past it there are always customers inside."

"Yeah, the nurses love the place, but hate it when we show up." Gage laughed, thinking of the group of nurses that reminded him of a flock of angry geese as they scattered.

"You guys have been going often?"

"I haven't, but the others have. I think Matteo has a crush on her. He doesn't have a chance since she's way out of his league, but I'll let him keep dreaming."

"She's very pretty, isn't she?"

He paused at his dad's comment. "Eh, she's okay. Do you have a crush on her too?"

"No, but I am always impressed by an independent, strong woman like her. It takes a lot for a single person, let alone a female, to move over a thousand miles away and start a successful business. She would make a good leader."

"Looking for my replacement already?"

Clay finally looked up from his tape measure and smiled softly at his son. "Never. It was only an observation. I'm glad you guys are going there often, she's a sweetheart and I would like to keep her in our community, but working nights like she does isn't safe. Speaking of which, the murder rate has increased lately, and I've been hearing a lot about other vampires entering our territory. I haven't seen any myself, but I wanted you aware. Your Uncle Al has noticed his murder rate in Daytona increasing, too. Something's going on, but we're not sure what."

Gage's stomach tightened at the new information. "Do you think it's connected to Waldo?"

Clay's eyes took on a heavy sadness at the name of the Miami family leader. "Possibly, that's something you must look at. I know it won't be easy and will be opening old wounds, but we need to keep our territory safe. Part of being a good leader means keeping a level head even when dealing with people you want to kill." He hesitated, like he wanted to broach a subject he knew would be controversial. "I know you're still hurt by what Venice did."

"Please for the love of god, don't bring her up. I do not want to talk about that wench of a woman."

"Okay, but maybe think about moving on from her. You know I never liked her, and it makes me so angry to see how she's changed you. Now *Willow* I like. When I helped her set up her café, I noticed how patient she was when things would go wrong, and I think you need a girl who's going to be patient with your cranky ass."

"If she's as sweet and patient as you say, then you shouldn't want me with her."

"Every leader needs his woman to lean on, and occasionally get some sound advice from. Your mother was that support for me, and I hate to see you not have someone like that. I know your mother would be so sad to see you alone."

He knew his voice took on an aggravated tone. "Please don't play the dead mother card to guilt trip me into dating your coffee girl. I'm not interested in dating. If Waldo might be poking around our territory, then it's not safe for me to be associated with her anyway. Or did you forget that he was the reason Venice left me?"

Clay's lips turned into a thin line. "No, how could I forget? Her betrayal broke my son." He sighed and ran his hand through his hair, finally disrupting the perfect style. "I have to get going before the lumberyard closes for the night. I need you to finish the carpet so we can at least start on this trim tonight. I want this finished soon so the manager can move back in. As much as he's loving working from home right now, I'd prefer to keep him on the premises to keep an eye on the employees. Thanks to your lovely friend Horatio, one of my favorite employees fell into the water and almost drowned."

Gage perked up at the mention of the lumberyard. "Hey, are you going to the store off Palm Coast Highway? There's an old mechanic shop that's up for sale next door. It looks a little run-down, but it would be a good starter place for my shop."

"You don't want a place that needs updating. I'll get you a plot of land and you can build yourself a brand-new shop with the exact layout you want."

"Yeah, you've said that a few times now, but I'm still waiting. I'll still be able to help you manage all your properties, if that's what you're worried about."

"What I'm worried about is you losing focus on rebuilding the family. Why don't you talk to Nikolas about helping you run the shop? I already tried to get him to work for me at the marina, but he said he wasn't interested in the nautical life. It seems like motorcycles are more his thing, and you could use some support if you're going to start your own business. Do you think I built my property empire all on my own? Hell no, your Uncle Al was there every step of the way and is still there when I need him. We supported each other and were able to build strong families because of that."

Gage's eyes glazed over and he zoned out as his father began his lecture about not isolating himself. Instead of developing a traditional retirement hobby, like bird-watching or crafting, Clay was nagging Gage into rapidly gaining loyal followers to rebuild their family to its former glory. So far, he had three that had somehow found a way to become not only his roommates, but also his best friends.

In his glory days, Clay had been running one of the top families in Florida, but once everything collapsed he had given up his position early and passed it onto his son. Typically, sons didn't take over as the head unless their father died, so their situation was unique. No other heads of families had their fathers guiding them like puppets. Gage was grateful to still have his father for advice, but it affected his confidence in his leadership skills, since he felt like he couldn't make a decision on his own.

"Also, since we're on the topic of Uncle Al, I need you to stop sleeping around." Clay's comment broke Gage out of his trance.

"Huh?"

"You hooked up with one of his boy's vassals and he was pissed. I think her name was Delilah or Denice."

Gage wasn't surprised to hear that another woman had been two-timing him. "Destiny?"

"That sounds right. Thank god you didn't kill her, or else you could have started a fight. This is another reason I need you to settle down with a good girl. I've been waiting almost forty years for grandbabies to spoil."

"Okay first of all, why are you trying to get the term vassal to come back? That's old-school slang that hasn't been used since the 80's. Second of all, he didn't mark her with his bite, so how was I supposed to know she was claimed?"

Clay shrugged. "If you stuck to one girl, you wouldn't run into this problem. Okay, I have to get going for real this time. I'll see you later."

Clay left and Gage returned to his cleanup. The silence in the office was making his ears ring, and his thoughts returned to the woman who not only broke his heart, but stabbed him in the back by running off with the enemy. He pulled out his phone and picked the loudest, angriest music he could find to help him through the night.

ɔɔɔɔ

Gage threw the head onto the pile of decaying, bloodless flesh that was piling up in the back of the cave. Nikolas appeared to be slacking on feeding his pets. He had caught his latest victim in the middle of torturing a kitten to death as he was leaving the marina for the night.

He had been walking down the dock when he'd heard high-pitched meows coming from one of the boats. At first, he thought it was someone's cat locked up safely in one of the rooms of the house boats, but the closer he listened the more it sounded like the creature was in pain. A splash sounded and the crying ceased, so he'd quickly run to where the noise came from. Expecting to find a kitten swimming in the water, he'd instead found a scrawny young man bent over a bucket on one of the boats. He'd looked like a rich kid with his name-brand shoes, freshly pressed slacks, and a new hoodie displaying a fraternity's symbol.

"The fuck you doing? This is private property." Gage called.

The guy had snapped his head up with round eyes and quickly stood up with his hands behind his back. "My dad owns this boat, sir."

"That doesn't explain what you're doing."

"Nothing, I was cleaning something. That's all."

"What are you cleaning?"

His expression had shifted from shock to irritation. "Mind your own business, bro."

He'd turned his back to Gage and bent down to pick up the bucket. Annoyed by the guy's attitude, aggravated by his father's lack of help with setting up a shop, and still raging at the recently constant reminders of his ex-girlfriend, Gage had quickly hopped over the boat's railing and landed with a loud thud behind the man.

"Now what the hell are you doing?" The guy had shouted and spun around. He'd taken a step back once he'd noticed how close Gage was, and tripped over the bucket.

To Gage's horror, the bucket had spilled out and a small, white creature had tumbled out of it, not moving. For a second he'd thought it was a rat, but he'd noticed its thin tail had fur and its face was not as long.

"Did you drown that kitten, you fucking psycho?" He asked and took another step forward. He'd felt saliva starting to build in his mouth and his fangs had ached with the desire to rip into flesh.

"N-no, it fell into the bucket and I was getting it out." He'd swallowed and his eyes had shifted to the dock.

"Liar. There's one thing I hate more than preppy assholes with piss-poor attitudes, and that's people that kill animals for fun." He'd smiled and known that in the moonlight he looked terrifying. His face had been shadowed, making his eyes look black, his sharp fangs had been on full display, and his shirt had highlighted his muscled arms. Arms that could easily rip this guy's head off his shoulders.

"I-if you kill me, m-my dad will hunt you down."

"Oh? What, is he a vampire, too?"

"No, he owns Highland Car Lot and has a lot of money. He'll hire a hunter to find you."

Gage had let out a sharp laugh. "I'm not scared of a used car salesman. Especially one that rents his building from my father."

The boy had taken off and tried to run around Gage to jump to the dock. Gage had been quicker and grabbed him by the back of the shirt, pulling him to his chest.

"Where are you going?" Gage whined like a friend was leaving his party. "I'm starved and could really use some fresh blood."

The guy had let out a high-pitched scream as Gage had bit down into the tender flesh of his neck. He'd torn a chunk of flesh out, and blood had poured down, covering the golden fraternity letters on the hoodie. Gage had been tempted to stick the boy's head into the salt water to increase his pain and drown him, much like he'd done to the kitten, but his hunger had taken over and he'd drained his blood quickly. The guy had thrashed around for a few minutes, trying to loosen Gage's grip, but eventually his strength had begun to fade away and he'd slumped to the ground, resigned to his fate.

Gage had loaded the dead body into his truck. He'd been grateful he'd driven it tonight since hauling a body seemed rather impossible on a bike. Before leaving, Gage had gone back to the boat to discard the kitten.

"Sorry little one," he had murmured to the limp clump of wet fur. He had squeezed it around its middle as he picked it up and a gush of water had come out of the tiny, pink mouth. Two blue eyes had squinted open, followed by a raspy mew.

"Oh, oh my god." Gage had panicked, not knowing what to do with the pocket-sized creature. "You're alive."

The kitten had sneezed, and a small spray of water and snot had covered Gage's hand. He'd felt bad releasing the kitten back in the marina and assumed she would die if he did that, so he'd taken off his shirt and rolled her up in the warm fabric to bring her home with him.

When he'd arrived at his house, Nikolas hadn't questioned why he'd walked through the front door shirtless and with a kitten. He'd simply nodded at Gage and taken the bundle from his arms.

"Her name is Buffy. Can you take care of her for a bit while I clean up a body?" Gage asked.

"Sure thing boss. I'll text Matteo and ask him to pick up some kitten food on his way home." With that, Nikolas had turned and taken her into the kitchen to find some warm milk.

Five

Willow

Willow flopped onto her couch as soon as she walked into her apartment. She was covered in a film of sweat that was caused by a combination of the high humidity of Florida's weather and the workout she'd just completed.

She attended a yoga class biweekly in an attempt to change up her schedule and give her something to look forward to. When she'd first moved to Florida, before she opened her coffee shop, she had been attending weekly yoga classes to tone up her body while making friends. The yoga gave her back some of the confidence that her ex-boyfriend had taken from her, but she was still unable to connect with others.

She had met one girl in class that she would make small talk with, but no one else in the class was overly eager to converse. It seemed that everyone had the mindset that they were there to work out and nothing more. The class had a Zen, non-judgmental vibe, but there was also a loneliness she felt afterward.

She frowned at the thought of friends. Willow had tried her best to build friendships and social connections throughout her life, but it was hard when she had moved around so much when she was younger. And now after her ex had broken her, she wondered if it was even worth it. People, no matter if it was a platonic friendship or romantic relationship, could change you. She was finally developing a sense of safety and trust in herself and didn't want to risk it even if she was lonely. She found her social connections within her regulars, and that was good enough.

To help ease the loneliness and give her something to look forward to other than work, she had planned to attend the upcoming music festival, friends or no friends. She was nervous beyond belief and assumed the night would end with her being uncomfortable, awkward, and drunk. Deep down she hoped she would meet someone there that would change the course of her current life, but she knew better. Reality wasn't like that.

Before she could get too comfortable on the couch, she forced herself up and over to the two-story rabbit cage that took up most of the corner by the balcony door. Her rabbit, Snickers, was waiting patiently and stood up on his hind legs when she approached, like he knew it was dinner time.

"What do you think of having a new brother or sister?" She threw a scoop of pellets and a handful of fresh hay on top of his feeder.

The rabbit didn't move, but continued his empty stare.

"Yeah, okay. Maybe not."

He turned quickly and started munching on the hay. She'd always wanted to add a new furry friend to her family, but was concerned about how Snickers would react. He had been an only child for as long as she had owned him.

After cleaning up his cage, she immediately jumped into the shower to avoid getting couch lock. She could feel herself losing steam, but still had a full night of running a coffee house ahead of her.

Once at work, Willow managed to drop an entire gallon of milk on the floor, opened a case of vanilla syrup only to find a bottle had cracked open, and did not receive tips all night long. She sighed in relief as she watched John and Ryan walk in. At least she knew she would get a few dollars and have a pleasant conversation.

"Hey guys, are you having the usual?"

"Yes ma'am," John stated with a lopsided smile. Ryan nodded briskly.

"I haven't seen you guys in a while, what have you been up to?"

John's smile became larger and a slight blush reddened his cheeks. "Well, I was on a mini-vacation. I took the girlfriend to Disney World to propose." He chuckled and his eyes sparkled. "She said yes!"

Willow's stomach flipped at the realization that she didn't know these two boys at all. She'd thought she did since they were regulars, but as mean as it was, she'd assumed they were single since they were both nerdy and awkward. She never knew John had a girlfriend, let alone was planning on proposing to her.

She wasn't necessarily upset, but her loneliness from earlier returned, heavier and more suffocating. There was also a pinprick of jealousy that he had found someone he loved enough to marry. She wondered what having that kind of relationship with another person was like.

"Oh, that's wonderful!" She kept her feelings hidden inside and plastered on her best customer service smile. "I didn't know you were seeing anyone, tell me all about her."

"Well, she grew up down the street from Ryan and they went to high school together, so I guess I have him to thank for introducing us." He patted his friend on the shoulder.

"So he set you two up on a date?"

"Not exactly. I was at a music festival two years ago when I ran into him with his group of friends. She was with the group and instantly caught my eye, so I ended up ditching my friends for the night to hang out with her. I guess she found me charming enough to give me her number, and the rest is history. We usually attend the festival to celebrate our anniversary."

"Are you talking about the same festival they're having next week?"

"Yeah, that's the one. We're not going this year since we will be in Colorado to break the news of the engagement to some of her friends who live there. Are you going, Ryan?" He turned to his friend, who shook his head and sipped the coffee Willow had just placed in front of him.

John continued, "The lineup didn't seem that good this year, so I don't think we will miss out on much."

Willow shrugged, not feeling like taking offense that one of the bands on the lineup was her favorite. "I'm planning on going, this will be my first-ever music festival on a beach. I'm looking forward to getting drunk, playing some slots, and rocking out with sand between my toes."

Ryan raised his eyebrows. "Slots?"

"Oh, the man can speak! Yeah, I saw a flyer on the boardwalk that the casino is going to have a tent set up and had a few slot machines brought in for people to play."

John's smile disappeared. "Oh yeah, I know what you're talking about. I'm not trying to sound like your dad or anything, but I wouldn't recommend going to that tent. A man name Clay owns it and his—"

"I know Clay!" She cut him off with a smile. "He's my landlord and has been so sweet to me."

"So you know he owns half of Vista Maria and is friends with the people who own the other half? He's mega rich, like billionaire rich, which makes him untouchable. He can do anything and get away with it."

"Clearly you are all for the 'eat the rich' idea." Willow smirked. "Clay doesn't seem like the type to be evil, though. He helped me fix up this place and checks up on me every once in a while."

"That makes me really nervous." John frowned. "He's probably trying to get close to you so he can eat you."

Willow gave a confused laugh. "What an odd thing to say. I thought *we* were supposed to eat the rich."

John gave her an equally confused look back, but before he could explain, the bell on the front door chimed and all three looked up to watch a pair of nurses walk in, signaling the beginning of the breaks at the hospital.

"I'm about to start getting busy and won't have time to talk soon. Here, keep this." She tossed the money they had paid her back at John. "Your coffee is on the house today as a way to celebrate your engagement. Congrats!"

The nurses that had walked up to the register cooed at the news they overheard before placing their orders. John's blush returned and the two left before the hospital rush could overwhelm them.

The rest of the night flew by, and before she knew it the sun was beginning to rise. Things had slowed down, and Willow was pleasantly surprised to find her tip jar close to full. She was so pleased that she did not even mind when a girl walked in as she was going to lock up for the day.

"I'm sorry! I didn't realize you were closing so early. I forgot you have odd hours."

"That's alright, you can be my last customer." Willow smiled. "I don't think I've seen you here before, is this your first time in?"

"It is. I couldn't resist stopping in once I saw the name Coffee House Bunny. I just adore bunnies."

"Aw thanks, I named it in honor of my pet bunny, Snickers. There's been a few creepy male customers that try to make a joke about me being a Playboy Bunny, so sometimes I regret picking out the name."

"Well, I think it's adorable. Actually, this whole place is adorable. I love the retro vibe it gives off. It's refreshing compared to the normal hipster places I usually go."

Willow beamed at the compliment—refreshing was exactly the vibe she was looking to create. "My name is Willow, by the way. So, what can I get for you?"

"I'm Marla, it's nice to meet you! I'll take a caramel macchiato if that's not too much trouble. Again, I'm really sorry. I used to work in food service and absolutely hated when people would come in last minute. You know what, I can always just go to the café down the street."

"Nonsense, their caramel is not as good as mine. A macchiato is easy enough to make, and I have zero plans after work, so it's not like you're keeping me from something."

Marla chewed on her lip and watched Willow make the drink. "Hey, this is probably going to seem super bold, and maybe even super weird, but I was on my way to this new pottery shop that opened down the street. Since you said you don't have any plans and you seem like a pretty cool person, would you want to go with me?"

Willow looked at her, but before she could respond Marla waved her hands in the air. "Actually, forget it. That was super weird of me, I am so sorry. My therapist has been pushing me to be more outgoing and make friends, but it's been royally backfiring."

"Girl, calm down. I was just trying to think of what pottery store you were talking about. I would be more than happy to go. I'm somewhat new to the area and work too much, so I don't have any friends either. Let me lock up really quick." Willow handed her the drink and untied her apron, throwing it on the counter.

"You don't have to clean up?" Marla looked at her like she couldn't believe what was happening.

"Nah, I'll come in early tomorrow to clean up. For now I'm going to worry about making a new friend and going home after to pass out on my cozy bed."

"Are you the only one who works here?" Marla asked as Willow followed her out and locked the door behind them.

"Yeah, just me. I know I should look into hiring someone, but that's a lot of trust to put into a stranger, plus it requires a lot of time to interview. Then there's the whole legal aspect, with taxes and employee benefits. I don't know how any of that works, and could really use a mentor."

Marla scrunched her face. "None of that sounds particularly fun, I think I'll stay an employee instead of an employer. How long have you been running The Coffee House Bunny?"

"Not long, only about two months I think. My time is running together and every day is the same, but I can't afford to take a break and shut down my café for very long. How does that saying go? No rest for the wicked?"

"You don't seem like a wicked person."

Willow clenched her jaw, but didn't respond. She stared ahead at the sidewalk that was beginning to fill up with pedestrians as people walked into their various jobs. The street her café was located on was mostly filled with businesses, from flooring stores to small law offices.

"So where do you work?"

"A boring old retail job. I used to work three jobs, one at a small boutique, the other as a waitress, and the third was a night shift at a gas station. I didn't stay at the station long, though. I had one too many scary interactions with some creeps. As burned out as I was back then, I do miss all the money I had. It was easy to save it since I didn't have the time to spend it!"

Willow nodded and gave a lopsided grin. "I used to work at a gas station, too! I guess that's one way to look at working yourself to death—it's a great way to save up money."

They rounded the corner and the pottery shop came into view.

They were about to open the door when a short, bearded man grabbed Marla by the shoulder.

"Don't go in there! You're supporting *them*."

She shook him off. "Ew, get off of me!"

"Leave us alone." Willow scowled at him and threaded her arm through Marla's arm.

"I mean no harm, I only want to save your soul. If you support them by buying their goods, you're basically letting the devil right into our own backyard. We have to keep our land safe from those filthy leeches."

Willow scoffed and went into the shop, noticing a Mexican male was behind the counter watching the ordeal. "I'm sorry about that. You shouldn't have to put up with racist old men like him."

"Racist? He wasn't talking about me, he was referring to the owner. Unfortunately there's some close-minded people out there that don't like her kind. But me, I don't mind. She's never hurt me."

Willow wanted to ask what he meant by "her kind," but was pulled down an aisle by Marla. The strange encounter quickly left her mind as she watched as the girl's face lit up at the sight of an entire row of mugs decorated to look like they were covered in ombre dragon scales. They were organized from dark to light, and the forest-green one caught her eye.

"I think I might need this." Willow began to reach out for the mug but stopped when she heard Marla gasp behind her. She turned to find a mug decorated in fat rabbits two inches away from her face.

"No, you need *this*."

"Holy crap, that's adorable."

The two grinned at each other and continued their exploration of the store, constantly showing each other the prettiest items they could find. It wasn't long before they each had a handful of pottery to purchase.

"I didn't know retail therapy was what I needed, but I think this has cured my burnout," Willow said.

"Shopping and making a new friend can really cure anything," Marla added.

"Hey, I really don't feel like making anything to eat when I go home, so I was thinking of stopping by that restaurant across the street. Would you want to join me?"

"Heck yeah, do you think it's too early for a beer, though?"

"Well technically this is my dinner time, so I won't judge you if you order one."

"Sweet, I'm getting a large then."

While at the restaurant, the two girls realized they had more in common than either of them thought was possible. They both were somewhat new to the area, though Marla was from Missouri whereas Willow was from Michigan; both were boyfriendless and friendless; and both were hopeless romantics obsessed with anything in the romance genre. It was obvious to Willow that the two were meant to meet, so they swapped numbers and decided on a day to check out a Mexican restaurant that supposedly had the best-of-the-best Verde sauce. It was so delicious, the reviews claimed you could pour it straight into your mouth.

What Willow was most looking forward to, though, was that she could finally say that she made a friend, not just a new regular.

Six

Gage

By the time they were done setting up, not only was the casino's tent the biggest, but it was also the most eye-catching. They made use of colorful lights that glittered in the night and rugs to make the tent look like a miniature casino on the beach, complete with a roulette table and multiple slot machines for people to play. Figuring out the electrical component was the hardest part, but Nikolas was able to work his electrician magic and found a way to plug everything in while also hiding any extension cords so as not to trip people. The last thing they needed was a lawsuit.

Since Nikolas had put in most of the work, Gage let him enjoy the festival and didn't schedule him to work the tent at all. Matteo, on the other hand, had pressed a few buttons to turn on the slot machines and then proceeded to make nooses out of the string lights, pretending to strangle himself. He was scheduled to work the tent all night long.

The table at the front was set up with coupons and flyers advertising all the different events the casino offered, and plenty of free merchandise for people to take home. Free pens, bags, and stickers were the best form of advertising—the boys would constantly see them all over town.

The night of the festival brought a wave of people from all over Florida. The crowd was intense, and Gage realized he didn't mind being stuck behind a table the majority of the night. It kept people a nice distance away from him. All he had to do was hand out flyers and convince them to play the slots.

Matteo hit Gage on the shoulder to get his attention. "Look out, a hottie with a body is coming your way."

Gage looked up from restocking the flyers to see a blonde, Playboy Bunny wannabe walking toward the tent. Matteo was right that she did have a body. She had an hourglass shape, long supermodel legs, and tits the size of basketballs strapped to her chest.

"There is no way those are real," Matteo stated as he watched the basketballs bounce around inside of her yellow sundress.

"Of course not." Gage smiled, but it was half-hearted. He preferred dark hair, not the platinum blonde currently sauntering toward him, but he was more interested in her blood than her attention. "Watch the tent for me, will you? I've got some business to attend to."

"Have fun and wear a condom!" Matteo shouted after him.

As he rolled his eyes and left the safety of the tent, he noticed the blonde looked him up and down and smiled at what she saw. He sauntered up to her with confidence and arrogance radiating off him. He knew damn well what he was doing when his arms flexed as he crossed them across his chest, and was validated when her eyes glanced toward them.

"Now what's a pretty girl like you doing all alone at this festival?" He asked in a smooth voice. Since this was not a traditional hunt where he planned on killing her, he knew he had to romance her to willing give up blood.

She giggled and shrugged, looking up at him from underneath her lashes. "Looking for a handsome boy to hang out with, I guess."

He smiled. She was going to be the easiest thing he did all night. "Well, I just so happen to know a handsome boy that's looking for a pretty lady to hang out with."

"Let me guess, is it you?" She took a few steps forward and placed her pointer finger lightly on his chest.

As she stepped closer he could smell the alcohol on her breath. She stood on her tiptoes to whisper in his ear. "Want to hang out with me back in my car?"

His smile grew even bigger. She was turning out to be the easiest thing he ever did in his life. "You lead, I'll follow."

She led him back to a blue Honda Civic and crawled into the back seat, exposing the white underwear that was underneath her dress. The spaghetti straps were already starting to slink down her shoulders and show off more of her cleavage. Gage sat down next to her and shut the door. Before he could say anything, she already had two lines of coke set up on the center console.

Gage scrunched up his face. "Well that was quick."

"It's just a little appetizer before the main course." She winked and snorted up one of the lines. She signaled for him to take the other, but he shook his head.

She shrugged and snorted the second line. "More for me then! Now, where were we?"

With dilated pupils, she scooted over to him and rested her hand on his thigh. She awkwardly shoved a finger from her other hand into his mouth and touched a canine.

He jerked his head away and tried to resist the urge to spit. Her finger tasted like salt and something bitter. "What the hell?"

She covered her mouth with her rejected hand and giggled. "I heard what a bite feels like from your kind. So what's a girl gotta do to try that wild ride?"

"How are you not concerned that I might kill you?"

She shrugged and began petting his thigh. "I don't know. I took some molly earlier and I think it's starting to kick in. Your pants feel nice."

Gage grew irritated with her drug use. Typically he had no problem drinking the blood of someone high on drugs, since it would cause him to feel that same high. But tonight he didn't want to be on whatever mixture she had in her system while trying to work the casino tent. He had to be sober, responsible, and on his best behavior so he didn't piss off his father.

Sometimes being the new leader was a drag.

"Oh, what's this?" She purred as she quickly slid her hand across his thigh and up to the zipper of his pants.

For a split second, he wished more than anything that the hand was attached to a dark haired barista instead of a drugged up airhead. He quickly shoved that thought aside and tapped his fingers in annoyance on the car door as the blonde struggled to undo the metal button of his jeans. She gave up and broke out into laughter.

"Sorry, I'm really messed up. I wanna go dance! What about you? Wanna dance with me?"

The idea of having a bloody treat was long gone. He rolled his eyes before getting out of the car. "I don't dance. Enjoy your night, sugar."

He slammed the door behind him, leaving her alone in her car. She didn't seem all that disappointed as she prepared another line.

Gage approached the tent and frowned at Matteo who was shocked to see him back so soon. "She's a druggie. I don't feel like getting high tonight."

"Is she now? Where did you leave her at? I wouldn't mind a quick bump."

"Good luck, she was going to go dancing. She probably went over to the EDM stage."

Matteo rubbed his hands together in anticipation and headed off on his mission, completing forgetting the fact he was supposed to work all night. Gage went back to tending the tent and kept his eye out for a girl that would be able to get rid of his hunger. To his disappointment, all the women who came up to the tent had partners or were old enough to be his grandmother - and the thought of draining a granny didn't sit right with him. It wasn't until an hour had passed that there was a girl who approached the tent alone.

"Fancy seeing you here."

His charming smile melted away when he looked down to see who it was. "Oh shit, it's you."

Willow looked different tonight, dressed in a distressed classic rock band shirt that hung off one round shoulder, black frayed shorts, and plain black flip flops that looked like they came from a dollar store. Her thick hair was up in a high ponytail, and she had winged eyeliner emphasizing her hazel eyes.

The blonde may not have turned him on earlier, but he sure as hell was now.

He was tempted to flirt with her and get her down on her knees to take care of the tension resting in his pants, but something about picturing her like that made him feel gross. She was too sweet to be treated like that. She deserved someone who would take her on a proper date first, not a vampire that was only interested in one thing.

"Uh, yeah it's me." She said.

He realized he had been staring at her for an uncomfortably long time as he analyzed her new look. "Sorry, you just look different."

"In a good way or a bad way?"

"Well, you're not ugly." Gage bit his tongue and felt himself growing frustrated at his awkward comment. He was always cool and in control during situations with women, but something about her destroyed that.

"What, am I usually ugly?" She tried to fake offense but ended up laughing. "It's okay, I know I'm not the prettiest girl in the world. But hey, at least I've got nice hair."

She fluffed up her ponytail and Gage gritted his teeth as an image of his hand tangled up in the velvety mess crossed his mind.

"I didn't mean that. I just meant that you…you don't look ugly right now." He threw a hand up in defeat and let his awkwardness take control.

"Aw, are you trying to compliment me? Is that why you look like you're in pain? I honestly thought you were about to have a stroke when you said you liked my coffee the other day. I noticed you haven't been back since."

"I've been busy. With work and stuff."

She looked around at the tent. "Do you work at the casino?"

"Kind of, my father owns it and I help him out when he needs it."

Her eyes turned into wide saucers and he held back a laugh at her comical look. "Wait. Holy crap. *Clay* is your dad?"

"Yeah, why do you seem so shocked?"

"Because he's so nice and sweet and you're, well…not. Although, having him as your father explains the asshole energy you give off. You're a rich brat."

"What?"

Her face reddened and she covered her mouth to giggle. "Sorry, I'm a little tipsy and sometimes things slip out a little more freely than they should."

He remembered his discussion with his father about the murder rate increasing. He hadn't found out yet if it was due to vampire attacks, but he wasn't stupid. Especially if there were rumors of Waldo being spotted around Vista Maria, he wouldn't put it past the man to start having his men hunt freely on his territory. And a festival this large would be a prime hunting ground for hostile vampires.

"You really shouldn't be wandering around here drunk, especially if you're alone."

"Calm down, I'll be fine. I'm used to being by myself anyway. I did see my friend Marla here but she was…busy. I was wandering around when I saw all the lights from off in the distance and was drawn to this tent."

"You sound like a moth."

"Moths are cool." She smiled up at him but her eyes were drawn to a slot machine that began flashing and blasting music. The man at it shouted in joy as he won fifty dollars.

"Can I play?" She asked Gage.

"That's what they're there for. Tell you what, I'll let you spin for free if you go get me a beer."

"Deal!" She did her excited clap before running off into the crowd outside the tent. It took her a surprisingly short amount of time for how busy the beach was before she came back with two clear plastic cups of golden liquid.

"I got overly excited and forgot to ask you what you drink. I figured this was a safe choice. Oh, and I did a shot of tequila while I was there so I'm a little tipsier than I was before. I'm not an alcoholic, though! I swear! I don't get to drink often, so tonight is my night to celebrate."

Gage grimaced at the lite beer but took it anyway. "Who's running the coffee shop tonight if you're here?"

She took a loud sip out of her cup and glanced around at all the slots that were flashing. "No one. I closed it for the night so I can have some fun. Speaking of which, can I play a slot now?"

"Sure." He threw her a few tokens that could be used in place of cash and she bounced off to the nearest open slot. As she played, he unsuccessfully tried to keep his attention on the people who walked in. He found his eyes slowly slipping back over to her every few seconds, taking in her round ass that looked like it would fit perfectly in his hands. It didn't help that she played the slots with as much enthusiasm as a child at Disney World.

By the time she had run out of tokens, he had finished his beer and had given up on controlling his wandering gaze. He walked over to her to see how much she had won for the night, only to notice that any winnings she had were put right back into the machine.

"I better go find Marla so I don't walk around unsupervised and drunk for the rest of the night." She giggled.

"Why do I get the feeling you're the type of person to wander into trouble when you're unsupervised?"

"Because I am." She downed the last of her beer then looked at her phone. "Oh! It's almost time for my favorite band to start, too. I really do have to get going, thanks for the free spins."

She hopped up on her tiptoes and gave him a quick peck on the cheek. He froze in his spot as his cheek started to burn where she kissed him. The scent of her washed over him. It was similar to something he had smelled once before, yet better. Sweeter. She smelled like candy with an undertone of warm vanilla. The last time he had smelt a girl that delicious was with Venice.

ↄↄↄ

The four boys walked into the coffee house the next day to find Willow in yoga pants and a beat up gray t-shirt, with dark bags under her eyes. Gage had decided to join them tonight in order to help him procrastinate on installing new carpeting in one of his father's rentals. Plus, he wanted to get another look at Willow to confirm it was only lust that made him look at her differently last night. Unfortunately for him, the homeless person chic was working for her.

"Let me guess, you had a little too much fun at the music fest?" Matteo grinned as he leaned against the counter and looked her up and down.

"I think so. I also remember now why I don't drink often. Are you guys getting your usual?"

"Yes ma'am," Matteo responded.

She looked over to Gage and raised one eyebrow but didn't bother to smile. "Still no beer, so do you want black coffee or the drink I made you last time?"

As much as he did not want to order the unmasculine, frilly drink she had made him, it had been pretty delicious. Plus, he deserved a treat if he was going to be doing hard labor all night long. "Does that drink have a name?"

"Why yes, actually, it does." She moved aside and pointed to the chalk board hanging behind her. Drawn in different shades of brown and white was the drink of the month, labeled "The Rich Brat."

"Hey, that's you!" Horatio laughed and slapped Gage on the back.

Gage kept his face expressionless as he stared at her. "Yeah, I'm not going to say that. Can you put it in a to-go cup, though? I can't stay long."

"His rich daddy has him working on a big project tonight." Horatio joked, but flinched when Gage turned his gaze on him.

"No problem, I'll bring it to your table when it's ready." Willow said. She turned her back to the boys as they headed over to the booth that had become their usual spot.

"Did you ever find that blonde?" Gage asked Matteo as the boys sat down. Like clockwork, the nurses sitting next to them got up and left, this time giving them dirty looks like they had forced them to end their breaks so early.

"Nah man, she disappeared. I was hoping to turn her into a vassal, but yet again my hopes were crushed."

Horatio snorted at his brother's reference. "A vassal? What the hell are you, some kind of pimp? No one has vassals anymore, it's the twenty-first century. We have what's called *bloody booty calls*. You get some girls that are into getting their blood sucked and have them saved in your favorites for easy access when you're horny and hungry."

"Hey, retro things are coming back in style and I'm making sure vassals make a comeback. I mean, who doesn't want a hoard of naked women living in your bedroom, eagerly waiting to please your every desire?"

Nikolas squinted at Matteo. "Dude, that's a harem. A vassal is just a person who agrees to let you drink their blood as long as you don't kill them."

"Also, having a hoard of women sounds expensive. Sammy damn near cost me forty dollars in food last night, so just imagine having to feed ten women. That's like four hundred dollars' worth of food every single night. Don't forget all the little gifts you'll have to buy for every holiday and birthday. No way, I'm good with just one girl," Horatio added.

Willow came up balancing all four drinks on a platter and looked at Horatio. "Not to be a creep, but I saw you and your girlfriend last night. You two were cute together."

Horatio's smile split across his face. "Thanks, she's a cutie, ain't she? I think I'll keep her."

"And I saw you met my friend Marla last night." Willow looked toward Matteo with a knowing smile.

"Who?"

"Marla, the little brunette girl that was following you around all night and kept looking at you like she was in love."

Matteo's face went pale as he clearly remembered the girl she was referring to. "Oh yeah, that chick was weird. I told her I wasn't interested, but she was determined to change my mind."

Willow's brow scrunched up and her smile turned into a frown. "Don't call her weird. You just don't know her well enough yet."

Nikolas laughed. "You're the one who wants to start a harem, might as well kick it off by adding her."

Matteo's eyes grew round and he chuckled, quickly looking at Willow and blushing. She simply shook her head and walked away.

"He's just joking! I'm not a pervert like that," he called after her.

"Well, as much as I'm enjoying listening to you idiots swoon over girls like a bunch of high schoolers, I have work that needs to get done," Gage said.

He stood up from the booth and headed out to his truck, which was loaded with tools and rolls of carpeting. He sat in the darkness of the cab and watched Willow through the window as she yawned and walked around the shop lazily talking to her regulars. He had been annoyed to discover that he was still intrigued by the woman and his lust from last night had nothing to do with it.

Seven

Gage

After a long night of carpentry, Gage decided to take the next night off and relaxed in his art studio. He was reclined in his dark blue velvet chair, feet propped up on his desk and a drawing pad balanced on his knees. Earlier he had been sprawled out on the hardwood floor, then stretched out on the velvet couch, then stood at his desk by the window unable to find a comfortable position. Being a vampire did come with perks, like being stronger and having a higher pain tolerance than the average human, but the occasional aches and stiff muscles from installing flooring all night still happened.

And it annoyed him.

It was Sunday night, which meant The Coffee House Bunny was closed, and he was strangely disappointed in not being able to see Willow. He wondered what she did with her days off and assumed it was probably something silly, like watching cartoons or coloring those adult coloring books that were everywhere lately. He frowned and nodded to himself.

"Yeah, she seems like the type to color," he mumbled.

He chewed at the end of his colored pencil and looked at his sketch, the irony completely lost on him.

Gage put up his drawing tools and set aside the commissioned forest scene he had been working on. Buffy unraveled herself from around the base of his chair, stretched, then jumped up on the desk to curl herself into a ball. He was absentmindedly petting her when he felt someone approach behind him.

"That's turning out good," Nikolas stated, walking into Gage's studio.

He studied the drawing, then sat down in a paint-splattered folding chair that was propped up in the corner of the room. He rested his elbows on his knees as he leaned forward. Gage knew this pose all too well. It meant that Nikolas wanted to talk about something serious.

Out of all three boys in his group, Nikolas was the one who Gage considered to be his co-pilot. Not that he did not trust Horatio and Matteo, but they were younger vampires and still a little naïve, whereas Nikolas was calmer, wiser, and more in control of his emotions. He was the first one Gage had enlisted to start his new family, and quickly took his place as Gage's best friend. He also was not afraid to address difficult situations.

The most recent situation being what had happened with Waldo and Venice.

Nikolas was the one who had intervened after Gage discovered Venice had been sleeping with Waldo for weeks before running away with him on the night Gage was going to propose. Nikolas had been able to stop him from going on a full-on rampage and hunting them both down to rip them apart limb by limb. He had also been there the night Gage got violently drunk and ended up in a sobbing mess on the bathroom floor. He had been able to pick up his drunk ass, clean off the vomit that covered his entire front, and put him to bed to recover.

Venice's betrayal was a blow that had fully broken Gage's already half-broken soul, as it happened not long after his father's family was slaughtered at the hands of Waldo's father, Gerald. Not only did she cheat, she sided with the enemy that had destroyed everything he loved.

Gerald had done more than kill the people that helped raised him— he changed his father in a way that nothing could repair. He had never seen such a strong man shatter like he did the night he lost his family - the night his father became a shell of his former self.

But he still had his son, and Gage was determined to become a leader that would make him proud.

"What version of Gage are you today? Are you feeling cranky or calm?" Nikolas asked.

"Well I was calm, but I'm guessing you're about to tell me something that's going to ruin that." He quit petting Buffy, with a small glare from her, and relaxed back into his chair.

"I'm going to tell you two things that will probably ruin that. Actually, one of them is kind of worrisome and the other could be good depending on how you look at it. Which one do you want first?"

"Give me the good news first. I want to enjoy my calmness for a little bit longer."

"Well, Clay called me today. He told me how he thought it would be a good idea if both you and I run the bike shop together. He went and looked at the garage you told him about and it wasn't as run-down as he thought it would be. He's willing to buy it for you, but you have to agree to have me be a co-owner."

Gage groaned. "Why can't he let me do this myself. It's like he doesn't trust me or think I'm capable enough to run my own business. He had no problem with Willow, some random-ass girl who isn't even from here, running her own café, but God forbid he lets me get my own shop."

"I don't think it has anything to do with trust or doubting you. I think it's more of a lesson he's trying to teach you to help you become the best leader you can be. He wants you to learn how to rely on and work with us. That's what running a family is all about. It's safer learning how to do that with a business where if it tanks then the worst that happens is we lose money. If our family fails—" Nikolas' voice grew softer "—then the humans of Vista Maria die."

It occurred to Gage that he never seriously thought about how important his role was. Being the head of a family was more than being rich and well-known in the city, he had to create and enforce rules that protected both his kind and humans. Most families believed in only killing those who deserved it, or consensually feeding off people without killing them. But there were still less civilized families, like the Miami family, that followed the old ways of killing anyone they desired. They wanted to return to the Victorian age where humans lived in fear of the monsters of the night. They thought fear brought more power, but in reality, all it brought was war.

Nikolas continued, "I've thought about it and I'm down to help with paperwork and finances, but ultimately you would be running the place."

Gage steepled his hands in front of his face as he thought. It was not an entirely bad idea, Nikolas was easy enough to work with and would keep his promise of working behind the scenes. Plus, this was the closest he had ever been to actually getting his own shop.

"Yeah, I'm good with it. We're not going to do any weird shit like putting both our names as the shop's name, though. I don't need people thinking we're a couple."

"Aw, but we would be so cute together—like yin and yang. You're the blond with a bad attitude and I'm the dark haired, handsome one with the friendly smile."

Nikolas cracked his signature heart-melting smile that made even the most suspicious person trust him. It was part of his hunting technique. All he had to do was look at a victim with his big, brown eyes and smile, and they would be putty in his hands.

Gage rolled his eyes. "Yeah, and I'm sure our children would come out absolutely adorable. Now, what's the bad thing you have to tell me?"

"Okay, thing number two is pretty bad. Do you remember Jesse James?"

Gage rolled his eyes even harder the second time. "Who? Do you mean Waldo, the little weasel that didn't think his name was badass enough so he had to change it to an even cringier name? The self-absorbed turd that is the head of the Miami vampire family? The pea-brained idiot whose own family cannot stand him but sticks by him anyway because he gives them free drugs and money? Of course I remember him, I fucking hate him."

"Trust me, every vampire in the Florida region hates him. To top off all his wonderful characteristics, Clay said there's been rumors of him appearing in our territory again. I don't get why the guy can't stay on his side of the state."

"Because he's an evil prick that finds joy in tormenting me. Clay informed me about the murder rates increasing and now I have no doubt that it's connected to Waldo."

"Well, the reason why Clay brought him up is because he's worried about Willow working nights. He wants us to keep a close eye on her and specifically requested that you start spending more time there." Nikolas squinted his eyes and raised his brows. "He was very adamant that *you* are the one that spends the most time there."

"Yeah, he's trying to play matchmaker." A burning sensation bubbled up in Gage's chest at the thought of Waldo hurting Willow. "Why don't we set up a schedule with Matteo and Horatio so that someone is always in the area? We don't have to be in the café, but I want someone close enough that if an attack happens they can get there within minutes."

Nikolas nodded his agreement. "Clay also suggested that we should mark her so other vampires that pass through know she's off limits. Again, he was very adamant that *you* do that."

"Okay, now he's just getting desperate."

Nikolas laughed. "I do have to admit that she does smell good and that could be tempting, especially for a new vampire with less self-control. I'm sure Matteo would be more than willing to mark her if you don't want to."

A flair of jealousy ran through him, but it was quickly extinguished. "Matteo doesn't have a chance in hell after insulting her friend the other night." He paused before continuing, "So you noticed her scent, too? She smells like candy."

"At first I thought it was all the syrups and sugars in the café, but I guess it's her blood that smells that way. I dig it, she's like a little portable air freshener smelling up the place wherever she goes. It's rare to find someone with blood as sweet as hers—it must be all the sugar she consumes."

"Nah, Venice smelled similar and all the bitch ever ate was lettuce and tofu. Maybe the scent is a trick, like how sirens sing beautiful songs to lure pirates to their deaths."

Nikolas looked at his friend with pity in his eyes. "Don't let one awful girl ruin you. Not all girls are untrustworthy. Look at Sammy, she and Horatio have only been dating for a few weeks and they're both so in love it's gross. Hell, she's already willing to give up her mortality and turn for him."

"Maybe she's just an exception."

"Or maybe Venice was the exception?"

Gage stood up and stretched. "Whatever. I'm going down to the beach to see if there are any bums that want to lose their lives tonight. I'm feeling a little hungry after all that work yesterday. Want to join me?"

"I can't, I promised Matteo I would help him change the oil on his bike tonight."

"By help, do you mean you're going to do it while he sits there and watches?"

"Probably, I don't trust him not to break something."

ↄↄↄↄ

It was getting close to two a.m. when Gage arrived on his motorcycle at the empty beach that ran alongside the Atlantic Ocean. Soon the bars would be closing and plenty of mean drunks would be wandering home, which made easy prey for a night like tonight.

There was something otherworldly about the ocean at night. No lights were allowed on the beach so that the sea turtles that hatched could find their way home by using the moonlight. But tonight there was no moon. The sky was an empty, black void sprinkled with stars, and all that could be heard was the soothing sound of the waves on the pale, sandy shore.

Gage parked his bike on the sandy asphalt and took a lazy stroll toward the gentle water. As he approached it, he realized he was not alone and the sweet smell that mixed with the salty air easily identified her.

Willow was faced away from him, waist-deep in the water, her hair cascading down the length of her bare back as she stared up at the night sky. She did not hear him approach behind her, or notice when he picked up her pile of clothing that was laying in the sand.

He observed her for a second, taking in everything that he saw. The water lapped at her back, almost touching the tips of her hair so dark it looked black in the night. Even without any moonlight, she appeared to be glowing against the surrounding darkness. She was like a smooth, pale goddess of the Atlantic, content in her natural environment. He wondered what that felt like, being so at peace.

He smirked and held out the lavender panties that were hanging from his pointer finger. "Skinny dipping, are we?" He relished in breaking the peaceful scene with his gravelly voice.

Willow spun around and covered her chest with her arms, her hair becoming entangled with them. With his ability to see in the dark, he noticed her face was flushed and her eyes were so large they took up half her face. His cock stirred as he noticed the flesh of her breasts brimming over her arms.

"What are you doing here!" She shrieked.

"I was taking a relaxing walk along the beach. What are you doing standing in the ocean butt-ass naked?"

Her face became contorted with anxiety when she saw he was holding all her clothes. "I-I was… Can you please stop playing with my underwear like that? They're not a toy. Those were expensive, which is why I'm not wearing them in the water!"

Gage paused his twirling and looked at the label printed on the small, silk cloth. "Michael Kors, huh? I thought he only made purses. I guess the old pervert is designing underwear now, too."

"The only pervert I know of is you! Please put my clothes down and leave me alone."

She hugged her arms around herself even tighter as his smirk turned into a full-on grin. He eyed her body and let his eyes rest on the belly button ring where a diamond moon dangled above the water, making him wish the tide would go out just a bit further so he could see what the moon was pointing at.

He partially complied with her request and placed all but the underwear back down. He stepped close to the water and held them just above the liquid surface. "If you want them, come get them."

"I'm not playing this game with you, Gage!" She buried her face into the hair tangled among her arms. She peeked up at him through the strands and he about came undone.

He quickly turned his wicked grin into a tight-lipped smile, hiding the sharp canines that were aching to sink into her tender flesh and taste her blood that smelled so sweet as she screamed his name in ecstasy. He suddenly grew worried that if that fantasy came true, something would change in him. That he could easily fall for this girl. He reminded himself that he was not the dating type.

But he *was* the type to tease a pretty girl.

"Aw, but I like games. You're no fun," he taunted, and pretended to drop the expensive silk into the water.

She lunged forward, reaching only one arm out to catch her underwear. Gage grew hard when he saw the soft, milky-white skin right underneath her breasts. It looked like a lovely place to mark her. He quickly caught the underwear and held them up high over his head.

"Oops, too slow," he purred.

"You're being childish, please just give them to me."

"You have to come get them. I'm wearing leather boots, there's no way I'm walking into the water."

"Can't you put them down on the ground and turn around? Or at least close your eyes?"

"Nope, not an option."

She let out a small, frustrated scream and slapped the water with her free hand. "You're intolerable. See if I make you any more special drinks the next time you come into my coffee shop."

He chuckled at her little tantrum. He took a few steps back from the water, hoping to trigger another frustrated scream. "The longer you wait to get them, the farther away I'll be from the water."

Her irritation boiled over and she took a deep breath before covering her lower region with her free hand and running out of the water toward him. She stood in front of him, glaring daggers up at him. He'd never realized how short she was until she was this close. She barely came up to his shoulders. There was no way she would be able to reach the underwear that was still being held up over his head.

"Well, hello there." He was impressed at himself for resisting the urge to peer over her shoulder and look at her exposed rear.

"Give me my fucking underwear."

He lowered his eyelids and leaned down, inches away from her face. "Beg me for them," he whispered.

She stood her ground and squinted her eyes back at him. "Go to hell, I will do no such thing."

"Don't worry honey, I'm already planning on going there." He smirked and dropped her panties onto the top of her head, turning around to head to the sidewalk and begin his hunt for the night.

ↄↄↄↄ

Gage returned home full and satisfied. Before he went to bed, he began a new drawing that was not commissioned.

He originally was going to draw the ocean with a star filled sky, but ended up adding in an hourglass-shaped silhouette standing in the gentle waves. He did not mean to include her, but sometimes art had a mind of its own and would unfold in a way the artist was not expecting.

For the first time in a while, he went to sleep that morning in a good mood.

Eight

Willow

Willow was curled up on her bed in the fetal position, hugging a pillow to her chest and wondering why life seemed to hate her. She crushed her face into the pillow and let out a frustrated scream. She was not normally the type to rip off her clothes and take a dip in the ocean, but she had been having a great night and decided to do a little bit of mindfulness in a natural setting completely devoid of people.

Only for Gage to show up.

"Stupid, moron, rich brat, idiot!" She screamed any insult that came to her mind, but was unsure if it was aimed at Gage or herself.

Willow threw the pillow back to its original spot against her headboard and sat up. She propped her hair up on top of her head in a messy bun and decided to end the night on a better note. After lighting a candle and plopping in a rose scented bath bomb, she stripped off her sandy clothes and sunk into the warm waters of her bath.

The first thing to pop into her mind, of course, was Gage's face. And that stupid, smug smirk he had as he swung her panties around on his finger.

Instead of letting out another stream of curse words, she wondered what her mother would have done in her situation. Her mother never had a consistent relationship after her father passed, and would rarely bring around any men she did date. Love wasn't a high priority for her, she was more concerned about raising a daughter and finding new places to live.

She thought about a time when she was young when her and her mother went shopping for groceries during a thunderstorm and the store's power went out. Willow could still remember the comforting smell of the store she could never fully describe, the sound of the thunder as it cracked in the darkened sky, and the feel of her mother's hand gently, but securely, wrapped around her own. She also remembered how her mother had tucked a few small items into her purse since the cameras were out of commission. It was the first time she saw her mother be bad, the first time she saw a different side of her. The theft made her seem more human, and less like the perfect adult all young children see their parents as.

It was a memory that reminded her that it was okay to mess up sometimes, that not everyone could be perfect. She tried to remind herself of that as the embarrassment from tonight crept back in.

She was not entirely sure how she felt about Gage prior to this incident. He was attractive, no doubt, but not very friendly. But then there was the music festival where he was tolerable, though she was drunk. She was starting to become slightly interested in him, but some internal instinct told her to keep her distance.

As much as she wanted love, she was influenced by her mother to not make it a priority. She had also learned the hard way by her ex-boyfriend that some men could not be trusted.

ɔɔɔɔ

The next night at the coffee house, Gage walked in and propped himself against the counter, his three friends trailing behind him. She could feel him watching her as she finished a cappuccino for a customer, but she purposely ignored him and only addressed the other three, asking if they wanted their usual beverages. When it was his turn, her warm smile turned into a glare.

"So are you going to make me my special drink?" He asked with a smirk.

The other three must have sensed the weird tension radiating off her, and went to their booth without question. Only Nikolas looked back with an amused glance.

"Actually, I have a different one I want to make you. Congrats, you got a second drink named after you." She pointed behind her to a new drink of the month that she'd drawn on the chalkboard. This one was simply labeled "Asshat."

"Mmm, I'm excited to try it."

"The secret ingredient is rat poison. I hope you like it."

"Ah yes, my favorite flavor. Please put an extra shot of it in there for me."

She bit back her smile. "Go sit down with your frat brothers, I'll bring it out when it's ready."

"Yes ma'am." He followed her orders and sat with his group. For once, the nurses next to them finished their drinks before getting up and leaving.

As Willow brought over their coffees, she noticed Matteo's face turned pale, and he froze in place. "Oh shit, don't look now, but there's that girl from the music festival that's obsessed with me."

He groaned as all three boys plus Willow turned around and stared at her friend that had just walked into the café.

"Hi Marla!" Willow dropped the tray onto the table, spilling the drinks a little, and eagerly waved her hand toward the girl with her mousy brown hair twisted into a braid down her spine and thick black plastic glasses.

Marla gave a matching wave back, but her face broke into an even larger smile when she noticed Matteo slinking down in the booth. His face turned red as she began to make her way over.

"You know what, guys? I think I have to go. I forgot that um, Clay wanted me to run an errand for him. Move, Horatio." Matteo attempted to push his brother out of the way so he could exit the booth, but Horatio did not budge.

"I thought I was Clay's errand boy? What does he have you doing tonight?" Gage questioned the anxious man.

"He, um, he wanted me to go check out something. Some rental property. I guess they had the police over there the other night for disturbing the peace or something. I don't know man, just let me out!" He began aggressively pushing his brother as Marla approached and gave Willow a hug.

Matteo began to slide underneath the table to escape that way, but Nikolas, who was sitting across from him, blocked him with his legs.

Gage faked a serious tone. "I didn't hear anything about that. Clay would have for sure asked me to deal with it if that were true. You're not lying to me, Matteo, are you?"

Marla giggled. "Aw, Matteo doesn't seem like the type to lie." She turned her attention to the red-faced man whose body was halfway under the table. "It's kind of funny seeing you here, I didn't know you would like a place like this. It doesn't really seem like your scene."

"Actually, I was just leaving. I have something I've got to do tonight." Matteo tried to push his brother out of the way again, still not able to make him budge. "Come on bro, let me out," he whined.

"Oh, well I wanted to ask you something really quick." Marla looked up to Willow nervously, who gave her a kind smile and a nudge. "Me and Willow were going to the Pink Flamingo Club next Sunday night, if you wanted to go with us?"

Horatio raised his eyebrows in interest. "Are we all invited? That sounds like something Sammy would be into."

"Of course," Willow answered. "I would love to meet her! I don't have many friends down here yet, and I'm always looking forward to meeting new people. We're meeting up at nine o'clock if that works for you guys."

"Sweet, we'll be there!" Horatio responded.

"Speak for yourself," Matteo mumbled.

Willow clapped. "Oh, this is going to be so much fun. I've been needing to get out more and see the nightlife of Vista Maria. I only get a tiny sliver of it in here."

"Are you two coming?" Marla nodded toward Nikolas and Gage.

Nikolas looked at the blond like he was waiting for his answer. Willow didn't realize that she was holding her breath as she watched him raise an eyebrow and look back at Nikolas.

"I'll go if you go," Gage said.

"That's up to you, boss."

Willow released her pent-up breath as he shrugged. "Sure."

Suddenly, Sunday couldn't come soon enough. She said her good-byes and led Marla up to the counter to make her a drink.

"I don't think Matteo likes me." Marla slid her money over to Willow slowly as she began steaming some milk. "He's everything I want in a man, but for some reason I never seem to attract the type of men I'm attracted to. I only attract the old, crusty-looking ones that are missing teeth."

"I think he needs to get to know you before he can decide not to like you. And if it turns out you two are not a good match, we'll find you someone else at the club. It will be full of hot, available guys who will be into you."

"Nah, I'm too plain for a hot guy. Maybe I need to lower my

standards and settle already."

A pang of sadness went through Willow as she looked at her friend's disheartened face. "You are not plain."

"Yes, I am."

"Fine, if you truly want to think of yourself that way, then guess what? That's changeable, all it would take is a little bit of makeup, a new dress, and some curls in that hair to make yourself stand out like a supermodel. How about you come over early on Sunday and we can get ready together? I have this gorgeous dress I've never worn and I think it would fit you perfectly."

"Really? That sounds like fun, I'll bring some snacks and we can turn it into a whole girl's night."

"Don't forget wine, we really should pregame so we don't spend too much money on drinks at the club."

"If our makeovers are as good as I think they're going to be, we won't spend a single dollar on alcohol. Men will be bending over backwards to buy us a drink."

"There's my confident girl!" Willow grinned and handed her a steaming cup of coffee.

ɔɔɔɔ

The next night was slow, and her last two customers left the café with a generous tip. Willow heard the vibration of metal coming from the back room, so she decided it would be okay to take a quick break and leave the front counter. She had a chime on the door and would be able to hear if anyone walked in.

"Are you bored?" Willow cooed to the brown-and-black speckled rabbit that was gnawing at the cage he was currently trapped in.

The cage was large, but only about half the size of the one in her apartment. He would normally get to free-range when she was home, so being cooped up in this metal prison all night was probably boring. She undid the latch of the cage and scooped the large rabbit into her arms.

"I figured you were getting lonely and wanted to come to work with Mama." She placed a gentle kiss on top of the rabbit's head.

It wasn't often that she would bring Snickers to work, but with how often she was here she would sometimes feel guilty leaving him home alone all the time. Plus, she missed him. She knew it was probably against health code to have a rabbit holed up in the storage room, but she was willing to take that risk to have her pet nearby.

She heard the chimes jingle and headed up front with the rabbit still pressed against her chest, his lop ears resting over her arms and her face nuzzled into its plush neck. She didn't care if it was a health code inspector, she missed her bunny.

"Why are you holding a rabbit?" Gage asked.

She unburied her nose from the fluff and smiled at him with love glittering in her eyes. "This is Snickers, he's my baby and the inspiration behind the name of my shop. I usually keep him at home, but he looked lonely tonight, so I decided to bring him with me."

The rabbit sat in her arms and looked at Gage with empty, black eyes and a nose that was constantly twitching. She took her black shawl that was draped over her shoulders and wrapped it around Snickers.

"Even though I'm still mad at you for the beach incident, I'll let you pet him if you want." She held the bundled furball out to him.

He continued to stare at those soulless black eyes. "I think I'll pass."

"What? Do you not like bunnies?"

"All they do is poop and act scared all the time. What is there to like?"

"Their soft ears, their fluffy cotton tails, binkies when they're excited, the chin wipe they do when they love you, and their little asshole personalities. In fact, you and a bunny would get along really well."

She placed a kiss on Snicker's forehead.

"I'll still pass, I don't want him peeing on me."

Willow scoffed. "He has never peed on me. He's litter box trained."

"Rabbits use litter boxes?"

"Yes, much like a cat would. They're very similar to cats, only smaller and sassier."

"I guarantee cats are better."

"You don't strike me as the type of person who owns a pet, so how would you know?"

"I have a cat."

Willow's mouth rounded into a surprised "o" shape at the information he shared. "For real? You really don't strike me as a cat guy."

He shrugged. "Cats are cool. They mind their own business and have bad attitudes, which like you said previously, fits me well."

"I bet he's named something basic like Fluffy or Mr. Kitty," she teased.

"Actually, her name is Buffy and she hates people more than I do."

"She sounds perfect for you." Willow began to take Snickers back to his cage, but a new customer walked in. The man froze and raised a copper-tinted eyebrow at the scene.

"Am I interrupting something?" He asked.

She shifted her voice to her customer service tone, sweet and professional. "No, I was about to put him away. Give me one second and I'll be right with you."

She quickly returned Snickers to his prison with an apology and a head scratch. When she came back up, she noticed the man was at the counter but leaning away from Gage.

"What can I get for you?" She asked.

"I think he was here first." The man slid his eyes over to Gage and watched him with a bored expression.

Gage looked back at him, not breaking eye contact. The stool made a loud scraping noise as he pulled it closer and took a seat. "It's alright, I was planning on staying awhile."

The copper haired man nodded and returned his gaze to Willow. "Then I will take a cappuccino, please."

Even the relaxing music filtering through the speakers didn't ease the tension in the café. As she started the espresso machine, she turned to Gage, eager to talk about anything to make it a little more comfortable.

"So Sunday Marla is coming over early to get ready for the club. I was wondering if you knew what Matteo was into? Like what does he find attractive?"

"I don't know, boobs?"

"Wow thanks, that was so helpful. I'll make sure she doesn't wear a top then."

Gage snorted. "We're guys, we don't sit around painting our nails and talking about what we think is hot. I have noticed that he has a stack of Playboy magazines in his room if that helps."

Willow chewed her lip as she carefully topped the cappuccino with foam. The dress she was going to lend Marla was cinched in the waist and showed a lot of cleavage. With the right bra, she could end up with a Playboy vibe.

"That does give me an idea. Here you go." She slid the paper cup to the man and noticed a new ten dollar bill was in her tip jar. He left with only a nod and Gage watched him through the window until he was out of sight.

"Well that was weird, do you know who he is?" She asked.

"No, not a clue." He grabbed a napkin and pen from the register and scrawled with his number across it. "Call me if you need me. I have to go."

He began to walk out the door, forgetting to order a drink, and looked over his shoulder. "I'll see you Sunday, Willow."

The sound of her name rolling off his tongue caused a blush to bloom from her chest to her cheeks. "Okay, I'll see you Sunday, Gage."

Nine

Willow

It was early Sunday afternoon and Willow was already starting to prepare for the night. To help her confidence, she decided to take care of the bush growing between her legs. She hadn't had sex in over a year, and had stopped caring about her appearance down there. No one was seeing it except herself, but tonight she wanted to feel sexy.

She stripped off her clothes and sat on the edge of her bathtub as she began shaving from her ankles on up. Most beauty care like this she had to teach herself, since her mother was against normal beauty standards and preferred parading around with hairy legs.

By now, she was a pro at shaving. She sat on the edge of her tub, naked and spread-eagle, and her nipples began to harden at the sensation of her hand touching herself. But she had work to take care of.

She took her time making sure not to miss any stray hair and soon she was smooth and slippery. She spread her legs a little further apart and used the handheld shower head to rinse off the cream.

She took her time running the water over her sensitive area, making sure to rub her fingers around to get all the cream off. She slid her hand up her stomach to grab her breast and massaged her nipple as she continued to spray herself with the shower head. Everything on her was slick and she'd never felt so sexy.

She looked down at her bright pink center and her face flushed red as an image of Gage flashed into her mind. She told herself she was not going to have sex with him. She wasn't even sure how he felt about her, but it sure didn't hurt to *imagine* having sex with him. He was attractive and after him giving her his phone number, she was very conflicted about her own feelings. She had never ended up calling or messaging him, but something about him offering to help if she ever needed it turned her on.

She wondered if he had a six-pack under the black t-shirts he wore all the time, and pictured what the rest of his rosary tattoo looked like on his chest. He seemed like the type of guy to scoff at the idea of giving a girl head, but this was her fantasy and right now she wanted to visualize his shaggy blonde head between her legs.

She turned off the water and used the tip of her finger to trace around her opening, pretending it was his tongue exploring the most secretive part of her. In her fantasy, he told her he liked the way she tasted and ran his hands up her thighs, holding them further apart so he could get more of her pressed against his mouth.

She let out a small moan of pleasure as she stuck one finger into herself. She was surprised to feel how wet she was from thinking about him. She stuck in another finger and began thrusting them as her other hand rubbed her clit. She closed her eyes and pictured Gage sucking her sensitive bundle of nerves as he hand-fucked her, bringing her to climax. She bent her head back and let out a deep, throaty moan as pleasure exploded within her, her hands picking up speed. Once she peaked, she opened her eyes and leaned against the wall of the shower, breathing heavily.

"Fuck," she whispered.

She was sad to see that he wasn't there, just a figment of her imagination. She grew frustrated at herself for feeling that way, and reminded herself that she was not going to have sex with him. At least, not any time soon.

cccc

"You look so pretty!" Marla cried as Willow opened the door to her apartment.

Willow had decided to start her own makeover early and had already applied her makeup. She was currently wearing black yoga shorts and a ratty grey t-shirt, but apparently the makeup overshadowed that.

"Thanks!" Willow beamed and took the wine bottle Marla was holding out. She noticed a sack of snacks hanging from her other hand and her stomach growled.

"Sounds like you're ready to break into these chips, I also grabbed some chocolate and a few protein bars because we need something solid in us if we're drinking all night."

Willow popped open the wine bottle and began pouring them each a glass. "Good thinking. So, I found out what Matteo is into to help us plan your outfit."

Marla paused and looked down into the glass of wine Willow handed her. "I feel stupid. I'm not his type and even with me all glammed up he still won't be interested in me."

"How much would you like to bet I can get him interested in you?" Willow hopped off to her bedroom and returned with a blood-red dress dangling from a hanger. "Give me two hours and I'll have you looking like you're ready for a centerfold photo shoot with Playboy."

Marla's mouth hung open and her eyes sparkled. "Yes please! Even if Matteo doesn't notice me, someone will with that gorgeous dress!"

It took them two hours to complete their looks. Marla had undone her braid and straightened her hair so it hung down past her round ass that the dress accentuated. She put in her contacts and wore the only pushup bra she owned. She had large breasts and the bra made them almost spill out of the deep V. Willow gave her a pair of fishnet stockings and black stilettos that added another layer of sexy to the look.

Willow wore a skintight lavender dress with a triangle cut out just underneath her breasts. She wore silver heels that matched the silver hoops dangling from her earlobes, and put her hair up in a curled ponytail. She didn't mean to do it on purpose, but she was also wearing the lavender silk panties from the beach incident. She'd only picked them because they matched the color of her dress. She told herself that Gage wasn't going to see them, anyway.

"Ooh, I'm getting me a boyfriend tonight!" Marla declared as she gazed at herself in the mirror and did a spin. "I've never felt so pretty before. Is this what it's like to be you?"

Willow frowned at Marla's reflection. "I'm not that pretty, I'm just average. Actually, growing up my bullies got me to believe I was the ugliest girl that ever existed."

Marla's eyes grew wide. "You used to be bullied? There's no way, you're so kind and sweet, how could anyone be mean to you?"

"Teenagers can be brutal, but I turned out the way I did because of them, so I guess I can't be mad. Feeling like trash all the time made me want to reach out to others and make them feel good, because you never know the crap they have to deal with on a daily basis."

"I like that. I want to be like you when I grow up."

"Marla, we're the same age."

Marla shrugged in response and downed the last of the wine. Soon, they were ordering a ride to the club to start their night.

By the time they arrived, the place was packed. It wasn't hard to find the four boys, though. They stood out, huddled up outside smoking cigarettes and talking to another group of six guys. One of them looked like a shorter and heavier version of Gage with short hair. Willow wondered if they were related.

She began to feel her flight or fight response kick in as she looked at the large group of testosterone-laden men. Ashamed that her ex-boyfriend could still control her emotions like this, she reminded herself that she was safe and approached the group.

"Hey," she said as she eyed the strangers. Even with the bravery she used to push through the fear her ex had instilled in her, something about them made her nervous. She stood close to Marla and wrapped her arm around hers.

"Oh, you must be Willow!" A tiny girl, with a slight Southern accent, popped up from behind Horatio.

She was the same beauty Willow had seen with him at the music festival. Tonight, she wore a golden septum ring that matched the gold sequin dress that hugged her tiny frame. Her hair was styled in tight curls that barely touched her narrow shoulders, which had a light dusting of gold powder that covered her brown skin. Her brown eyes were lined with thick eyeliner, making her resemble a modern-day Cleopatra. She could see why Horatio was drawn to the striking beauty—she had an electric energy you felt just by looking at her.

"And you must be Sammy." Willow smiled and felt her fear begin to fade at the sight of another girl, one who could hopefully control at least one of the boys.

"That's me! Horse here told me you run that midnight coffee shop." She pointed her thumb toward Horatio. "I used to be a barista before I worked at the marina and absolutely loved making drinks. I didn't like working for a chain coffee shop, though. Too much politics and not enough respect for their staff. I'm glad I left. It was better for my stress levels, and I found a cute boyfriend at my new job."

Horatio gave a shy smile and wrapped his arm around her waist. "Ready to go inside?"

"Absolutely!" Sammy tugged on Horatio's sleeve and he obediently followed as she led the way into the darkened club.

Willow was about to follow them when the man who resembled Gage stepped forward and offered her his hand. Unlike Gage, he had a friendly smile and she felt comfortable enough to take his hand. He bent down and pressed a light kiss on the back of her hand and she silently thanked herself for remembering to put lotion on her rough skin earlier.

"I'm Robert, but you can just call me Robby. Uncle Clay has said a lot about you. He's always impressed by young people who have a good work ethic."

Willow gently slid her hand out of his and covered her mouth as she giggled. "Aw, Clay's the best. I'm so glad he was willing to rent me the space. So, if Clay's your uncle, that must mean Gage is your cousin?"

Gage snorted. "Unfortunately."

"Oh stop it, you love me." Robby attempted to smother his cousin with a hug, but Gage quickly stepped to the side.

Gage glared at him. "Don't you have to go inside and harasses some unsuspecting men?"

"Yes, actually, I do." Robby patted him on the shoulder and strode inside the club. All the men she did not know followed him like ducklings, and nodded a greeting to her as they passed.

The pulsing music could be heard when the door opened and a stray strobe light lit up the doorway before the door came gliding closed. She looked at Marla, who had obviously been avoiding looking at Matteo since they arrived. She wasn't sure how to handle the situation, since Matteo was also very obviously looking anywhere but at Marla.

"Well, we should probably join them," Willow stated as she pulled

Marla by the arm into the club.

Once inside, a surge of excitement tore through Willow. The music, the lights, the crowds of people dancing all around her made her feel so alive. It also helped that she had pre-gamed and was feeling the effects of the wine. She didn't care that there was a line wrapped around the bar, or that twenty women were waiting to access the bathrooms, or even that some young guy had thrown up all down the front of his white button-up shirt due to a mix of drugs and beer.

She ran to the dance floor, and the blue and purple lights made her skin match the color of her dress and her dark hair even darker. The silver hoops she had chosen flashed when they reflected the lights, and brought attention to her face full of wonder and happiness as she bounced along to the beat.

It didn't take long for her to lose Marla among the tightly packed crowd. Willow had stopped her dancing and was scanning the club when she spotted her friend's red dress. She was grinding against a guy, but Willow couldn't tell what the man looked like from her position. She ducked down and made her way through the swinging arms around her to try to get a glimpse.

A man stepped back and knocked into her, causing her to almost fall to the ground. He caught her before she could be stepped on and pulled her back up on her heels.

"Oh crap, you okay?" He yelled above the music.

She smiled and gave him a thumbs up, continuing to snake her way off the dance floor. She found shelter in a corner by the bar where it was a little bit quieter. The man that had accidentally pushed her followed her to the spot with an embarrassed grin on his face.

"Sorry again about that, but maybe it was fate? You're really pretty and I would love to buy you a drink." He spoke to her in a more relaxed tone now that the music wasn't so blaringly loud.

Willow smiled and batted her eyelashes at the handsome man. "Aw, you're such a sweetie, you don't have to do that!"

"Of course I do, it's the least I can do for almost getting you trampled to death."

His smile showed a set of perfectly straight teeth which appeared blue due to how white they were. He had dark hair styled with a wave in it, which fit the aesthetic of the white suit and light pink V-neck shirt he was wearing. Settled against his tanned chest was a silver chain with the Sagittarius symbol on a charm. Normally his style would not have appealed to her, but not being one to turn down free alcohol, she decided to give him a try.

"Well, if you insist." She took his arm so he could lead her over to the bartender.

Willow took one last look out onto the dance floor to try to spot who Marla was dancing with, and stopped dead in her tracks. There she was, face-to-face with Matteo, with her hands wrapped in his hair and their lips inches away from each other.

"Damn, I should have become a matchmaker!"

"What was that?" The man turned back around, but she shook her head and continued toward the bar.

He didn't turn back around to ask her what she wanted, and proceeded to squeeze his way through the crowd to order their drinks. While she was waiting, she looked around the dance floor for a familiar blond head of hair, but was disappointed to not find it. The club was a decent size, so there was no telling where Gage might have gone. But, he didn't seem like the dancing type, so she assumed he had gone to the patio.

The patio would be quieter with fewer people. And fewer people meant fewer girls to grind their ass on him. Not that she was jealous.

But maybe once she was done with this drink, she would make her way out there.

While she was still looking out at the crowd, the man had found a coveted spot at an open high-top and waved his hand to get her attention. Willow took a seat across from him and stirred the pink, bubbly drink that was between her hands. It was in a traditional margarita glass but was not any kind of margarita Willow knew. She took a sip from the black straw. It tasted of strawberries, watermelon, and citrus with a slightly bitter aftertaste that reminded her of an orange peel.

"I hope you like fruity things, I asked the bartender to make whatever she would like. I'm not positive, but you don't really strike me as a gin and tonic kind of girl, so I needed help from a professional."

"It's not half bad! It kind of tastes like summer."

The two sat in silence as Willow wracked her brain trying to figure out what to say to him. Small talk was not her strong suit, but she felt like a club was not the place to get into deep, philosophical discussions.

She chewed on the side of her lip. "My name's Willow, by the way."

"Thomas." He held his hand out and she shook it. "So what do you do for work? You look like you could be a model or an actress."

"Oh stop," she giggled. "You're being cheesy. I actually own a coffee house. I specialize with the graveyard shift crowd, so I'm open at weird hours to make sure our nurses and cops have access to the caffeine they so desperately need at two a.m."

"Do you get much business?"

"Enough to keep me afloat. I'm lucky I moved to an area with a lot of overnight workers. I used to live in Michigan and I was sick of the winter weather, so here I am in Florida."

"You're originally from Michigan?"

"Kind of. I come from a long line of Travellers, so we never stayed in one place for too long and lived out of an RV."

Thomas scrunched up his face. "You lived in an RV? Like you were homeless? You definitely don't look like you came from homeless parents."

Willow bit back her irritation at the ignorant comment and re-minded herself she was only going to use him for drinks tonight. "No, we weren't homeless, our RV was our home. Think of it like a trailer."

"Ah, so you're trailer trash," he laughed, amused by his own joke. "I'm just messing with you."

She stared at him, not giving him any sort of response. She picked the piece of pineapple off the rim and studied it, noticing the edge of it had turned pink, before popping it into her mouth. She wiped pineapple juice off her chin, hoping she looked cute rather than like a messy child who needed a bib.

"Are you originally from Florida?" She asked, unable to handle the awkward silence.

"Born and raised, baby. Tampa's my hometown and I'll never leave it no matter how dangerous it may become. I'm standing my ground and protecting my home. I refuse to let these stupid leeches kill off my people and take our jobs, turning my city into ruin." He shook his fist in the air like he was giving a powerful, though unsolicited, speech. "As much as I love a creative business idea like your coffee house, you better not cater to those filthy vermin. I don't trust them, they'll wait until you feel comfortable and as soon as you turn around, they'll kill you."

Willow had stopped chewing her pineapple and started planning a way out of this situation. She was interested in him, but he had instantly flipped that switch to the off position with his random rant. She knew the South was known for keeping racist ideals alive and well, but was not expecting to come across someone with those beliefs in a modern beachside club.

The energy around him had changed and she felt that he could become dangerous if angered, so she planned to get herself out of the situation safely. She started taking large sips of her drink, hoping to finish it off quickly so she could use the excuse of having to use the restroom to ditch him.

"I'm glad you like it, drink it up baby."

Her drink felt the urge to make its way back up at his little line. There was something about his tone of voice that put a pit in her stomach. She decided to lighten the mood until her drink was low enough.

"What's your favorite movie?" She asked.

"That's a tough one, but I'd probably have to say it's a tie between *Silence of the Lambs* and *American Psycho*. Both are iconic with amazing male leads. What about you?"

"*The Lost Boys*, for sure."

"The 80's movie with punk vampires that drive motorcycles? Really? That whole concept was so stupid and it was a poorly executed movie. Terrible acting, terrible plot, and terrible costume design."

She smiled flatly and stood up. "Okay, I'm going to go."

Just as she feared, things escalated. He grabbed her arm and tried to pull her back into her seat.

"Where are you going? You haven't finished your drink yet. That cost me a lot of money and you didn't even drink half of it."

"Oh, you're right. How rude of me." She grabbed the glass and chugged the remainder of the liquid, burping loudly and slamming down the glass. She hoped he was as offended by her gas as she was of his whole personality.

"I gotta piss, have a nice night." She spun around and headed back to the dance floor to find a man with better movie preferences and a more attractive personality.

"Alright, I'll see you later," Thomas called behind her. The hairs on the back of her neck rose as his tone made it seem like a statement, not a question.

Ten

Gage

Gage hated clubs. The Pink Flamingo wasn't as bad as some of the others as it was mostly humans who came here. The only reason he decided to come was because it didn't feel safe for Willow to come alone, especially after that weird interaction in her café. He had no idea who the copper-haired man was, but he smelled human, which meant he was not part of Waldo's family. The stress of not knowing where Waldo currently was or what he was planning was making him paranoid.

He was off to the side, hidden in the shadows as he scanned the crowd trying to find that dress that drove him mad. Maybe that was another reason he'd agreed to come—he wanted to see her dressed up, and she did not disappoint.

That fucking dress. *Fuck.*

While he was searching, he noticed Marla and Matteo were quickly becoming acquainted as they attempted to suck each other's faces off in the corner. When she and Willow had first arrived, neither he nor Matteo had recognized Marla at first due to her new look. It seemed

Willow took his comment about Playboy and ran with it.

"Clay didn't tell me how pretty she was. I was expecting some kind of hipster girl with a shaved head and a horrible sense of style," Robby said as he appeared next to him.

"Who?"

"The girl you're desperately looking for, Willow. Last I saw she was talking to some dude near the bar. But don't freak out, she looked offended by something he said so your odds with her are still good."

"I'm not desperate." Gage turned away and headed toward the fully-packed bar with Robby close behind. A sharp spike of concern ran through him when he couldn't find her there.

"By the bathroom."

"What?" He hissed at his cousin.

"Now she's by the bathroom. See, she's waiting in line."

The panic subsided when he laid his eyes on her. She was bouncing from foot to foot, looking bored and annoyed with the long line. To his delight, she was alone again, with no man in sight.

The bar was separated from the dance floor and a little bit quieter which, to Gage's dismay, made it easier for Robby to continue talking. "I'm surprised you haven't marked her yet. I know how quickly you can fall in love."

Gage's jaw clenched at his cousin's accusation, but he chose to ignore it and not let him ruin the night that had just begun. When the two approached the bar, the thick crowd that was encapsulating it parted like the Red Sea.

The bartender was a young blonde girl, barely twenty-one, but smart enough to know that these two required her full attention. She looked nervous as she served each of them a beer and a shot of top shelf whiskey, but looked relieved to find that they both tipped her twenty dollars and left her alone to attend to her more human guests.

They found a table that was recently abandoned and Robby started up his conversation again, not afraid to approach the subject that most people were smart enough to avoid. "I'm shocked that you actually came tonight. Every time I've invited you to the club you always told me it wasn't your thing. Willow must have some kind of hold on you, huh?"

Gage gritted his teeth. "I'm not here because of her, I can do fun things sometimes."

"Clubbing is not your idea of fun, my dude. You hate dancing, can't stand drunk people, and hate good music. She's the only reason why I can assume you came out tonight. You're in love, just admit it."

"Shut up. I don't know her well enough, and I've told you before I'm done dating. I learned that lesson real quick."

Robby rolled his eyes. "You have to get over Venice, she was a snake from the start. Never trust a stripper."

"I really wish people would stop bringing her up. I've heard that name one too many times lately."

"It's because she changed you, and we all hate this new Gage. You have never been a douche like this before. Sure, you've been an unfriendly loner your whole life, but you've never been a *douchebag* unfriendly loner. Venice took off with Waldo over a year ago, how many women have you used since then?"

"I've lost count."

"See! That's what I mean! The Gage I knew always treated women with respect, not as a useless sex toys."

Gage ignored his comment and turned back to watching Willow as she inched closer to the bathroom doors. A smile broke across her face when a black-haired, bearded man slid up next to her. His jaw clenched as he watched the man put his hands on her hips and try to guide her back to the dance floor to grind against his crotch. Willow pushed him away, too gently for his liking, and shook her head. Luckily for the man, he took the hint and left.

Gage stood up from the table and ran both of his hands through his hair. If he continued to sit here and watch her he was pretty sure he would end up killing an innocent human. "I'm going outside for a smoke, don't follow me. I'm not in the mood for a lecture about being a douche."

"Oh, don't get all testy with me. Someone needed to have this conversation with you." Robby shrugged his shoulders, downed his beer, and rejoined the mass of gyrating people.

Gage grabbed his drink and made his way to the outdoor patio, which seemed eerily quiet compared to the loud club. He found Nikolas smoking a joint with a small brunette girl with a bored expression. Neither of them seemed like they were enjoying each other's company, so he did not feel bad interrupting them.

"I have to go." The girl eyed Gage and quickly slipped back inside the club.

"Thank you," Nikolas sighed. He stubbed out the joint and dropped it into the pocket of his black dress shirt.

Another reason why he would label Nikolas as his best friend was because they both hated socializing. He knew the only reason why he was here was because he felt a sense of loyalty to suffer through the night with him.

"Your dad bought that garage."

Gage's eyebrows shot up. "So I guess this is really happening."

"Yeah, I told him we agreed to work together and he put a bid on the property. It went through this morning. Did you not know?"

He shook his head and took a drink to hide his giddy smile.

Nikolas frowned. "Shit, I hope I didn't ruin a surprise."

"You probably did, but that's okay. Guess we have to start buying tools and advertising our business."

"Have we picked a name yet?"

"Nope. We could do something basic like Vista Maria Custom Shop."

Nikolas looked at him with a scowl. "You're much more creative than that. Keep trying."

Gage thought for a moment. "What about Bloodsuckers Inc.?"

They both laughed and Nikolas nodded his head. "That's stupid, I love it. Maybe one day we can have our own TV show like *American Chopper* and vampires from all across the country will come visit our shop."

The smile melted away from Gage's face. "You know they don't let our kind on TV."

Nikolas shrugged. "It's a nice dream."

They wandered over to some empty patio chairs and pulled out their phones to start researching all the supplies they would need to renovate the new shop.

He didn't want to admit it, but his heart was racing at the thought that he would soon be the proud owner of a motorcycle garage. He knew there was a lot of work that would have to be put into it, starting with building his portfolio of custom designs to post on their website, but had no doubt that with Nikolas helping him they would succeed.

Willow

Between her last drink and the wine from earlier, Willow wasn't lying when she said she had to piss. She stood in the bathroom line for what felt like an hour, then started to make her way through the dance floor to the patio. Halfway there, she spotted Marla as she pressed Matteo up against a wall, thrusting her pelvis harshly into his with a leg wrapped around his waist. His right hand grabbed a handful of her left ass cheek and his left arm gripped her tightly around the waist.

Willow worried that Matteo would turn out to be a dick and make it a one-night stand, causing Marla undeserved heartbreak. She was tempted to pull them apart, but didn't want to ruin her friend's night, either.

She cursed her ex-boyfriend for turning her so bitter. It was hard, but she tried to convince herself that maybe not all men were bad, and to cut Matteo some slack. Plus, Marla was a grown woman and knew what she was doing.

Willow wiggled her way through the crowd until she was in the middle of the mass of sweaty bodies. A fast-paced song came on that she was not familiar with, but everyone around her seemed to know it as they lost their minds all at once and began jumping up and down.

One girl dressed in a neon-green string bikini with glitter coating her entire body spun into the side of her. Willow caught her and spun her back in the opposite direction, suddenly feeling a weird sensation overtaking her. The lights seemed brighter and she developed tunnel vision. She felt her heart rate pick up and her breathing become shorter and shallower. She thought a panic attack was starting due to the claustrophobic tightness of the crowd.

She pushed her way through and continued to make her way to the outside patio, hoping the fresh air would calm her down. And if Gage were out there, maybe he could take her home. She suddenly didn't feel like clubbing anymore.

She was unsteady on her feet and held her arms out to keep herself stable. The feeling was growing more intense and her eyelids began to feel heavy. Even though she was at a nightclub surrounded by people with high energy and EDM blaring, she could sit down on the floor and fall asleep instantly. Even her limbs were starting to grow heavy, making it that much harder to quickly get out to the patio.

When she reached the heavy metal door, she had to apply her full body weight for it to open. A man's hand appeared on the door as she was leaning against it.

"Need some help there, beautiful?" Thomas' voice whispered in her ear.

"No, I'm good." It was an effort to push those few words out of her mouth.

Her panic was in full force as she felt herself slowly lose control of her body. Her mind was starting to lose focus, no matter how important she knew it was that she needed to stay aware of her surroundings. She had never had a panic attack this bad before, and wanted to get somewhere safe where she could finish it out alone.

"You don't look so good. I have a hotel room reserved across the street, how about you go with me and lay down for a bit?"

The thought of a quiet room with a comfy bed and a toilet that was easy to access sounded so appealing to her right then that she almost agreed. But the cloud of haziness cleared for one second and she realized that being alone with him sounded like a horrible idea.

"No," she said in an airy voice, "I'm good. I need to...sit." She struggled to finish her sentence.

She slipped through the half-opened door and looked around her. The world was spinning and she had to lean against the wall. From across the patio, she saw a familiar looking head of shaggy blond hair slouched in a metal patio chair, nursing a drink while scrolling through his phone.

Thomas grabbed her shoulder and gave it a hard squeeze, trying to direct her to the gate in the patio's fence. "Let's sit down in my hotel. There are too many people here and you look like you're about to pass out. I don't want you to cause a scene."

A flashback of her mother squatting down in front of her eight-year-old self popped into her mind. Her mother had her finger in her face and was scolding her for almost going off with a stranger at the grocery store. He had been forceful with her, stating that she appeared lost, and demanded that she follow him so he could take her to a police station.

"You have to trust your gut, mo stóirín. If that man made you feel funny, you listen to that feeling and you get the hell away. I don't care if you have

to kick, bite, or scream—you do what you have to to get somewhere safe."

Using her mother's voice as a motivator, she mustered up the last of her energy and shook his hand off her. She headed over to Gage, keeping her full attention on staying upright even though she felt as if she were on a boat in a storm. His blond hair appeared to be glowing like a halo due to the blurriness that was happening with her vision.

As she got closer, Gage looked up and raised an eyebrow at the film of glitter that was covering her front half. "What did you do in there? Make out with Tinker Bell?"

The weakness was becoming too strong and she fell to her knees as she continued to crawl her way over to him. She propped herself up on his chair and looked at him with pure panic in her eyes.

"Gage, I wanna go…I don't feel good. I'm scared, please take me home." She leaned her face against his knee. "Please," she whispered as she focused on taking deep breaths.

She was determined not to pass out, but the black stars on the edge of her vision were taking over and Gage's hand that came to rest on the top of her head felt so warm and comforting. She could hear people talking, but couldn't understand what they were saying as she slipped into unconsciousness.

Gage

Anger and panic at not knowing how to help her were rolling beneath his calm exterior as a man in a white suit approached them, wringing his hands together. Willow's eyes slipped closed and he could tell at the weight of her head on his lap that she'd passed out.

"Hi, I'm so sorry about this. My girlfriend had a little bit too much to drink tonight. I really need to get her out of here and take her home."

"She's your girlfriend, huh?" He asked, not releasing the hand that was entangled in her hair.

"Yup, she's not really a drinker, as you can probably tell. So, let me just help her up here and we'll be out of your way, sir." He reached out to grab her, but Gage didn't move.

"What's her name?"

The man paused as he tried to recall it. He shifted his gaze away from Gage.

Gage grew deadly still, like a predator preparing to pounce. "You don't know your own girlfriend's name?"

"Kim, her name is Kim. Now if you would please let me take her-"

"Kim, huh? That's odd, I could have sworn her name was Willow. And I could have sworn she came to this club with me, not you."

Thomas's face blanched and he chuckled in a high-pitched voice. "I'm so sorry, I didn't know she was taken, since she was making moves on me and flirting. You two have a nice night."

He tried to wave goodbye and retreat into the club, only to be stopped by Nikolas. He had moved with feline grace as he quickly stood up from his chair and slinked behind Thomas.

"What do you think, boss?" Nikolas gave a wide smile that displayed a full set of straight white teeth, with two fangs glistening in the moonlight.

"I'm thinking it's a shame our little friend here was about to leave before we could invite him to our after-party in the alley." Gage reflected a similar smile.

"Oh no, friend!" Nikolas slapped the shaking man on the shoulder and dug his nails into his skin. "You can't miss that, that's going to be the best part of the whole night. Tell you what, you can be our guest of honor!"

Thomas's Adam's apple bobbed in his throat. "No, I really should be going. I need to go check into my hotel room since I need to be up early tomorrow for something. Thanks for the offer, but I'll have to take a rain check."

He tried to walk around Nikolas, but Nikolas' grip on his shoulder never let up. Robby walked out to the patio and looked at the death grip Nikolas had on the man. Gage nodded his head toward his cousin, summoning him over to join the fun they would soon be having.

"Oh, what's this? Are we planning an after-party?" Robby's face lit up. He put his beer down on one of the patio tables, abandoning it for the other type of drink they would soon be consuming.

"You two are, I'm afraid I'm going to have to pass and get this thing home." Gage lifted Willow's ponytail and dropped it back down. She didn't even twitch at the motion.

"Speaking of going home," the man began his sentence, but was quickly shut down by Nikolas' glare.

"Robby, did you drive your bike or the Mustang tonight?"

"Do you need to use my car?" Robby asked, already getting the keys out of his back pocket.

Gage sighed. "I can't believe I'm trusting you with my bike, but yes. Can we swap rides for the night?"

"Anything for you, cuz!" Robby's vicious smile grew inhumanly large. Gage never trusted anyone with his most cherished possession, but tonight he was entrusting it to his cousin since there was no way he was going to be able to put Willow on the back of his bike.

Gage picked Willow up bridal-style and followed the boys out of the patio gate while they shuffled a sweaty and panicked Thomas between them. He was babbling about paying them money and finding them an endless supply of beautiful women for them to kill in exchange for his life.

"Hey Nikolas?" Gage paused and looked over his shoulders. "Make sure it hurts, yeah?"

Nikolas nodded and reached up quickly, tearing off the man's nose. "I'll tear him apart piece by piece, just for you."

The man stared at his nose in Nikolas's hand as the gaping hole in the middle of his face began pouring blood. As Gage carried Willow to the blue Mustang that was inconveniently parked in the very back of the parking lot, he heard the beautiful sound of the man's screams floating through the midnight air.

ↄↄↄↄ

Gage gently placed Willow on her back in his bed and observed her sleeping form. He could have easily texted his father for her address, since he was the one who'd found her the apartment, but he couldn't resist having her close to him tonight. He felt like he was truly going mad now.

She looked so peaceful and happy, even though she had barely escaped a traumatizing night. Part of him wondered if she looked this way due to passing out near him, knowing he would keep her safe. The thought brought a comforting warmness.

The thought of the potential rapist ignited his fury again, but it soon dissolved when he looked at the smooth, white skin the triangular hole in her dress exposed. It was the same section of skin he had noticed at the beach, the part of her his fangs were aching to mark. He wanted his bite there, not only to signal to other vampires that she was not food, but to prove that she belonged to him and only him.

The thought crossed his mind that he could bite her right now and she wouldn't feel a thing with how drugged she was, but then how would he explain where the mark came from? He could blame the white suit and she would have no reason to not believe him, since she had passed out so early in the night, but he didn't want her to think that she had been raped, either.

He gently passed his fingertips over her exposed skin, and a lightening bolt of desire ran through him at how soft and warm she was. He placed his palm flat against her and felt the rising of her chest as she took deep, peaceful breaths while she made her way through whatever dream she was having.

She moaned slightly and rolled over onto her side, grabbing the pillow that was next to her and snuggling it against her face. He decided to think of that as a moan of pleasure as she dreamt about him, and left her to her fantasy.

Eleven

Willow

Willow woke up disoriented, with cotton mouth and a pounding headache. She looked at the clock next to her bed that read 5:00 pm. She tried to recall her night, but was distracted by the black-and-gold comforter she was tucked under. Her comforter was covered in blue paisley.

The room was decorated in a dark color scheme with a Victorian era flair. There was an ornate bookcase across the room full of dusty, leather-bound books, and a matching loveseat at the base of the bed. The flooring was dark oak with a red-and-gold oriental rug taking up half of the room and black drapes hung from the large bay window to her left, concealing the darkening sky behind it.

This was not her cheap, little bedroom.

"What the hell?" She whispered to herself as she looked around the large room.

She slipped out of the bed quietly and padded over to the door. She heard rustling behind her and spun around to see a man curled up in a ball on the loveseat. He had a thin blanket thrown over him with no pillow, and looked extremely uncomfortable.

"Gage?" She spoke in a loud voice, hoping to wake him from his restless sleep, but he did not move.

She coughed, trying to clear her throat, but all it did was worsen her dry mouth. "Gage?"

He uncurled himself and slowly sat up, looking as disheveled as she felt.

"What time is it?" He croaked.

"It's five at night, how long have I been sleeping? And where am I?" She croaked back. She swallowed, trying to rid herself of the disgusting taste in her mouth. "Is there water somewhere?"

He yawned and ran his hand through his messy hair before stretching. His black t-shirt rose up as he lifted his arms above his head to reveal a sliver of skin. Willow looked away, feeling even more uncomfortable with the situation.

"In the kitchen. Follow me." He sighed and stood up slowly, sounding like an elderly man struggling to get out of bed. "Why did you have to wake me up so early?'

Willow didn't want to argue with him that five p.m. was the opposite of waking up early, so she followed behind him without saying anything. She stuck close to him as he led her through a hallway that felt more like a museum than anything else. Oil paintings of bloody war scenes hung from the walls, and a sapphire-blue floor runner trailed down the oak hallway, leading them to a flight of stairs.

Gage seemed to glide down them and she struggled to keep up with him. She was weak and shaky, and desperately craved something to drink. It wasn't until her feet touched the cold marble flooring that she realized her heels were missing.

"Where are my shoes?"

"I threw them on the floor by the bed."

"You took off my shoes?"

"Sorry, I didn't realize you wanted to sleep in those stilts. I thought it was a safety hazard. I couldn't have my guest stabbing herself in her sleep."

She was taken aback by the simple, thoughtful gesture. Not once would her ex-boyfriend have ever thought to do something like that. Her comfort had been the least of his worries.

They turned a corner and entered a kitchen flooded in the setting sunlight.

"Oh shit!" He quickly retreated around the corner. "I forgot to close the blinds last night. Be a doll and shut them for me, will you? It's giving me a headache."

Willow found his extreme reaction odd, but the light was also increasing the pounding in *her* head. Once she followed his command, he came back in and grabbed a crystal glass from a cabinet to fill with water. It only took her a few seconds to down the whole glass after he handed it to her.

"What the hell happened last night? The last thing I remember was seeing Marla with Matteo and…" She trailed off, remembering the guy who had bought her a drink. "I must have been way too drunk. I've never been blackout drunk before. Please tell me I did not embarrass myself."

Gage leaned against the granite island that was in the middle of the room and watched as Willow covered her face with her hand. She was silently pleading that she did not swing from the ceiling screaming *Wonder Wall* lyrics.

"Oh, you definitely embarrassed yourself," he grinned. "You came to me for help. That's pretty embarrassing."

Willow peeked at him from around her fingers. "Why would I go to you for help?"

"You really don't remember anything?"

"No, I really don't."

"I'm pretty sure you were drugged and almost raped, but thankfully your knight in shining armor was there." He pointed to himself, widening his grin.

"What?" She slid her hand down her face and stared at him in horror. "That's really not funny and inappropriate to joke about. What the hell do you mean I was drugged and almost raped?"

"Chill, I'm not joking. Some guy said your name was Kim and he was trying to take you home while you were unconscious on the floor. Don't worry, I made sure nothing happened, and he's been taken care of."

"Did you call the police?"

"I said he was taken care of." Gage stood up and retrieved her glass to refill it with water. He dug around in a drawer and handed her a bottle of aspirin along with the refilled glass.

"Thanks," she mumbled, yet again thrown off by a thoughtful gesture. "Is this your house? How did you get me here?"

"You sure are full of questions today."

"Well excuse me for trying to fill in the blanks. It's not like my memory was impaired or anything," she snapped.

"I let you use my bed for the night and get a kink in my back from squeezing myself onto that tiny couch, and this is the attitude I have to deal with? Yeah, this is my house and I brought you here in Robby's car. Which reminds me, he has my bike." Gage pulled out his phone from his back pocket and swiftly started texting.

She felt her face redden, so she kept her head down and stared at the bottle of pills she rolled around in her hands as she pushed herself to apologize. "I'm sorry. I don't feel good. Something like this has never happened to me before and I'm not the nicest person when I'm confused. Nothing bad happened to me, right? I mean, besides the drug part?"

"You don't believe me?" His tone wasn't unkind, but more hurt.

Willow bit her lip as she thought over his question. She had heard it before in a nastier tone when her ex-boyfriend would gaslight her. This time, coming from Gage's voice, a part of her wanted to believe him. Clay had proven himself to be a kind individual, so wouldn't his son have some of those traits? Her delayed answer caused him to look up from his phone.

"I guess I don't really know you well enough to answer that, but for the sake of my sanity I'm going to believe you. Can you take me home now, please? I really appreciate everything, but I want to take a shower and curl up in my own bed for a while before work."

"Let me take a shower really quick and we can go. I need to get the smell of cigarettes and beer off me before I puke. Clubs are not my scene."

"Then why did you go?"

He shrugged. "I was bored."

He started to walk out of the kitchen and she followed behind. Halfway to the stairway he turned and looked at her. "Are you going to take a shower with me?"

"Oh! No, I'm sorry. I guess I can wait for you here." She quickly returned to her spot back in the kitchen.

It was not long before she grew bored and began to explore her surroundings. She felt odd being here. A few weeks ago he was only her customer, a rude one at that, and now she was wandering around his extravagant home. Being in someone's home was like being in their mind—it revealed a lot about who they were. And from what she could see, he had a *very* interesting mind.

Everywhere she looked there were oil paintings depicting dark and gloomy scenes, or portraits of people long since deceased. One of the portraits was of Marie Antoinette—after her beheading. Willow frowned at the detached head of the Queen. Blood had been painted dripping from the stem of her neck, her eyes were cloudy with a glazed expression, and her tongue was bloated and sticking out of her mouth. The attention to detail was so good, it made her feel nauseous. She stepped closer to see that the bottom corner of the painting was signed with the single letter G.

She continued her exploration and came across a door that was partially opened. She knew it was wrong, but her curiosity would not let her ignore it, so she pushed it open and stepped inside to find a room full of drawings. Most were half-done sketches of wilderness scenes, but in the corner of the room was a painting of a beach scene painted in hues of black and purple. As she approached it, she noticed the silhouette of a woman standing in the ocean.

"Holy hell!" Something brushed up against her leg, but she stopped herself from kicking it when she looked down and saw a fluffy white cat wrapped around her feet.

"Hi there! You scared me." She bent down to pet the fluffy creature. "You must be Buffy."

The cat purred in response and rolled over onto her back, allowing Willow to pet her soft belly.

The smell of mahogany and black teakwood filled the room as Gage walked in on the two. "What a fucking slut."

Willow looked up at him, reveling in the pride of having his cat like her, but was thrown off by the fact that he was shirtless. He was wearing low-cut black jeans with the black-and-gray waistband of his underwear peeking over the edge. She let her eyes linger on the trail of dark blond hair that led from his belly button to the top of his pants before snapping her attention back to Buffy.

"She usually hates people. You must have bribed her with a treat or something," he said as he grabbed a t-shirt with Clay's rental company logo off the back of a chair.

"Or maybe she just likes me." Willow gave Buffy a few more pats on her tummy before standing up. "Is this all your artwork? It's amazing."

He looked down and picked some cat fur off his shirt, avoiding all eye contact with her as he ignored her question. "Listen, I have to pick up my bike before I drop you off. I don't trust Robby with it for much longer and I have to get to work soon. Have you ever ridden on a bike before?"

"Nope."

"Okay, well there's a first time for everything. Just know that if you fall off I'm not coming back for you." He headed out of the room not waiting for her to catch up.

"Hold on! Can I at least get my shoes?"

"Make it quick."

She was positive he would leave her here if she took too long, so she quickly ran up the stairs, gritting her teeth against the pounding in her head. She was breathing heavily by the time she slipped into the Mustang idling outside.

She did a double take when she looked behind her and noticed that his house was more of a mansion. While inside, it did not seem as massive, but she realized she had barely seen a third of it.

She couldn't believe someone so young could own a place so extravagant. "Is that your place, or Clay's?"

"Technically Clay's, but he lets us live here."

"Us? Who else lives with you?"

"Matteo, Horatio, and Nikolas."

She nodded and they fell into a comfortable silence. She wanted to know more about him, but between the headache and leftover fogginess from the drug, she decided to listen to the music and not talk. She had to admit, his playlist was not bad. Most of it was 80's metal songs with a few current ones thrown in.

They approached a neighborhood made up of brick townhomes. The streets were made of matching brick with streetlights that looked like antique gaslights. They pulled up next to one that had a motorcycle parked in front, and both climbed out of the car.

"Wait here, I'm going to swap keys really quick."

She watched him stalk up the set of stairs and open the red-painted door. She noticed the curtains in the front window stir and Robby's head popped up between them as he waved to her vigorously. She waved back, but his head jerked out of the window, almost like someone had pulled him backward.

She chuckled and eyed the motorcycle next to her. It was a matte black Yamaha Bolt with intricate glossy black flames decorating the tank. It was a subtle detail you had to be close enough to notice. The back seat was small, with no backrest and she was certain her blood pressure would rise as soon as she sat on the back.

She also wondered how she was going to manage sitting on the bike with the tight dress she had on.

"Do you trust me not to kill you?" Gage whispered in her ear.

He had snuck up behind her quietly, his body mere centimeters from hers. A chill ran down her spine and she involuntarily took a step forward to distance herself.

"Can you promise me not to drive like an asshole?"

"I guess I can be on my best behavior. Get on." He swung his leg over the bike and held out his hand to help her on the back.

She followed his cue and took his hand, using her other one to keep her dress down as she straddled the leather seat. Luckily, her dress was tight enough that she wouldn't have to worry about it flying up, and she fit against him snugly so that she wasn't flashing anyone.

She told him her address and he started the bike and jerked forward, causing her to grab him around the waist. She noticed his cocky grin in the mirror.

"I thought you were going to be on your best behavior?" She mumbled.

"I am."

Contrary to what she had been expecting, Gage ended up being a decent driver. After a few minutes, she was able to loosen the death grip she had around his chest and enjoyed the ride. There was something exhilarating about the wind blowing through her already-tangled hair.

She was a little bit disappointed as he pulled into her parking lot and propped his bike up on the kickstand. He turned to look at her and she could feel butterflies causing havoc in her stomach.

"Are you getting off?"

She felt her face flush. "Oh, yeah."

She slid off the back and stood next to him, looking down at her heels as she toyed with the belly button ring she could feel under her dress. He didn't make any movement like he was about to leave, so she looked up to find him looking at the opening in her dress underneath her breasts. When he looked up, his eyes were lustful.

A shiver went down her spine.

"Thanks for everything. Next time you stop in at the Coffee House Bunny, your drink is on me."

She started to walk away, but his quiet, rough voice caused her to pause. "Hey, Willow?"

"Yeah?"

"What are you doing next Sunday?"

"Nothing, why?"

"Do you maybe want to grab dinner?"

She thought about it for a second. His eyes grew hard at her silence, so she smiled to reassure him.

"Sure."

Twelve

Gage

Gage couldn't believe that he asked Willow to dinner. It went against everything he had been saying: he wasn't the dating type. But he felt like a man possessed as he watched her stand next to him awkwardly like a teenager on her first date. He couldn't think in the moment—all he knew was that he wanted to see her again, and not behind the counter at her coffee house. So he asked her on a date.

Curse that fucking dress.

He didn't curse the fact that he had to play hero, though. There was something satisfying about breaking stereotypical ideals of vampires, and the fact that he'd saved a pretty girl fulfilled his age-old desire of being a knight in shining armor. Only he preferred black leather, and to ride in on a bike.

The next few nights dragged on, with Sunday feeling like it was a lifetime away. He wanted to join his boys at the Coffee House Bunny, but he also wasn't sure if he could face her in front of them. He felt that they would be able to tell that something was up, and the last thing he wanted was their harassment over his love life.

By the third night he felt like he was going to go insane.

He decided to go hunting in hopes that a fresh kill would ease whatever the hell was stirring in him. Gage pulled into Cass Corridor, a neighborhood well-known for how dangerous it was. This was the boys' prime hunting place since most of it was filled with registered sex-offenders, abusive substance users, and sex workers willing to sell some blood. The sad reality was that the police did not care what happened here.

He parked his bike under a maple tree that was slowly dying outside of a burned-down home. He tried to see if there were any people staying inside the boarded-up brick building, but only found the remains of a fast food dinner and used needles. He proceeded to walk the streets, hoping to find one desperate junkie out looking for a fix.

He ignored the part of him that was begging to turn around and go home. No matter how long he had been hunting humans, there was still that small voice inside that berated him. People with addictions were just like him, looking for the next high to calm that drive within them just as he was looking for fresh blood to quench his thirst.

"Motherfucker," he sighed, and kicked a rock that was on the sidewalk.

That voice was going to win tonight. It wasn't often that he let it win, but tonight it had the advantage with his emotions roiling over Willow. He could go a few more nights without blood.

Gage paused his stroll and turned to a bush where the sound of crying was quietly emanating from it. He came around the other side to reveal a small girl, only about five years old, huddled up among the dirt and leaves. His stomach dropped. It was odd to see a young child out this late at night.

"You good, little one?"

Without responding, she tucked her head in between her knees which were pulled up against her chest, trying her best to turn invisible.

"Hey, are you okay?" He asked again.

Slowly, the girl lifted up her head, but still didn't respond.

"If you need help or something, I can get that for you."

"My sissy... I don't want daddy to hurt her no more," the girl mumbled.

"Where is she?"

The girl pointed behind her to a two-story house that was dark except for one glowing window upstairs. Gage stood up and decided to take a peek around the house to see if he could find where the little girl had escaped from. The back door was unlocked, and he found it easy to slip inside as there were no dogs to alert the homeowner of his presence. He heard groaning and muffled crying coming down the stairs into the living room.

He slithered up the stairs, being careful to avoid any creaking steps, and paused at the top. He quickly slipped around the corner when he heard the groaning stop, and then heavy footsteps made their way to the bathroom. The shower turned on and he risked a peak around the corner to find the hallway dark and empty.

On the way to the bathroom, he passed the room the groaning had been coming from and saw a teenage girl curled up on her bed, crying softer now than she had been.

His adrenaline began pulsing through his veins as he approached the bathroom door.

He loved this part of the hunt.

He heard some faint whistling, like the monster was proud of what he did. An evil smile curled Gage's lips as he let *his* inner monster out.

He swiftly closed the bathroom door behind him and felt the humidity of the running shower begin to dampen his clothes. His mouth began to water and his teeth ached as he stepped closer to the shower, anticipating the metallic blood that would soon be running down his chin. The best part was that the monster didn't even know there was a bigger, badder monster on the other side of the thin shower curtain.

The shock made the blood so much sweeter. Gage made sure to cover the man's mouth with his hand when he ripped open the curtain to reveal his naked prize. The man's scream was muffled as Gage sank his teeth into his hairy shoulder. He ripped off a piece of the man's flesh and watched as bright-red blood began to pour down his back.

"You should really learn to lock your doors, you never know what might creep in at night," Gage whispered.

The man shifted his eyes to look at the creature that had a death grip on him. Gage thought about prolonging the kill, but decided a quick ending was better. He didn't want to make too much noise to scare the already traumatized girls. He bit into the man's neck this time, creating a large gash he could easily drink from. Within a matter of minutes, the man was dead and Gage was satisfied.

He propped the man so it looked like he had died from a slip in the shower. He knew the ripped skin and lack of blood would be suspicious to the police, but he highly doubted they would look any further into it. Especially once the man's daughter told them what he had been doing to her. It helped that some on the force were vampires themselves and followed the rules of hunting set by Clay.

After feeding, Gage always felt a high of excitement. It was times like these when he realized that killing wasn't so bad, as long as he killed the right ones. He could easily continue living his life, destroying one sack of shit at a time.

ↄↃↄↄ

Gage sat in his darkened truck, wearing sunglasses even though the sun was setting and he had the darkest tint possible covering his windows. He usually didn't leave his house until the sun was fully set, but he wanted to see Willow before she left for work. And now he knew where she lived.

He was parked in a gas station's parking lot, nestled up against the building so anyone passing by would assume it was the clerk's car. He was at the perfect angle to watch the TV flicker inside her apartment next door.

It took some trial and error for him to find the right balcony since he had not been inside to find where exactly her apartment was located. He shuddered at the memory of the naked old woman he'd accidentally spied on earlier. He was not certain why she was sitting in her living room butt-ass naked, but he was not about to continue watching to find out.

He was a little disappointed to find Willow was the complete opposite. She was fully clothed in pajama shorts and a t-shirt with a blanket partially covering her legs.

He wasn't being a total creep. Clay had requested he check in on her since Waldo had been officially spotted in their territory last night. He just didn't clarify if he was supposed to check in on her at home or work.

Waldo had come into the casino and played a few rounds of blackjack for no other apparent reason than to taunt them. By the time Clay had arrived, he was long gone with no hint as to where he went other than telling the dealer he was heading north. But north could be anywhere from Georgia to Canada.

No one was sure why Waldo kept appearing on their territory, and it had everyone on edge. Even Uncle Al, who was the head of the Daytona territory, felt uneasy. Not only was he concerned because he and Clay brothers, but any time a neighboring territory was under attack, the closest leaders were expected to help out. It helped keep local families on good terms with each other, and most vampires had abided by that unwritten rule for centuries.

Gage watched as Willow went to the kitchen and returned with a bowl of popcorn. She flopped down on her couch in the most unattractive way possible, with her feet propped on her coffee table, her knees wide apart, and the bowl resting on her scrunched stomach.

She made it look adorable.

He paused at her knees, wondering what it would be like to be in between them. Or what it would be like to bite her during sex and taste her blood, which smelled so sweet. Venice sometimes would let him do that right as they were climaxing. There was nothing better than her blood gushing into his mouth at the same time his cock was gushing into her.

His thoughts were pulled from his fantasies when Willow stood up and walked onto her balcony. She was looking out into the distance, and he grew nervous that she would recognize his truck from the few times he'd driven it to the café.

Luck was on his side as she stretched her arms above her head, her breasts moving in a way that made him realize she was not wearing a bra. She bent over and let her arms hang loosely from her shoulders. He knew in the way she was positioned those little shorts would not be covering much.

She slowly bent back up in a fluid movement. She wasn't doing anything overly sexual, but the way she was moving had him transfixed. She was slow and methodical, probably paying attention to every muscle in her body. He wanted her on top of him, moving that way as she rode him.

As soon as he started to get hard, she turned around and went back inside her apartment. He was about to leave, but she reappeared before he could start the truck's engine. She rolled out a thin mat and bent over again into the only yoga position he knew—downward dog. This time, he could see the side profile of her round ass cheeks.

Gage slid down in his seat, debating if he wanted to pull out his dick to start stroking it. The only thing holding him back was that he was in a public parking lot and the last thing he wanted was a cop to come knocking on his window. He could handle the ticket, but wouldn't be able to live with the humiliation his boys would surely bring him if they found out he was put on a registry. So he kept his dick in his pants even though it was straining against the zipper.

But Willow certainly wasn't making this easy for him. She slid her body to the ground sensually and arched her back so her stomach was lying flush to the wood and her face was pointing to the sky. He imagined her bare back from the night on the beach and running his hand down her soft skin. Then he imagined himself grabbing those plump cheeks and smashing his face between them, knowing that her arousal would taste as sweet as her blood.

She lifted herself off the ground and folded her knees under herself, placing her forehead against the mat. Gage bit his finger, drawing blood, hoping that the metallic flavor would distract him from the uncomfortable pressure in his jeans. It worked for a second, until she was on her hands and knees squirming her body like she was a cat in heat. She arched her back, then wiggled her ass as she slowly curved her stomach to the ground. She did this a few times in a row, almost like she was putting on a show for someone.

By now, Gage's whole body was throbbing. He took the risk and slipped his cock out of his pants to run his hands up and down the firm structure as she continued her writhing. He spit in his hand, wishing more than anything that it was her own saliva he was using to slicken his length. His pace matched her fluid contortions and he tightened his grip.

He felt the tension build in himself as she returned to that sexy downward dog position, this time lifting up a leg to reveal her sex to the sky. Her shorts covered her slit, but exposed her lips and he came as he envisioned himself coming up behind her and slamming himself into her warm folds.

He was breathing heavy as she toppled over onto her side. They both laughed at the same time, but Gage was quick to quiet his. He felt a warmth come over him after his orgasm, instead of the normal satisfied, yet cold, feeling he normally felt.

He groaned as he accidentally wiped his hand through the cum on his steering wheel. There was no way in hell he would be able to walk into the café tonight and make eye contact with her after what he just did. He texted Matteo and Horatio to have them check in on her and pick him up a coffee.

Thirteen

Willow

"So when are you going to start serving muffins? I could really use some carbs right now," John asked as he and Ryan finished the last of their coffees. The night was busy, so she had not been able to talk to them much, but it had finally seemed to plateau.

"That's funny you bring that up, because serving baked goods has been in the back of my mind lately. I don't have the time to bake or look for a supplier, though. I would love to support a local bakery and sell their items, but I also want to make my own, so I guess I first have to decide on that."

"There used to be a bakery down the street from here, but the owner went missing and his family closed it up. The news said he had mental health issues, but I think he was killed. A lot of good people have been dying recently." The corners of John's mouth turned down and he made an expression like he smelled something rotten.

"That's so sad, it seems like it's always the good ones whose lives end way too soon." She grabbed a rag and wiped up some sticky spots.

"That's why I want you to stay safe and watch yourself with those four men that come in here. I think they have something to do with it, though they act like they don't. It's all a sham."

She stopped cleaning and looked up at him. "Why would they kill innocent people?"

"For fun. We have to get back, see you later Willow." He stood up and pushed his cup toward her. Ryan mirrored his actions and the two left Willow with her thoughts.

Something was weird here. Back in Detroit there were always murders and violence that was blamed on gangs, but here all of that seemed to be blamed on something else. She felt like John blamed Clay and the others because they were rich, and probably powerful from owning so much of the city. There was no way she could picture any of them murdering people for fun, though.

But she had been wrong about men before.

If Clay or Gage turned out to be cold-blooded killers, she didn't know what she would do. They were her last hope of rebuilding her trust in not only men, but in herself as well. Her instincts had been wrong with her ex-boyfriend and she'd paid a terrible price for that. Self-doubt could be a damaging, isolating thing.

Like they knew she was thinking of them, Horatio and Matteo walked through her door. "Hello Matteo." Willow gave him a tight smile.

"What? No hello for me?" Horatio pouted.

She turned to him and gave him a much more pleasant smile. "Hello Horatio. Are you having your usual?"

"Yes, ma'am."

She began making one drink, completely ignoring Matteo. She had heard from Marla the other night and was disappointed, yet not surprised, that she and Matteo turned into a one-night stand. Marla even texted him the next night, but never got a response. She had gushed to Willow about her leg-shaking orgasm, but couldn't hide the hurt tone that was in her voice.

Matteo raised an eyebrow. "Do I get a drink?"

"Nope. What are you up to tonight, Horatio?"

Horatio glanced at his brother and tried to hide his amused smile. "Literally nothing. Sammy's working at the marina and I'm so tired of hanging out all night with this asshole—" he motioned toward his brother "—so I'm planning on parking my butt on the sofa to binge watch some 90's sitcoms. I wasn't even planning on coming here, but Gage asked us to."

Willow paused mid-stir. "Why didn't he just come here himself? He hasn't been here in a while."

Horatio shrugged. "He said he was busy installing some security system at a rental and didn't have time to stop by to pick up a coffee, so he sent us to get him one."

"Technically, he just sent Horatio, but I was bored and decided to tag along," Matteo added.

Willow decided to bring up the topic that was sitting on the tip of her tongue. "Are you sure you didn't stop by to see if Marla was here?"

Matteo looked down and began fidgeting with a straw wrapper that was left on the counter. "Ah, so that's what the cold shoulder is about. I didn't mean to lead her on, I thought we were on the same page about it being a one-time thing."

"You clearly knew she had a crush on you, and still you slept with her with no intention of anything else. You're a slimeball." She slammed Horatio's drink down in front of him and noticed that he seemed to be enjoying watching his brother get scolded.

"I am not!"

"Are too. But I suppose it's for the best, because she deserves someone that will treat her like a princess."

"Oh my god, if I message her back will you like me again? I don't like it when you're mean to me."

Willow pursed her lips and stared at him. She wanted Marla to be happy, and for Matteo to actually get to know her beyond the bedroom, but she was worried he would lead her on again. "If you promise to only have a conversation with her and not use her for sex."

"What am I supposed to converse with her about? Can't I apologize and leave it at that?"

"You can talk about your weird anime obsession," Horatio mumbled.

Willow clapped her hands together. "She loves anime! She's watching one right now about vampires."

Matteo rolled his eyes. "I hate vampire ones, they're so unrealistic."

"Very funny. I'm sure there's others that you have both watched. That's the point of a conversation, to discover stuff like that. If it ends up that you two have absolutely nothing in common, then go your separate ways. But at least give her a chance."

"Fine. Can I have a coffee now?"

Willow nodded and began making his usual. "What is the rich brat going to drink tonight?"

"He would drink whatever you made him. At this point I don't think he comes here for the coffee," Horatio answered.

Willow's face flushed. Before she could ask what he meant by that, the two boys tensed as a male customer walked in.

He was a short man sporting a light-brown buzz cut, with a neck too long for his spray-tanned body and arms too muscular to be natural. His face was small and weasel-like, which would have been adorable on a nerdy tech guy like John or Ryan, but did not fit the gym-rat aesthetic this man was displaying. He strutted up to the counter and flashed a brilliant white smile with abnormally long canines at Willow, completely ignoring the two men that were already standing there.

"Well hello there gorgeous, how is the night treating you?"

Willow held back a sneeze at the overpowering scent of his spicey cologne and put on her best customer service smile. "Hello, it's been pretty good. How has yours been?"

"It's been good, but I'm sure it's about to get better after I have one of your coffees. I've heard nothing but good things about your café, so I decided to make a trip over here."

"This is a pretty far drive from Miami just for a cup of coffee," Horatio stated.

Willow turned to see the brothers giving identical death stares, and a pit of fear blossomed in her stomach. Their eyes were dark, their lips set in a hard line, and they didn't feel like the two goofy brothers she was used to. They felt dangerous.

The man, however, continued to look at her with a smile on his face. "I've had some business up here. I'm so glad I stopped in. You have to be the prettiest girl I've seen in a while. The name's Jesse James, by the way."

She took his outstretched hand and shook it. This was turning into such an odd encounter, which grew even odder when he leaned forward and took a loose strand of her hair, wrapping it through his fingers.

"You smell delicious."

Horatio grabbed him by the wrist and ripped her hair out of his hand. He had moved so fast, Willow barely had time to flinch at the movement.

"I don't know what business you have here in Vista Maria, *Waldo,* but it's probably best that you end it and get the fuck out of our territory."

He growled, "My business is none of your concern, now let me go."

Willow interrupted the two when she saw Horatio dig his nails into the guy's wrist to the point blood trickled down his arm. "Yeah, I'm going to put a stop to this before you guys end up in a fight."

Her breath caught in her throat when Horatio turned his death stare on to her. It was like he snapped out of a trance with his eyes losing his hard glare and a sheepish grin sprouting across his face.

"Sorry, Willow." He threw the man's hand down and picked up his coffee. "I just really don't like it when people cut in line. Can you make Gage whatever he had last time?"

"I'll come back another night when these brutes are not here." Waldo winked at Willow. "You enjoy the rest of your night, sweetheart."

"The fuck you will," Matteo growled. "You're not welcome here, and if we catch you here again, you'll regret it."

Waldo rolled his eyes. "Yeah, sure." He turned away and disappeared into the night.

Once he was gone, Willow looked at the two boys with raised eyebrows. "Are you two going to tell me what that was all about?"

"I think Gage should be the one to tell you. I will say that 'Jesse James'—" Matteo made a face and used air quotes "—is not his real name. It's Waldo. Make sure you're never alone with him."

"You know, someone else told me to never be alone with you guys. I'm starting to think I need to pack up and move to a different city. Stuff is getting weird here."

Horatio stuck out his bottom lip. "Aw, but we would miss you. You can't leave us! Who would make our coffee this late at night?"

"You know you can buy a Keurig and some flavors and make it yourself, right?"

Matteo scoffed. "It's not the same. You add that special little touch that makes it so much sweeter."

Willow felt herself grow more at ease now that the brothers were back to their normal selves. While waiting for the milk to steam for Gage's drink, she doodled a picture of a floppy eared bunny and a cat that looked more like a cloud than a feline on his cup.

She thought back to the room full of intricate, well-done artwork in the mansion. Her scribbles were nowhere near as good as what she assumed were Gage's paintings, but she hoped they brought a small smile to him all the same.

The boys left and she continued on with her work, organizing her excess stock and making orders as customers came in. It was a few hours before closing and she was in the backroom, surrounded by empty boxes she was in the process of breaking down when she heard the bells on the door chime. When she walked up front her face automatically broke into a smile.

"I was wondering when you were going to stop in. I was beginning to think I scared you away."

"You are the least scary creature I know, I was just busy." Gage stuffed his hands in his pants pockets and took a casual stance at the counter.

"My boys told me that you got to meet the charming Waldo earlier. I figured I would stop by and make sure everything was okay here. He is not a good guy, Willow, and it makes me concerned that he seems to be interested in you."

She blushed and wondered if his concern stemmed more from jealousy than fear for her safety. "If it helps put you at ease, please know that he is not my type. In fact, I'm rather insulted you think I would be into his fake tan and steroid arms. I have better taste than that."

"Willow." He leaned forward and the rest of the café seemed to disappear as she focused on his face. "I don't want to talk about it here, but please understand that he is dangerous. I want you to stay away from him and to promise to call me if he ever comes back."

"I promise," she whispered.

He returned to his normal stance and broke the tension between them. "Speaking of being insulted, I showed Buffy the picture you drew of her and she wanted me to tell you she is not that fat."

Willow bit her lip. "Snickers thought I did an excellent job on the drawings and said they were very realistic. Next time I'll make her a little slimmer, though."

"She would appreciate that." He leaned against the counter, "We're still on for dinner Sunday, right?"

"Of course. I'm curious, where do you plan on taking me?"

"What's your favorite type of food?"

"Mexican. I heard there's a really good restaurant across the street from the yoga studio I go to. Would you want to go there?"

She noticed a small spark in his eyes at the mention of yoga. "Yeah, I'm good with that. Do you want me to pick you up on the bike or the truck?"

She grinned. "The bike."

"Hmm, so I guess I wasn't *that* bad of a driver then if you're willing to get back on it."

"No, you were pretty decent. I'll see you Sunday."

A small smile that she hadn't seen before on him snuck across his face. "Good night, Willow."

She liked the way he said her name. It made her tingle in all the right places. "Good night, Gage."

Fourteen

Willow

Willow spent more time on her outfit for tonight than she did when they were going to the club. She went with black skinny jeans, knee-high leather boots, and a leopard print V-neck. She wore minimalist gold jewelry and kept her hair in a braid down her back to prevent it from tangling in the wind. She was originally going to rock her Fran Fine outfit with a black mini skirt and fishnet stockings, but remembered the awkwardness of getting on the bike in her tight dress.

She stood outside her apartment complex, listening as the sound of the motorcycle engine drew closer in the night. She bounced on her feet as his headlight illuminated the full parking lot and came up beside her.

"It looks like you're ready to go," he said as he leaned his bike against the kickstand.

"I've been waiting all week for another ride, yeah I'm definitely ready to go."

She placed her hand on his shoulder and hopped onto the back, wrapping her arms around his waist. It was strange to her how naturally she fit against him.

She watched as Vista Maria sped past them, surprisingly large numbers of people still outside for almost nine p.m., wandering the street on their way home from dinner or work. That was the thing about Vista Maria, it never shut down no matter the time or day. It slowed down around midnight, but even then people were still out working or drinking at the numerous bars that lined the streets. It made her feel comfortable to be a part of a town that was so alive.

Just like last time, he proved himself to be a good driver. She didn't release her hold on him, though. Every time they would pull up to a red light, he would absentmindedly touch her knee, which sent an electric current through her body. She didn't want that feeling to stop, and was disappointed to find them pulling into the parking lot of the restaurant way too soon.

"Don't look so sad, we'll go for a longer ride after dinner." He helped her off the bike and they made their way into the restaurant. She noticed his hand twitch toward hers like he was going to hold it, but thought better of it at the last minute.

As soon as they sat at their table, Gage groaned as his phone vibrated in his pocket. He glanced at it, but whoever was calling was sent to his voicemail.

"Is it work related?" She asked.

"Probably, it was my dad. I don't have a set schedule, so he calls me whenever to assign me things."

"It sounds like we both don't have a great work-life balance. Do you at least like working with your dad?"

"Kind of. I see him a lot, maybe a little bit too much, and sometimes I feel like I'm the only one he talks to. If he's not calling me about a project, then he's calling to tell me about some stupid sale that's going on at the hardware store. I really need to get that man a girlfriend, he's lonely and needs someone to talk to who's not me."

She nodded. "I noticed your dad didn't have a wedding ring on. Where's your mom?"

He looked at her, a ghost of a smile playing on his lips. "What were you looking at his hand for? Are you interested? I can totally hook you two up."

"I'll pass. He's a little too old for me, don't you think?"

"No, you seem like the type to have a sugar daddy."

She was about to make a smart remark when she noticed the waitress who approached them. She flashed them a smile that caused Willow to do a double take. She swore it looked like the girl had fangs.

"Hi Gage, what can I get you two tonight?"

He looked at Willow and raised an eyebrow. "Are you a margarita or a beer girl?"

"Margarita, strawberry to be exact." Once the waitress left with their order, Willow turned her suspicious glare to him. "How does she know you?"

"My dad owns half the city, we're pretty well-known around here."

She thought about how Clay seemed to have so many connections, so much money, and so many enemies. Something clicked and Willow gasped.

"Oh my god, it all makes sense now. Why customers told me to stay away, why you have random beef with a dude from Miami, and why Matteo and Horatio referred to Vista Maria as their *territory*. You're not just a rich family, you're a *mafia* family."

Gage choked on his water. "Not quite. People hate us because of what we are. I think that's why my dad took such a liking to you— you came in with no expectations of us and treated us like any other person."

"I pride myself on being open-minded. It helps that you guys seem pretty down to earth, too. You don't live up to that stereotype of being evil, power-hungry villains that want to hoard money while other people suffer."

Gage nodded and played with an ice cube in his water. "Yeah, that's actually a rule my dad set, if a vampire wants to live in Vista Maria, then they have to contribute to the community in some way. Most help at homeless shelters, but some have started community gardens, donated to the library, or started local businesses like you."

Willow watched as he toyed with the ice cube, the frozen square bobbing up and down in the water. The condensation ran down the glass in almost slow motion as she processed his words. He seemed unaware of her shock, or that her mind was frozen on the word he'd just said. He looked up at her finally, his green eyes wide and curious.

"Is something wrong?"

"I'm sorry, but did you say if a *vampire* wants to live here?"

"Yes, we're not the only ones around here. There's quite a few, a lot of whom make up your customer base. I thought you knew? My dad told me you got the idea for a midnight coffee house because your ex worked the night shift. Was he not a vampire, too?"

Her voice came out in a shaky whisper. "No."

Sudden realization drifted across his face. "Oh, you're one of those that didn't know." He nodded his head slowly. "That makes sense, there are a lot fewer families in the Midwest than other places, but still, you traveled around a lot. You never knew about vampires or met any?"

"What are you talking about? No!" She shook her head violently, trying to clear the mixed emotions that were tumbling around. "No! What the hell do you mean? Of course I've never met a vampire, they're not real!"

"Last time I checked, I was pretty sure I was real." He lifted his lip to reveal a canine tooth that was more pointed than normal. Without even a wince, he pierced the tip of his finger and a needle point of blood bubbled up.

He dropped his lip and a sly grin formed. "Do you wanna try?"

"This isn't a joke, my whole world is turning upside down right now and you're asking me to poke your tooth?"

He shrugged, the grin not budging. "You could poke something else on me if you want."

"You better be glad that waitress didn't bring our drinks yet or else I would throw it in your face. Vampires are fairytales, made up in medieval times to explain why some decomposing bodies made noises or would sit up. They didn't know about gas or rigor mortis."

"Is that what they taught you in school?"

"If you're a vampire, then prove it."

"I thought I just did?"

She leaned across the table, anger taking over and making her bold. "Turn into a bat."

He barked a laugh. "We don't do that. Oh man, you really don't know anything about us, do you? Okay, let's restart. Hi, I'm Gage and I'll be your tour guide today as we go through Vampire Basics 101."

"Enough with the sarcasm."

"I'm sorry, I'm so amused though. I've never heard of someone accidentally going on a date with a vampire before. We've been coming into your shop for weeks now and nothing clued you in? You never noticed our fangs or the fact you only see us at night? Why did you think some people hated us?"

"Because you're rich! Everybody hates the rich."

The waitress arrived with their drinks and Willow put on her default customer service smile to place her order. Even though she didn't seem to understand anything anymore, she did know one thing: she was starving. And the least he could do after disrupting her whole life was buy her an enchilada.

The tone between them changed after the waitress left and reality settled over her. She was slowly coming to terms with the fact that there were real vampires out there, and she was sitting across the table from one. If he had wanted to hurt her, he'd had ample opportunities to do that already. Yet, he'd chosen to protect her. He'd worried for her safety at the music festival, rescued her from the rapist at the club, and even came back to check on her after Waldo. Didn't she say earlier that she was open-minded?

Her curiosity began to bubble to the surface and overwrite her anger. Not many people had the chance to sit down and interview a vampire, so she was going to take advantage of this situation. "So, is this like some new disease?"

All humor melted off his face and he looked like he was seriously thinking about that. "I guess it's kind of like a disease. I've never thought about it that way before, because to me it's always been a way of life. There was no other choice for me but to become one, since both my parents were vampires. It doesn't spread like an illness and it's not genetic. You must willingly choose to become one."

"People chose that?"

"You would be surprised how many people are interested in eternal youth. I don't say eternal life because we can still die. It's not like in the movies where the only way to kill one of us is with a stake through the heart. We can die in all sorts of ways. Burning, decapitation, drowning, explosions, etcetera. Speaking of movies, they don't portray us all that accurately. We can see ourselves in mirrors, we're not afraid of garlic, and," he narrowed his eyes at her, "we *don't* turn into bats. They do have it right that we can't go in the sun. We develop solar urticaria, where the sun gives us major migraines and a rash, but it won't kill us."

"So you, Horatio, Matteo, Nikolas, and Clay are all vampires. Who else?"

"Sammy recently turned, too. Vampires are sprinkled all around town. Pay attention to your customers better and see if you can find them. Most nurses and medical staff are not vampires, it can be too hard working around all that blood all the time."

"Next you're going to tell me zombies and werewolves are real."

He scoffed. "Now *those* are fairytales."

She took a bite of the steaming enchiladas that were placed before her, then peeked at the waitress who came over to deliver their food. Sure enough, those were fangs she saw in her smile. When she left, she decided to continue her interrogation.

"What are these rules you have to follow?"

"There are three main ones that are meant to keep everyone safe: don't prey on innocent people, don't add to the crime rate, and contribute to the community. These help keep the peace so humans don't have any reason to start killing us."

"Not many people like you guys, do they?"

"It's about 50/50, some like us and some hate us. The hate usually stems from fear and a lack of understanding."

"Isn't that where most hate comes from? That and an insane amount of stubbornness that keeps people close-minded."

"It's easier to be close-minded and full of hate than it is to change a belief you've held your whole life, particularly if it's a belief that society supports in media. We're shown as dangerous monsters that only care about killing humans, not as people who were once human and continue to live lives with the same human emotions and values. For them to understand that, they have to admit they were wrong and look at all the harmful, unjust things they have done in their life. That is painful, and one thing people try to avoid the most is pain, so they stay closed-minded, where it's nice, safe, and comfortable."

She looked up at him. "It's almost sad when you look at it that way. They keep themselves trapped in fear by not allowing themselves to feel pain and then growing from it."

"Yeah, but who likes to feel pain?" He whispered, more to himself than her. "Is it my turn to ask questions? I'm as curious about you as you are about me."

She cleared her throat, his blatant interest in knowing anything about her throwing her off. Not only was she going to have to get used to vampires, she was going to have to get used to a man who cared. "Sure."

"Why did you move away from Michigan?"

"That's a pretty deep question to ask."

"You started the deep questions by asking about my mom."

"Speaking of which, I noticed that you never answered me."

Gage shrugged. "I'm going to assume that you moved here to get away from something or someone."

"You're right, you caught me. I'm a felon." She paused, chewing on the side of her cheek, before giving him the true answer. "I did run away from someone. My ex-boyfriend was pretty horrible. I met him after my mom passed away from lung cancer. Well, the cancer didn't take her—she chose to end her life. The treatments didn't work, so she ended up committing suicide instead of slowly suffocating to death. She left me a note, rented a motel room, and took a bunch of pills. My mom was a very headstrong person and didn't want cancer to decide when she would die. That was her choice and I respect it, she was dying either way. But I hate that it happened.

"I stuck around for a little bit after, not really knowing what to do or where to go. I ended up selling the RV we lived in, which was how I met my ex. He worked at the auto lot that bought it. He was super sweet at first and was so supportive as I went through my grief. I fell in love way too quickly and moved in with him after he ended up getting a job in a factory in Detroit. I should have waited longer, then maybe I would have seen the real him. I never would have moved in with him if I knew how abusive and cruel he could be."

Gage frowned. "Don't blame yourself. I know how monsters work and it's a game to them. They lure you in at your most vulnerable. Has he tried to talk to you since you left?"

She shook her head and pushed a few stray pieces of rice around her plate. She felt lighter after having told him about some of her past, especially since he didn't seem to pity her or judge her for getting into an abusive relationship. But she wasn't ready to fully disclose all that happened the night she left.

"If you ever want me to take care of him…" He trailed off, raising an eyebrow.

"Don't worry, he won't be following me here. I told you about my mom, now tell me about yours."

"Besides being workaholics, we also have our mothers in common. My mom committed suicide, too. She wasn't sick, but not happy with how her life turned out I guess. It hurt like hell when it happened, but I also wasn't surprised since suicide is pretty common for our kind. Decades of killing people can start to add up."

The two sat in silence, both now pushing their food around the plates. She looked up at him, with his golden hair falling in his face etched with sadness. "Tell me something good so this doesn't turn out to be the most depressing date I've ever been on."

His mood shifted to something resembling hope, which was a new side to him she hadn't seen. She couldn't help smiling as his face broke into a boyish grin. "Me and Nikolas are finally opening our own custom motorcycle shop. That's been a goal of mine for a while now."

"Congrats! We'll have to celebrate your grand opening."

He pulled out his phone and showed her the blueprint of his future shop, along with some of the artwork he was going to use in his portfolio. His portraits of dark, emerald forests and cobalt mountains with smoke took her breath away.

"I really liked the unfinished painting in your room. It was a beach scene with the purple hues."

"You saw that?" A note of panic was in his voice.

"Yeah, it was probably the prettiest one there. It helped that I was in it." She grinned and stood up from the table, holding out her hand for him. "Are you almost done? I'm ready for another motorcycle ride."

His hand completely swallowed hers as it wrapped around protectively. "Damn princess, you're getting a little bit demanding now. I take it that means you're starting to feel more comfortable around me?"

"You seem pretty okay to me."

"Okay enough to hang out with again?"

"Yeah, I think tonight was tolerable enough that I could stand to do this again."

He laughed. "Sammy's throwing a party to celebrate her turning, so I was going to invite you. And before you even ask, Marla is also invited."

"That sounds like fun! Where is she having it, though? I don't know if I'm up for another club."

"Don't worry, it'll be at our house."

They left the restaurant walking side by side. Neither of them dropped their hands until they climbed on his bike.

Fifteen

Willow

Willow tied a bow around her middle with the strings from her dress and looked at herself in the mirror. Her dress was on the shorter side, stopping right above her knees and had a brightly colored pattern of sunflowers and bluebells. She had her hair up in a high ponytail and limited makeup on so as not to irritate her sunburn she accidentally received on her walk the previous day. She was getting tanner lately—the perks of moving to a sunny state.

Her intercom buzzed, alerting her that her friend had arrived. She ran downstairs and met Marla by her car. She wore red skinny jeans, black wedges, and a black long sleeved silk top. It was simple, but sexy.

"Look at you! Matteo won't be able to keep his hands off you again."

"Thanks, I figured I would wear these pants since they make my butt look good. Do you really think Matteo will still be interested in me? I haven't heard from him since the club, so I don't think he cares that much." Her tone grew sad. "I don't want to do another one-night stand, either."

She felt her eye twitch. Matteo had said he would text her, but clearly he was not a man of his word. That would be the last drink she ever made him.

"Maybe he's shy. Or stupid. Actually, he's probably both. Do you really want a shy, stupid man?"

Marla shrugged, not even breaking a small smile at her attempt at humor. "I don't think he's either of those things. I think he's a very handsome, silly guy with a great smile and he's got connections to the most powerful men in Vista Maria. I'm not surprised he wouldn't want me when he could get any girl he wants."

"His loss then, because you're pretty amazing. Maybe instead of shy and stupid, he's shallow. That's the worst type of guy to have in your life, so maybe you're dodging a bullet. There's plenty of better fish in the sea."

Marla tilted her head back and sighed with her eyes closed. "Yeah, but sexy, single, vampire fish are rare. I thought I finally found my Edward."

"Oh, so you *do* know he's a vampire. I was wondering, but didn't know how to bring it up. Gage informed me when we went on our date and it blew my mind."

"You didn't know? Welcome to the club, it's kind of hard to stay ignorant to them when you live down here. Speaking of your date, have you guys talked since then, or is he like his friend?"

"He's come in for coffees throughout the week, but I haven't texted him. I don't want to come on too strong or seem desperate, and he hasn't messaged me at all. Plus, I don't even know if I want to be in a relationship yet. My last one didn't end so well, and I feel safest by myself."

Marla's eyes widened. "You are living every girl's dream right now! I am so jealous. You have an attractive, rich, powerful vampire interested in you and you didn't even have to chase after him. If you turn him down before you give it a shot, I'll be disappointed in you."

"Yes ma'am." She smiled and linked her arm through Marla's. "Who's driving?"

"You can, I don't know where they live and apparently you've already spent the night there." She winked.

When they arrived, they were both surprised at the number of people that were attending this party. They had to circle the large block twice before finding a place to park, almost two streets over.

"I regret wearing heels," Marla moaned as they started their trek to the mansion.

Willow thanked herself quietly for wearing simple black flip-flops. "I didn't realize Sammy knew so many people. But then again, I don't really know her that well."

"Maybe tonight we can get to know her a little better and expand our friend group to three."

"If we can even find her tonight." Willow paused as they approached the mansion and observed the chaos in front of them.

The front was lined with cars parked bumper-to-bumper with groups of people huddled around the sportier ones, taking pictures and checking out the engines. The girls made their way through the impromptu car show to the backyard to find it packed with women in skimpy swimsuits, men sporting six-packs, and a whole pack of people wearing similar Baja hoodies sitting in a circle passing a joint. If they were younger, it would have felt like a cliché high school party from an 80's movie.

Not seeing anyone they knew in the yard, the girls decided to maneuver their way through the crowd to go inside the mansion. The interior was as packed as the exterior, with people in large groups huddled together, shouting over the stereo that was alternating between rap and rock songs.

"I am so glad you're here!" Sammy sprung out of nowhere and wrapped Willow into a tight hug as they entered into the kitchen. Willow could tell from the neurotic energy coming off her that she had probably been drinking before the party even started.

"What did you do, invite everyone you saw on the beach?"

"Yes." Sammy burped and waved her hand in front of her face. "Sorry, I chugged my rum and Coke and the carbonation makes me gassy. I don't have friends, so I invited anyone I saw on the beach. Hey, I need to make you two a drink!"

Willow and Marla grabbed each other's hands and followed Sammy to the kitchen island that was completely covered in red Solo cups, two liters of various pop, and glass alcohol bottles. It was the total opposite from how the tidy kitchen looked the last time she had been here. They pushed their way through the mass of people huddled around the island and once at the center, Sammy threw a few cups to the ground in search for clean ones.

"I can totally go for another rum and Coke, is that good for you two?" Sammy called over her shoulder as she dug through the bottles of various half-drunk alcohol.

"That's fine," Willow shouted over the music.

She noticed Marla hidden behind her looking like a small, scared rabbit caught in a trap. She couldn't blame her—this was extremely overwhelming, and all she wanted to do was go home and watch a movie on her couch. The vibe here was different from the club, with no dancing and people only wanting to get wasted and take selfies to show off that they were in a mansion.

"Where is Gage at?" Willow shouted over the music.

Sammy scrunched her face up. "Huh?"

"Gage! Where is he at?"

"I think he's sulking in his room like an antisocial creep. He got all pissy with me for inviting so many people, so you might want to avoid him. I don't know why he got so irritated with me. Horatio and Matteo live here too, and they're not mad."

Sammy finished the drinks and spun around to hand Marla one, a feline smile spread across her face. "Matteo should be in the living room. Here, take this shot for courage and some confidence. You look like you need it."

Sammy thrust a bottle of vodka into Marla's hand and all but poured it down her throat when she hesitated. She joined her with her own bottle of vodka that she then passed to Willow.

"We're here to get fucked up and have fun!" Sammy shouted. The people nearest to them cheered in agreement.

"I don't think we're going to stay too long," Willow began, but was cut off when Sammy put her finger to her lips.

"Don't say that, you just got here. Come on, don't be party poopers—do another shot, mingle a little bit, and let loose. You seemed to enjoy your night at the club. I heard you left with Gage." Sammy wiggled her eyebrows.

"He took me home because someone drugged my drink and tried to rape me."

Sammy sucked her bottom lip in. "Oh, well...I'm glad that didn't happen. I promise you'll be safe here, these people know better than to pull any crap like that cause we'll kill 'em." She cackled and revealed her new sharp canines. "Damn, it feels good to be powerful."

Sammy reached for another cup, forgetting she already held one in her hand. Willow put her vodka bottle back on the island and pulled Marla off to the side. "I think she's extremely wasted and I doubt we're going to get to know her very well tonight. What do you think about heading out, grabbing a pizza, and throwing on an old horror movie at my place?"

"She seems kind of mean anyway. Your idea sounds absolutely amazing, but I do want to see Matteo before we leave. My outfit looks pretty good, and I want him to see me in it."

"How about we finish our drinks she made us and then leave? That will give you time to find him and flirt a little."

"Whatcha guys whispering about?" Sammy joined them and leaned heavily on Willow. "You are so pretty, by the way."

"Thank you, but we were about to make our way into the living room to find Matteo. It was nice seeing you again, Sammy."

"I can help!" Her eyes grew big and she spilled part of her drink onto Willow's dress, leaving a large brown spot on her chest. Marla quickly grabbed a stray napkin off the counter and dabbed it up before it could get much worse.

"Matteo!" Sammy screamed and started pushing people out of the way as she made her way to the living room, pulling Willow with her.

"Oh my god," Marla whispered under her breath.

"Matteo! Your pretty little slut is here!"

"Sammy, what the hell?" Marla's face turned red.

"Relax, I'm only joking. You look more like a prude than a slut with all that material you have on." Sammy waved her hand up and down.

Willow could see the tears starting to well in Marla's eyes and pushed Sammy's arm off of her shoulder. She tried to keep her tone even, reminding herself that the girl was very drunk and not in full control of her words or actions. "I think we can find Matteo on our own, but thanks for your help."

She quickly pulled Marla away before Sammy could respond. As they made their way through the room, she spotted Matteo and Robby taking up residence on a beat-up leather couch that must have been brought in specifically for this party. Matteo looked up and his eyes were instantly drawn to Marla. He whispered something to Robby, who also looked over.

"Hey Matteo, Robby." Willow nodded and stood in front of them. "Have either of you seen Horatio? Sammy is getting a little too drunk and might need his help."

Matteo groaned. "That girl cannot seem to hold her liquor. Did she do anything embarrassing?"

Marla looked down at her heels and tucked a piece of hair behind her ear. "No. She's being kind of mean, though."

His face hardened. "Mean how?"

"I don't think she liked my outfit very much. I guess it *is* a little plain."

His eyes swept over her and a genuine look of confusion clouded his face. "What's wrong with your outfit? I think you look nice."

She peeked up at him. "Do you really?"

"Yeah, black and red are my favorite colors."

Joy pierced through Willow as she watched her friend's confidence come back. Marla suddenly stood up straighter and was making eye contact again, all due to one little compliment from a pretty boy. She nudged her and Marla took the hint, sinking down into the couch next to him. Matteo's face turned a light pink and he began fidgeting with the assortment of band pins he had attached to his vest.

Maybe he was just shy. She supposed she could forgive him for not messaging her this past week, and decided to make him his coffees again.

Robby's voice caught her attention. "Gage is up hiding in his room, he's not really a people person. Here," he leaned over to the table next to them and grabbed a red bowl, "take these chips to him. When he's cranky like this, food or sex seems to help."

Willow flushed but took the bowl. She made her way through the crowd again, holding onto the bowl with a death grip. Between the stoners eyeing it and the drunken people falling into it, she was surprised she made it up the stairs with half of it still intact.

She stood in front of his door and debating on knocking or walking straight in. She was curious to find what he would be doing if she barged in unannounced, but her manners outweighed her curiosity. She gave a few gentle raps and clutched the bowl tighter.

The door cracked open and one green eye peered out at her.

His eye glanced into the bowl. "Did Sammy send you up here with a peace offering?"

"No, Robby did. He said food helps when you're cranky."

The door widened and Gage stepped to the side to let her in, taking the bowl from her. "I'm not cranky, I'm fucking annoyed that my house has turned into a nightclub. When Sammy was planning this, she said she was going to invite people from the marina and a few people she knew from the beach to have a cookout in our backyard. She didn't tell me she was inviting all of Vista Maria."

"It is pretty intense down there. How's Buffy doing with all these strangers in her home?"

"She's terrified." He frowned and looked toward the bed. "She won't even come out for catnip."

"Poor baby."

She went over to the bed and crouched down on her hands and knees to peer underneath. Sure enough, there was a white ball of fur pressed up against the wall, shivering. While Willow murmured some soothing baby-talk to the kitten, she noticed the sound of the music quiet and become a distant thumping rhythm she could feel through the floorboards.

She sat up and watched as Gage walked away from the door he had closed. The energy of the room suddenly felt more intimate. She stood up and brushed her dress down, picking imaginary dirt off the front. She was happy to see that the brown stain from earlier had turned into a less noticeable off-white thanks to Marla's quick thinking. He placed the bowl on the nightstand and they stood in awkward silence, not looking at each other.

He shifted his weight from one foot to the other. "You uh, look nice."

"Thanks, I've been getting tanner since I've been talking walks outside before work. I've decided to take a break from my yoga classes, so that's how I stay active now."

"I'm glad you walk in the daytime. Don't go walking by yourself at night, it's not safe."

She scrunched up her face and tilted her head at him. "I thought the vampires that lived here follow your rules."

"They do, but sometimes a rogue one from another family will pass through. The death rate has increased, and I've confirmed it's from vampire attacks."

Willow thought back to John's comment about the missing baker. "Does this have something to do with that Waldo guy?"

"Yes, he's been letting his men kill people in both our territory and Daytona."

"How come?"

"That's a long story." He looked away and Willow could tell from the way his eyes grew glassy that it was a sad one, too.

"So how do I keep myself safe from these rouge vampires? I normally carry pepper spray, is that enough?"

His eyes refocused on her and he smirked. "I don't think that will help much against the monsters that roam these streets at night."

She took a step closer. "Then what do I need to protect myself from these nighttime monsters?"

"Me."

Willow's breath caught in her throat with a sudden desire to touch him. "And how are you going to protect me?"

His smirk widened, and she noticed the light glint off his sharp canines. "I'll rip their fucking throats out if they touch you. Don't forget, *I'm* the scariest monster on these streets."

He was the one to close the gap between them. Willow forgot to breathe as his lips crashed down onto hers and his tongue pried its way into her mouth. She shut her eyes and allowed his entrance into her body, his tongue gliding over her teeth. She tried to do the same, but he pushed her tongue out and filled her mouth more deeply. His hands ran up her sides and toward her back as she lifted her arms to capture his neck and pull him closer.

He lifted her off the ground and she wrapped her legs around his waist as he placed her on the bed. She continued to hold on to him as she ran one hand over the base of his neck and up into his soft, blond locks. She closed her hand, gripping a handful of hair tightly in her fist as he dropped down on her. She could feel the pressure of his entire body against hers and she spread her legs even further to allow the entire length of him to be pressed against her core.

He sat up, breaking their intense kiss, and ripped his shirt off to expose the full rosary tattoo and a chest that looked like it was chiseled by a Greek sculptor. Before lifting her dress above her head, he bent down and untied the bow laced against her midriff with his teeth.

Once her dress was off, he looked down at her laid out beneath him and gently dragged his fingers across her stomach. She flinched at the tickling sensation and watched as his eyes filled with lust and wonder.

"You're absolutely beautiful," he murmured.

He bent his head down to touch the soft place beneath her breasts and placed a light kiss. She shivered as he gently dragged his teeth along her sensitive flesh. She arched her back and she felt him tense like he was having to hold back.

In her new position, he was able to slide his hand under her back and unclasped her white bra that was hiding her rounded breasts. With his other hand, he slipped her matching lace underwear down and she was soon naked under his passionate gaze.

She couldn't believe her fantasy was becoming reality when he slid off the bed and knelt on his knees. He dipped his head between her thighs and let out a growl of approval as he dragged his tongue over her entrance and along her clit. He wrapped his hands around her thighs and pulled them apart further so he could properly bury his face between them.

She ground against him as he began to flick her clit with the tip of his tongue and inserted a finger into her opening. She gasped as a pleasant heat started at her core and worked its way into her lower belly as he sucked her clit into his mouth. He slipped another finger into her and began pumping both, filling the room with a wet sound as her juices soaked his hand.

She closed her eyes and tilted her head as she focused on the feeling of his fingers sliding in and out. In and out. His rhythm was smooth and delicious and she involuntarily whimpered as her hips thrusted up, wanting more.

His mouth let go of her and trailed a line of kisses from her navel up to her breasts while continuing to work his hand inside of her. He curved his fingers just enough to hit that precious spot.

"Oh, fuck me." She drew each word out in a sensual call and lifted one leg to grab it and fold it against her chest to give him room to go deeper.

His fingers were great, but she needed more now. She opened her eyes to drop her leg and grab his face. She pulled him to her lips.

"Fuck me," she begged again in between kisses.

He ripped his hand out of her, causing her to gasp from the unexpected emptiness, and yanked his zipper down revealing his hard length. She bit her lip and gazed at the appendage that would be worthy of starring in porn. Her toes curled, imagining how deep he would be able to fill her and wondering if all of him would even fit.

"You look nervous," he rumbled.

She didn't answer, only slid her body up further on the bed to allow him room to mount her. He smirked and slid his pants off, revealing his fully-naked form before climbing on top of her.

She ran her hands down his shoulders, appreciating the hard strength she felt, and gently ran her nails down his back. She grabbed both of her legs this time and brought them to her shoulders, fully exposing her opening to him. He looked at her like she was a valuable painting hanging in a museum.

He reached a hand down and helped himself inside. If she thought the feeling of his fingers in her was heavenly, this was otherworldly. She couldn't stop the moan as he fully sheathed himself in one slow push.

"Jesus, Willow." His breath caught and he cradled her face with his hand as he looked down at her.

It was too much for her, she wasn't used to a man looking at her with so much passion. She didn't know what to do or how to respond, and her discomfort was ruining the moment.

It was time to change things up.

"I know you're capable of more than this, so fuck me already." She whispered in his ear.

His dark laugh rumbled through her. "Your wish is my command."

Her breath was knocked out of her as he rammed himself into her wet chasm. As he dove into her roughly again, he placed a hand on her neck and leaned down next to her ear.

"You drive me fucking insane."

He tightened his hold on her neck, restricting her breathing slightly as he began pounding into her. Her eyes rolled back at the intense pleasure she was feeling, no longer thinking about anything other than him filling her. Her nails ran down his back again, this time digging in as her sex swallowed his entire length. He angled himself so that he was hitting her clit with each thrust against her. Her waves of ecstasy were building the same time stars began to dot her vision.

He loosened his grip and she gasped in air as the waves crashed over her and she screamed out in bliss. As soon as he heard her scream of pleasure, he came filling her with his warmth and crashed down on top of her.

Sixteen

Gage

Fuck, fuck, *fuck*.

Gage looked down at Willow's head resting against his shoulder and felt her naked body pressed against him fall into an even breathing pattern as she drifted off to sleep. Without speaking, they both curled up together under his duvet and became lost in their own thoughts.

His shifted to memories of Venice and her betrayal. He had met her in a strip club, selling her body to be able to afford the simplest necessities. He had been captivated by her fierce beauty with her pin straight black hair chopped off at her chin, her amber eyes that glowed in the stage lights, and the countless tattoos that wrapped around her entire body. Her smile was closer to a sneer and should have been a warning, but instead it pulled him in even more.

He had been at the club with Nikolas hunting down a sex offender who had been on the verge of reoffending again when he'd noticed her sensual dance on stage. She had approached him after—hindsight told him she'd known who he was and wanted a taste of the rich and powerful life—and used her charms to win him over.

Honestly, it didn't take much since he was still healing from the loss of his father's family.

They'd had a whirlwind romance, with plenty of fucking but also plenty of fighting. Within weeks she had moved in, which led to most of their fights revolving around Matteo and Horatio. She'd never complained about Nikolas - she had been smart enough to realize Gage would have never put up with that.

As much as the fighting had worn him down, there had been a small, self-deprecating part of him that loved it. He'd felt like he deserved it for letting his father down by not being able to save his family.

Even with their fighting growing more physical, with her slapping and spitting on him on more than one occasion, his love for her was intense. She had known all the right things to say to make him forgive her and believe she loved him. She was the perfect example of why women could not be trusted.

He'd trusted Venice to love him. To never leave him. Yet she had run off with Waldo.

He'd also trusted his mother to love him and always be there, and yet she'd ended her life. His love had not been enough to make either of them stay.

He looked down at the brown halo of hair outlining Willow's peaceful face. A hint of a smile was resting on her lips as her eyes slightly moved behind her lids, telling him she was dreaming of something happy. There was something different about her compared to Venice. She was sweeter, more accepting, and seemed to be the type to work through problems instead of screaming about them. Willow also got along well with the others, and Clay was fond of her.

How long would this last before she left him, too?

A deep ache bloomed in his chest. He was positive he wouldn't survive giving his love to someone again, only to have them throw it away like it meant nothing. Another heartbreak would push him over the edge and he knew he would become the monster that he feared he'd become.

The image of him almost killing Destiny flashed through his mind. He wouldn't let that happen to Willow. Now he had to figure out how to get her out of his bed and pretend like nothing had ever happened.

But that was going to be hard with the taste of candy imprinted on his tongue.

And the feel of her tightness clamped around his cock.

He shuffled out from under her before he became hard again and tried to get inside her one last time. He needed to get away from her since he couldn't trust himself not to do it again. And after learning that she tasted how she smelled, he *definitely* couldn't trust himself not to bite her during round two.

"I'm sorry, I didn't mean to fall asleep." She sat up and rubbed her eyes, her hair frizzy and tangled around her bare shoulders, giving her a freshly-fucked look that wasn't helping his self-control.

"It's fine. I should go and mingle with people since this is my house, after all."

"I guess Robby was right. Snacks and sex do pull you out of your cranky mood."

"Yeah, I guess so," he mumbled.

He dressed quickly and tossed her clothes toward her. She took the hint and began putting herself back together.

"Are we good?" She asked.

He looked up to her and his knees almost gave out. She looked close to tears, and he was causing them.

He knew he should say something, but the words were lost to him. Anger sparked at his inability to handle this situation, which was clearly causing her pain. He wondered how he was supposed to be the leader of his family when he couldn't even handle this situation in a dignified way.

His tone came out harsher than intended. "Yeah, we're good. This shouldn't have happened—this was a mistake on my part. I'm sorry."

"Oh." The tears finally came and her eyes glistened. "I should have listened to John weeks ago when he told me to be careful with you. It's not that you're a dangerous vampire. You're a user. I should have seen this coming, this was my fault."

She broke eye contact with him and pulled out her phone to order a cab. "There are a lot of people here, so I think I'm going to get going. Marla is with Matteo, Sammy's drunk as hell, and I don't really know anyone else here well enough to hang out with them all night. I guess I'll see you around."

She turned and dashed toward the door, not even bothering to retie the bow around her midsection. He didn't stop her. Instead, he sat on the bed and waited for Buffy to come soothe his tumultuous thoughts.

He waited and waited, but she never jumped up. He left to join the party instead of stewing in the isolating feeling of self-hate.

Gage entered the living room and immediately located his small troupe taking shots of something crimson in the corner. Nikolas was staring with an ashen face at the news program that was silently playing in the background. He followed his gaze to see a banner warning people of vicious dolphin attacks. If he were in a better mood, he would have taunted Nikolas for introducing the dolphins to human flesh during his nighttime feedings.

Next to Nikolas on the couch was Sammy, who was all but grinding on Horatio's lap as she sang along to the song that was playing. Horatio was casually leaned back, acting like this was a normal occurrence. Gage noticed that Matteo and Marla were missing and Robby was in Matteo's usual spot next to Horatio.

"You and Willow were gone for a while." Horatio gently pulled Sammy to the side. "What were you two kids up to?"

"That's none of your business."

A small gasp left Sammy's round mouth and she stopped her squirming. "Ooooh, you totally fucked."

"Shut up Sammy," Gage growled.

"She pretty much ran out of here like a ghost was chasing her. Why did she leave in such a hurry, cuz?" Robby asked.

"Oooh, I take back what I said earlier." Sammy leaned back and pointed her finger. "You didn't fuck her, you *fucked up.* You said something to piss her off, didn't you?"

He could feel himself losing his grip on his temper. "No! Nothing happened, she's fine, I'm fine, we are *all fine.* She wanted to leave this stupid-ass party you threw. That's all."

"Stupid-ass party? Well, if you would stop being such a stuck-up little—"

Horatio clamped his hand over her mouth and stood up. "I think it might be time for a glass of water and to chill out in our room."

"The fuck does that mean?" Sammy slurred from between his fingers.

"It means you're a drunken mess of a person," Gage hissed.

Robby stuck a refurbished wine bottle covered in gems between Gage and Sammy. "Hey cuz, want a shot? I found the perfect ratio of blood and vodka. I call these Shots of Death."

"That's a terrible name for a terrible drink." Gage tried to turn his attention back to Sammy to remind her whose house she was currently using as a nightclub.

"Come outside with me for a second, would you?" Robby grabbed Gage by the back of the neck and squeezed.

"Well I would, but I'm in the middle of something."

"Let me rephrase that. Come outside with me right now or I'll cut off your dick and throw it out the door so you have to chase after it."

Gage obliged, deciding that it was not worth causing a scene to put

Sammy in her place. Horatio wouldn't appreciate that, and the last thing he needed with Waldo sniffing around was to cause a rift in their family.

Once outside, Robby led him to a spot hidden away from the crowd. "I'm older than you so I have literally known you your whole life. I can tell something happened and everyone is not all right. You're a terrible liar, you get all twitchy and short tempered when you're upset. Look, your eye is twitching right now!"

"It's twitching because I want to punch you in the face."

"Then do it."

Gage didn't hesitate. He landed a blow right to his cousin's nose, feeling a tiny bit satisfied at the sickening crunch it created. The satisfaction didn't last long as Robby's fist came flying toward his right eye.

"What the fuck?" Gage grunted as he held his face.

"You didn't expect me to sit there and take that, did you?" Robby asked in a nasally voice.

A popping sound could be heard as he straightened his broken nose, holding it in place until it healed. For vampires, minor injuries like these would be healed before the next night, so Gage was not worried about his black eye. It was also why sometimes Robby and him ended up in fistfights, knowing that the damage they inflicted wouldn't last long. It was a satisfying, though animalistic, way to release tension.

Gage groaned and kicked the ground. "I fucking slept with her. Then I made her cry by telling her it was a mistake. I'm the biggest goddamn idiot in the world."

"I'm not disagreeing with you, that was extremely stupid."

"I promised myself I would never date again, yet there I was at a fucking Mexican restaurant buying her margaritas and enchiladas like a hypocrite. A dumbass hypocrite with memory loss. When I'm with her it's like I forget that woman are awful, manipulative creatures."

Robby frowned. "*Can be,* not *are.* Venice was horrible, I'm not denying that. I still think about that time I walked in to catch her slapping you and pulling your hair all because you wouldn't give her money for something."

"And I still remember how you pulled her out of the room by her hair."

Robby shrugged. "Doesn't the Bible say something about *an eye for an eye* or some shit? I was giving her a taste of her own medicine. But, that's not the point. The point is that I don't want you to use her as an example for all women. Especially with Willow, who seems like a sweetheart. I've only met her twice, but she seems like the total opposite of Venice."

Gage looked up at the night sky and let out a long, deep breath. "I don't think I'm ready."

"Is it that, or are you scared?"

"I'm not scared," he answered too quickly.

Robby gave a tight-lipped smile and nodded like he knew better. "It's okay to be scared sometimes. You have a lot happening with learning how to run your own family, starting your own custom shop, and dealing with Waldo coming back into the picture. Plus women, especially pretty ones like Willow, are scary. Why do you think I'm gay? I don't have to deal with those beautiful, intimidating creatures this way."

Gage rolled his eyes. "I don't even know what to say to her."

"She seems rational. I bet if you sat down and had a conversation with her, she would listen. Explain to her that tonight wasn't a mistake, you just suck at handling emotions. Make sure you do this sooner rather than later. Don't let her linger in that pain and embarrassment."

"I suppose I can stop at the coffee house tomorrow."

"Good." Robby smiled and wiped the drying blood from his face with his sleeve. "Since I brought up Waldo, the jackass killed off one of my new turns yesterday. The poor guy wasn't even a vampire for a full week before one of Waldo's men chopped him up and left him in a sewer. I think his plan is to dwindle down my numbers because he's planning on attacking you. He knows we would come to help if a fight broke out, and that there's no way he could fight off both our families."

Gage groaned. "Why does he keep wanting to start shit with me? This all started because of that bonfire."

Both men's face darkened at the memory of the night that had started everything. Gage had been attending a bonfire on the beach hosted by a few employees he knew from the casino. Waldo and his friends had been passing through Vista Maria when they'd stopped for dinner. They'd followed the old rules of killing innocents, and unfortunately their target had been the people at the bonfire.

Gage had been no match for protecting them by himself against four seasoned vampires, and Waldo had made sure to leave Gage broken and bleeding in the sand. Clay had found him dragging himself out of the sand and up onto the boardwalk a half hour before sunrise. He had never been so humiliated and angry at the loss of innocent lives.

Clay had lost his mind at seeing Gage so close to death. Gage knew it couldn't have been easy seeing his son—the last thing he had to connect him to his deceased wife—bloodied and broken.

Clay went to Miami for justified retribution and killed the three that were with Waldo that night. Most families respected the law that one is allowed to extract revenge however one sees fit, but the Miami family was never one to follow mainstream laws. So Waldo's father, Gerald, had attacked Clay and killed every last one of his family members. At the end of the fight, Clay had managed to kill Gerald and ripped his very lungs out of his chest. Gage had never seen his father act in such a brutal way before.

Robby frowned. "I think he's trying to play it off as revenge for his father, but deep down he's a psychopath that finds joy in causing you pain. You losing the fight at the bonfire wasn't enough. He wanted to completely destroy you. So he took Venice away, and now he's trying to take your territory and new family away, too."

"But why *me?*"

Robby shrugged. "Maybe because you tried to protect humans. Or because he views your territory as easy pickings since you've got the smallest family around. Before Uncle Clay's entire family was wiped out, he was running with a minimum of at least thirty men, not including their spouses. Your group of four makes you look like an easy target for someone wanting to expand their territory. You really need to start adding more people."

"I know, my dad's been on my ass about that, too. I'm not like you though, I can't add people I barely know to my family. We're tight-knit and that's the way I like it. Besides, being small doesn't mean that we're weak."

"I know you're not weak. My family is pretty tight-knit. I have my five guys I'm close to, and the rest are more like employees I barely interact with. I do a quick background check, confirm they know full well what being a vampire entails, then give them my blood."

Gage gave a sarcastic snarl. "What, do you post job openings online and filter through all the applicants?"

"Kind of. The internet opened so many doors for us to find those weirdos that think they're already vampires. All it takes is a couple messages and soon they're begging to be turned. Also, hit up those goth clubs. You'll find plenty of wannabe vampires there."

"I hate clubs."

"I don't. I can find you some potential members while I'm out next weekend. I was thinking of taking a drive down to Miami to hit up the clubs down there. What a shame it would be if I ran into one of Waldo's men and *accidentally* killed him."

"Think I can tag along? Not for the clubs, but I want to see if I can find out anything about Waldo when I'm down there. He told one of the casino employees that he was heading 'north' and I want to know what that means."

"Sure, I'm always down for a road trip buddy."

"Thanks." Gage turned around and began heading back. "If you need me, I'll be in my room working on some commissions."

Seventeen

A Note on Mental Health

Vampires may not be real, but domestic violence is. And as you learned from Willow and Gage's story, it can happen to anyone. I've included some resources below if you or someone you know may need help. And if you're a survivor, please remember that trauma and abuse may change the brain <u>but so does therapy.</u> You are not permanently broken, you are just different. And in time, you will heal.

https://www.thehotline.org/ (online chat available, but remember that internet history can be tracked)

800-799-7233 (National Domestic Violence Hotline)

https://ncadv.org/ (National Coalition Against Domestic Violence)

https://www.loveisrespect.org/ (one of my favorite resources to teach teens about healthy relationships)

If you feel unsafe verbally asking for help, I've included a blank space here. My hope is that you can write a note, give this book to a trusted person, and tell them to check out chapter 17.

ɔɔɔɔ

ɔɔɔɔ

Eighteen

Willow

It was a slow night at the Coffee House Bunny, with only a handful of customers stopping by. Willow handed the man with copper hair his black coffee and he dropped a five-dollar bill in her tip jar before leaving her alone in the café. He was the same man from a few days ago, but did not seem to be much of a threat. He just seemed tired. There was no need to contact Gage. Besides, she would rather cut off her own toe than text him.

She tried to convince herself that his rejection didn't hurt. She wasn't sure if she wanted a relationship, anyway. One thing she was glad about was that Gage had showed her his true colors *before* they'd started seriously dating. When she looked at it that way, he'd done her a favor. He'd saved her a lot of heartbreak, drama, and re-traumatization. Her ex had hurt her both verbally and physically, but by the end she didn't love him. With Gage, she wasn't so sure the same would hold true.

But she would never find out if she could love him now, because according to him she had been a mistake. Embarrassed by that one little word, she'd fled his bedroom before she could really give him a piece of her mind.

She had never been judged on her sexual abilities before, but she must have been bad if he was labeling what they had done a mistake. There was no other explanation she could come up with that would cause him to instantly regret sleeping with her.

Willow pulled out her clipboard from underneath the counter and sighed as she flipped through the pages. She hated doing inventory, but it was either this or continue to ruminate about Gage.

Before she could start, her phone dinged, alerting her that Marla had texted checking in again. Marla had sent a text after the party asking what had happened, but she'd ignored it and tucked herself into her couch with a blanket and a slasher film where the handsome male lead was sliced apart. Watching the carnage helped ease her anger, but did nothing for the sadness that was creeping into her soul.

Hey, sorry for ditching u. I'm ok. I couldnt find you and assumed you were w/ Matteo. How did that go?

She picked up the clipboard again, only to put it back down when her phone chirped with a response seconds later.

SO GOOD!!! We've been texting all night. We didn't even have sex last night, we hung out in his room & talked instead!! Hes even cooler than I thought, we're going to some fancy italian place 2nite.

A part of her was slightly jealous of Marla, wishing that Gage would have done the same instead of fucking her and then throwing her clothes at her.

Good, I'm happy for you. Keep me updated xx

Willow sighed and started counting the bundles of napkins, straws, and stirrers she had stored under the counter. The other part of her was truly happy for Marla, because she saw how much joy Matteo brought her.

Her mind kept wandering and after having to restart her count three times, she finally finished and stood up from behind the counter. She noticed the bells on her front door swinging slightly, but not enough to make them chime. She found it odd, since her air conditioner wasn't running, but returned to her tasks. She grabbed the spare bag of espresso beans to refill the machine, and chills ran up her spine when she turned around to throw out the bag. She had a feeling that someone was watching her.

She went over to the windows, wondering if some creep was staring at her from the sidewalk. Her anxiety told her she was going to see some lowlife man jerking off as he watched her inside the café, but the reality was that the streets were bare. Not even a car had driven past in the two minutes she had been looking out her windows.

"I should've brought Snickers to work," she mumbled to herself.

She went back to her dreaded inventory and began counting the syrups stacked against the wall. She was running low on vanilla, but had a surplus of raspberry flavoring. She turned back around to write down a note to create a special of the month that included raspberry, maybe something vampire-themed, but froze when she noticed a dark flash near the bathrooms out of the corner of her eye.

"Hello?"

She was beginning to feel like the star of her own slasher film. Contrary to what was expected in those movies, she decided to mind her own business and ignored the feeling of dread building in her stomach. Opposite of manifestation, she hoped that if she ignored something hard enough, it would go away.

Finishing her count of the items out front, she made her way to the storage room in the back. She felt safer here away from the windows and the open space of the café. There were fewer places for a masked serial killer to hide.

She placed her clipboard down on a nearby table to reach up and turn an unlabeled box around to figure out its contents. As soon as she stretched up on her tip-toes, the door behind her that she'd purposely left open clicked closed.

She spun around with eyes wide, ready to see a man in a hockey mask lunging toward her. Instead, a blond man stood leaning against the wall with his arms crossed and his piercing green gaze locked on her.

"What the hell, Gage?"

"We have to talk."

"Customers are not allowed back here." She tried to shoo him out of the room, but he didn't budge.

"I'm not here as a customer, Willow. We have to talk about last night."

"There's nothing to talk about. I was a mistake, you made that very clear, so I'll move on and find someone who likes me enough to not use me. Now please leave."

She whipped around, her ponytail having an attitude of its own with a satisfying swing as it came to rest on her shoulder, and continued her count. His hand snaked its way around her face and covered her mouth making her unable to scream as his other hand wrapped around her waist. Panic surged through her as she tried to wriggle her way free, but he tightened his hold even more to the point that she was sure there would be bruising on her sides.

His voice was dark and deep, the whisper of his breath tickling her ear. "Ever since I met you, you have consumed my every thought. You've even invaded my fucking dreams. I didn't sleep today because I couldn't get the thought of how you felt underneath me out of my mind."

His tongue flicked out and ran a line down her neck, his fangs trailing down her skin. He squeezed his hand that was clamped over her mouth to the point tears brimmed at the corner of her eyes, then let her go. She spun around and looked up to find pure desire burning in his eyes.

"I like how you look when you're scared because that's how you're supposed to look at me, instead of being naked and grinding against my face." He cornered her and put both hands against the wall, inches from her face, as he leaned toward her and growled. "Are you scared of me, Willow?"

Her breath was shallow and quick, and a cold shiver made the hairs on her arm stand up, but what she felt wasn't fear. No—she thought how broken she must be, because she was feeling a mix of desire and excitement. She slowly shook her head no.

"I guess I'll have to change that then."

He grabbed her by the shoulders and pulled her toward the table, roughly pushing her clipboard off onto the floor. She flinched at the loud crash as it collided with the tiles.

"Gage! What if a customer comes in?" She gasped when he bent her over the table, forcing her legs apart with his knee.

"Good thing I locked the door," he whispered before biting her ear.

The bite was gentle and didn't pierce her flesh, but sent shivers down her spine nonetheless. She felt his warm body pressed against her as he leaned over her, trapping her against the table. One hand held her shoulder down while the other traveled up her thigh, over her ass, to the top of her jeans. He inserted a finger between her pants and skin, sliding it around to the front to undo the button. The sound of her zipper filled the room.

"I really need to get back upfront. It was slow today and I don't want to miss a customer," she whispered as she tried to sit up.

It didn't take him much effort to push her back down.

He began leaving a trail of white-hot kisses down her neck as he slipped his hand into the front of her jeans. He massaged her clit through her underwear and she let out a deep moan as a warmth blanketed her. She instantly forgot about the potential customers.

"Still want to go back up front?" He asked.

Instead of an answer, she curved her back and thrust her ass against the hardness tight against his own zipper, begging to be let out. He groaned and removed his hand from her shoulder, allowing her to sit up a little. He continued to massage her as he undid his pants and released his cock. She bit her lip and closed her eyes, relishing the feeling of her pants slowly being dragged down her legs to pool around her ankles.

He pulled her pink thong taunt and to the side, revealing her soaking wet entry for him. He never quit his circling, and the pressure was starting to build in her stomach. She involuntarily kicked her hips back, helping him slip his tip into her entrance. She laid down completely flat on the table, moaning as he slowly entered her and filled her to max capacity. This time, his thrusts were slow and gentle.

Willow pressed her body hard against the cold metal table, wishing she was on her back so she could wrap her arms around him and dig her nails into his flesh. He was creating a storm within her, and she needed something to hold on to, afraid that the release would send her free-falling into space.

Each time he entered her she could feel her walls clinging to him, not wanting to let go. He picked up his pace while entangling her ponytail in his fingers, pulling back to lift her head off the table. As soon as they made eye contact, her storm finally exploded and her eyes rolled back as she let out an ungodly noise, pleasure flowing through her every limb.

"Oh fuck, Gage, fuck!" She screamed at the top of her lungs, knowing that no one would be able to hear her.

He kept rubbing her clit, forcing the orgasm to last longer than it should until he came. He thrust so hard and deep inside her as his storm poured over him that she was surprised he didn't wound her organs.

"Goddamn it, Willow." He pulled out of her and quickly pulled his pants back up. She looked over her shoulder in confusion and watched as his eyes landed on his cream seeping out of her pulsing center. He had a painful expression on his face before he abruptly turned and left the room, closing the door behind him.

"Wait!" She called after him, but by the time she put her pants back on and ran out front, he had left, the bells of the door tinkling behind him.

She stood in a haze, wondering what the appropriate reaction was to the situation she found herself in. One minute she thought she was terrible in bed, then the next she found out she had driven him crazy. She was as confused as he seemed to be.

She thought about texting him, but chastised herself for even considering chasing after a man. If he wanted more than sex from her, he would have to be the one to say something, because now she wasn't embarrassed.

She was pissed.

ꙅꙅꙅꙅ

The haze continued through the night and into the next day. It didn't help that she tossed and turned in bed. Every time she closed her eyes, she pictured his green ones looking down at her with lust. She knew she needed to clear her mind to survive the night at work, so she decided a run on the beach would reset her mind.

Fall—or what little fall Florida experienced—was approaching, and the air was still humid but was not so blazingly hot. It was perfect for running, since dry air usually made her throat burn, and the breeze would wick away the sweat. She put in her headphones and blasted a playlist of 70's disco music. There was something about the beat that got her pumped and increased her stamina.

Her feet pounded against the sidewalk as she watched the businesses slowly begin to turn off their lights and flip their signs to closed. Much of the town was beginning to shut down as a smaller part was coming alive.

She passed by a strip club whose lights began flashing and dancing around the sign that read that Cherry Bomb would be the star dancer tonight and that a drag show would be performing this weekend. She made a mental note to ask Marla if she would be interested in joining her for a wild time getting drunk and watching beautiful people lip-sync to Madonna.

A man came stumbling out of a bar like he had been thrown out and almost crashed into her. She deftly avoided him, giving him a small wave and smile. She turned the corner and watched a group of giggling girls go into a different bar. One had a sash around her that proudly stated she was a bride-to-be. Another group of girls were taking pictures of themselves in front of a vintage theater that was showing *The Rocky Horror Picture Show*. There was a line of eccentrically-dressed people behind them waiting for the doors to open.

Willow smiled at them all, loving how happy and carefree they seemed. That's all she ever wanted out of life—to feel safe, happy, and at home—and she was beginning to believe that she would get that here in Vista Maria.

Even with Gage toying with her emotions, she had Marla, her regulars like John and Ryan, a cozy little apartment close to the ocean, and the Coffee House Bunny. It was an amazing feeling to be a female business owner, knowing that her ancestors struggled to gain the right to have their own money, let alone own a business. Her little life was coming together, and she was starting to feel whole again after so much pain had marred her past.

Willow broke free of the city streets and stepped onto sand. The view took her breath away and she paused her workout. Before her was an ethereal sunset full of pink, purple, and red layers, with whisps of blues dispersed throughout. She sat down, brought her knees up to her chest, and wrapped her arms around them in a tight hug. Resting her chin on her knees, she could almost feel the presence of her mother's spirit sitting down beside her.

When she was alive, they used to watch sunsets together and mark them on a list to track how many states they saw them in. Now Willow could mark Florida off their list.

Mo stóirín.

A chill ran down Willow's back at the whisper of her nickname. She would hear her mother's voice in dreams, but never awake. And never so vividly.

She jumped when she felt a tapping on her shoulder and looked up, half expecting to see her mother. Instead, she saw the man that had stumbled out from the bar earlier. He had pockmarks scaring his face, a slight hunch to his shoulders, and his black hair was styled in a bowl-cut, giving him the look of Moe from the Three Stooges. The energy he gave off, though, made Willow realize he would be anything but funny.

"Excuse me, miss, but you do smell rather lovely. I was wondering if you were taken?"

The feral glint in the man's eyes warned her to lie. "Thanks, but I have a boyfriend and he's waiting for me at home. I promised him I wouldn't be out too late."

"That's wise. It's not safe after dark." His smile widened to the point it looked painful, revealing sharp canines among yellowed teeth. A shadow fell across his face as the sun completely fell below the horizon.

"Yeah, I better get going. Have a nice night." She tried to stand up, but the man pushed her down with one hand.

"You should let me walk you home, I promise I don't bite." He began cackling like a crazed clown and his eyes turned black. "Well, I don't bite *too* much. I don't want a big mess to clean up."

The man lunged at her, but she quickly rolled over and tried to crawl away from him, unable to find the coordination to get her legs under her to stand. He grabbed her by the ankle and pulled her back toward him, collapsing on the ground to try to bite her calf. She screamed and kicked him in the face, throwing fistfuls of sand hoping to blind him briefly so she could get away. All he did was snarl and bat the sand away.

"Give up, girly, you're no match for me." He lunged for her again, grabbed her hand, and attempted to pin her body down.

"Fuck you!" She spit in his face and grabbed him with her free hand, pressing her thumb into his eye. He let out a wet roar as she felt his eye pop like a grape under her adrenaline-fueled strength. Blood oozed down his cheek, and he released her to grab ahold of his face. She tried to scramble away from him again, but froze in horror when he revealed a normal-looking eye.

"That's the thing girly, I regenerate faster than you can hurt me. So give up."

She was in too deep of a panic to respond, but was able to stand up this time and begin running back toward the city. She let out a blood-curdling scream when he grabbed the back of her sports bra and pulled her back to the ground. Tears began streaming out of her eyes as she rolled over and looked up at him towering over her.

This was her end.

This was her reparation for the sin she'd committed the night she'd left her ex.

"Mama, I'm so sorry," she whimpered. She chose to keep her eyes open to stare down her murderer.

As quickly as he had pulled her down, his head disappeared and blood splattered the sand around her. His headless body stayed standing for a few moments before it began tipping toward her.

"Oops, don't want that to land on you," a man's voice said cheerfully.

The decapitated body flung over her and she watched as it soared through the air and out into the ocean. From her position on the ground, she watched as a pair of feet dressed in black slacks and dress shoes reared back and kicked the head like a bloodied soccer ball. A feeling of relief and comfort came over her as she realized the only well-dressed man she knew was Clay. He had come to her rescue like the father she never had.

She watched the head soar through the night sky and make a soft splash into the dark waters not far from the body.

"There we go, dear." He held out his large hand and helped her sit up.

Her legs were shaking and too weak to stand, so she had to look up at him from her spot on the ground. Her mind took a second to process who stood in front of her, for it was not the man she'd originally thought. Her voice came out in a breathless whisper as the man's face came into focus in the night.

"Waldo?"

Nineteen

Willow

"Hi Willow, it looks like you got yourself into some trouble tonight. I'm so glad I heard you scream and came running over here. Hasn't anyone told you not to be out on the streets at night?"

"Who was he?" She gasped out, clutching sand between her hands so hard it was about to turn into diamonds.

"A rogue vampire."

She gave him a blank stare and he let out a sad laugh, baring his sharp fangs and crouching down to be eye-level with her. "This is what happens when you're not protected by a family. You could've been his meal."

Willow's stomach rolled and she swallowed to keep back the nausea. She had been seconds away from dying and had freely given up her will to live in her last moments, with all desire to fight gone. Her mother would have been so disappointed.

The world began to close in around her as she hyperventilated, tears rolling freely down her cheeks. Waldo's face changed to a look of concern and he got down on the ground to tip her head between her knees.

"Just breathe, Willow, just breathe. Everything's okay and you're safe now." He rubbed slow circles on her back as she kept her head hung with her eyes clamped shut. Eventually, she was able to get her breathing back on track, her body began to calm down, and the nausea subsided.

"I'm so sorry about that." She wiped at the snot leaking down her top lip.

"There's nothing to be sorry about. You had a near death experience and are in shock. Let's get you home. Did you drive here?"

She shook her head and finally stood up with his aid. She didn't let go of his arm as she said, "I ran here. I needed to clear my mind of something and thought exercise would help."

"Ah, well look on the bright side, I'm guessing you're probably not thinking about whatever was bothering you before." He gave a small chuckle, but stopped quickly after glancing at her. "Sorry, too soon for humor?"

She tightened her grip on his arm as the image of the vampire's gaping mouth heading toward her flesh flashed through her mind. "Yeah, too soon. I don't live that far away, will you please walk me home?"

"Absolutely."

They walked in silence with the sound of sand crunching underfoot as they stepped on the boardwalk. She realized her nails were digging into his arm, and let go to find crescent shapes embedded into his skin.

"I'm sorry, I didn't realize I had a death grip on you like that."

"Don't worry about it, I didn't even notice. We have a high pain tolerance compared to humans."

"That explains why you didn't even flinch when Horatio made you bleed in my shop." She glanced at him out of the corner of her eye, remembering their warning. So far, he seemed to be the total opposite of what they portrayed him as. "Why do they hate you so badly, anyway?"

He huffed a bitter laugh. "I'm curious—what have they told you so far?"

"Not much except that you let your men hunt here. Oh, and that your name is Waldo, not Jesse James."

He scowled, "I loved my father, I really did, but I'll never understand why he gave me such an ugly name. I prefer to be called Jesse James, if you don't mind."

She nodded. "I can do that."

"Thank you. As for your little friends, they probably haven't told you much about me because they're ashamed of the part they played in our feud. I'll own up to my sins and admit that my friends and I did kill on Clay's territory. We were young and dumb and very drunk, but it's a night I will always regret.

"We had been partying our way up the coast for a few weeks, stopping at different beaches to meet locals and have fun. By the time we hit Vista Maria, we were starving and needed a fix. We were used to living in Miami under different rules—there, we have more freedom with who we can hunt—and forgot that not all families live that way."

He turned his head and looked at the ground, his voice growing soft. "We attacked a small group on the beach that night. They were innocent and didn't deserve that. I still have nightmares to this day about what we did, but I deserve to live with them for being such a...monster. Please don't let my past worry you. I have grown since then and changed my ways. Have you ever done something awful that you regret?"

She wrapped her arms around herself in a tight embrace, trying to block out the memories of her own past. "Yes, yes I have."

"Then you understand the guilt I've been living with."

"More than you know."

"If I knew I was going to lose my father and start a war over that appalling decision, I never would have done it. Clay came and killed my best friends, then my father tried to get revenge for me. I didn't want him to do it, but he was so protective of me and went to fight."

He took a deep, dramatic breath. "He lost his life in that battle. I am a son who has been grieving the loss of his beloved father and his friends since that night, all because of Clay's irrational punishment. To make the wound worse, Clay attempted to take over the Miami territory until I stepped up and took my father's place as the head. He went quiet after that, a little too quiet for my comfort, so I have been popping into Vista Maria to keep tabs on them. That's how I heard about your shop and why I stopped in. I'm so glad I did, because you are the most stunning woman I have ever seen." He glanced at her, but quickly looked away. "I'm sorry, now's not the time for my flirting. I sometimes have a hard time with my filter when I'm around pretty women."

She gave a halfhearted smile but didn't respond. They were almost to her apartment, and the realization that he would leave and she would be alone again made the nausea return.

She took in a big, shaking breath and murmured more to herself, "Will I ever feel safe again?"

He stopped walking and gave her a sad look. "Of course you will. Most vampires are not brutes like the one you met tonight. He was new, and didn't know how to control his urges. It's ones like him that have been hunting on Vista Maria's territory lately. Most of us are refined, rational people who only target the lowest of the low. You are too pure and kind to ever be a target."

He stepped forward and tucked a lose strand of hair behind her ear.

She didn't flinch from his touch, but instead leaned into it. After her attack, there was something comforting about having a muscular man treat her so gently. For a split second she wished it were Gage instead, but banished that thought with the memory of him leaving her bent over her table, confused and hurt.

Jesse James cupped her face and tilted her head up ever so slightly to look at him. "But, if you really want to feel protected, there is a way to ensure your safety."

"What's that?"

A thin smile spread across his face. "You can join my family. All it takes is one little bite from me to mark you, and other vampires will know that you are claimed. You don't have to move to Miami right away, since your café is here, but you'll officially belong to the Miami family. And if you're worried about Gage and his boys, they know they would be severely punished for ever hurting my property."

Now she flinched. She didn't like the idea of being labeled as property, especially after gaining her freedom from her ex. "I don't think I want that. I don't want to be a vampire."

"No, no." He shook his head and furrowed his brows like he was talking to a confused toddler. "That's not how you become a vampire. You must drink the blood of your leader to be turned. The bite just marks you as mine."

"I'm not a piece of property to be owned."

"Don't think of yourself as property, it's more like being cattle." He grimaced. "That's not any better, I suppose. It's an old way of thinking, but it's the history behind the bite. Humans used to be branded like cattle as a way for vampires to collect people who were willing to be used for their blood. Others knew to avoid those with a mark, or else they could be killed as justified retribution. Humans are not treated like that anymore, thankfully. I find it very demoralizing, but sometimes it comes in handy to keep humans safe. It's still a rule that is honored by every vampire, and I thought you might like the option of having that security."

"I can understand wanting safety from other vampires, but why would people be so willing to be fed off of?"

He smirked. "Because it feels incredible. It's like having the most intense orgasm you've ever felt."

Willow's face flushed and she looked away from him. "I'll think about it."

"That's fair. You had a very traumatizing night and need some rest. I'll be around Vista Maria for a while, so I'll check in on you in a few days and see if you have changed your mind."

She took out her key from her shorts pocket, shocked she didn't lose it in the attack, and made her way to her apartment. She paused before heading up the steps. "Thank you for everything. I do owe you—how does free coffee for life sound?"

"That sounds amazing, Miss Willow." They held each other's gaze for a moment before he developed a sheepish look and rubbed the back of his neck. "I'll be seeing you around, my dear."

She watched as he headed down the sidewalk and back toward the beach. As soon as she was alone in her apartment, the silence turned heavy and a surge of panic coursed through her veins. She ran to Snicker's cage, and held him against her chest as she collapsed onto the ground and sobbed into his fur.

She wasn't sure how long she was like that. She assumed it was a while since Snicker's entire back was damp from her tears and her own back ached from being curled over in her hysterics. Her panic subsided, replaced by numbness. In a state of autopilot, she took a hot shower that turned her skin red, then rubbed herself dry with a towel so harshly she was surprised she had skin left. She didn't feel any of it.

ꙅꙅꙅ

Willow still opened the Coffee House Bunny that night. She couldn't bear to be alone and wanted the comfort of her customers around her. She conversed with some of them, but she couldn't recall anything they talked about. She greeted them, made their drinks, smiled a lot, then cleaned up the mess. Over and over again. All while she tried to push back the thoughts of her attack.

"Everything okay there, Willow?"

She whipped her head up, the sound of Horatio's voice breaking her focus of stirring cream into a coffee. Both Matteo and Nikolas were standing next to him, but Gage was nowhere in sight.

"What?"

"You've been staring into that cup for, like, a whole-ass minute. Did you smoke something without me?" He gripped his chest and feigned a broken heart.

"No, I'll make your drinks."

"Oookay, then. Thanks." He paused and shared a look with his twin. "You sure everything is okay? You seem a little more off than normal."

"I'm fine."

Horatio nodded like he didn't believe her, but left the counter to sit at their usual booth.

Matteo stared at her for a second. "You're not still mad at me over Marla, right? I may not have messaged her back, but I did talk to her at the party and you were right. We do have a lot in common."

"She told me." She felt like she was moving like a robot as she turned to make their usual drinks. She tried to snap out of her daze, but felt like she was watching herself through a TV screen. It was more like she was playing a video game than being in reality.

He looked at Nikolas and shrugged before joining his brother at their booth. Nikolas stayed behind and watched her. "Hey Willow, look at me for a second."

She ignored his command and continued assembling the drinks. Her hands began to shake, spilling milk on the counter. She paused and stared at the white droplets. They looked fuzzy and almost dreamlike, and when she reached for the cloth to wipe them up, it felt like she was moving through mud.

Nikolas' voice grew softer and he leaned against the counter so that no one else in the café could hear. "Did something happen?"

She looked up at him and realized that he, too, seemed fuzzy. She blinked, thinking her eyes were dry, but nothing changed. Panic rose in her throat. "I don't feel good."

"You don't look good. Did you take something?"

"No. I don't want to be here." The panic that was bubbling earlier finally exploded as she convinced herself that nothing was real. She had never felt so disconnected before and was terrified she was going crazy. It was like she was free-falling with nothing to hold on to, and that she would soon be sucked into a dark, empty void of insanity.

"How about you come sit down with us? I'll flip the sign to closed."

She had no idea how to explain what she was experiencing to him, but knew she needed to get away from everyone before they realized she was losing it. A panic attack rushed through her, causing her dreamlike state to feel even worse. She couldn't answer him, her mind searching for a safe place away from the audience of customers.

She ran from behind the counter, spilling a drink in her haste, and locked herself in the storage room. Even in here she didn't feel safe. A loud, uncontrolled wailing erupted from her. Nothing was safe, and she would never feel comfortable again.

Just as with Snickers, she wasn't sure how long she kept herself locked in the room, crying. It could have been minutes, hours, or even all night. Her panic had shrunk but the feeling of time and her surroundings not being real stayed. She had heard shuffling and whispering on the other side of the door, then a small knock.

"Willow, honey, it's Clay. The boys told me something really upset you tonight and you have us all worried. I wanted to check and make sure you are okay. Is there something I can do to help?"

She sat up from the fetal position she had curled into and rubbed her face with her apron. The cold metal of the lock brought her awareness to her hands. She was surprised that she could feel it since her body had felt dull and separate from herself for so long. She cracked open the door to look at Clay's kind face. He appeared calm, yet the slight flush to his cheeks hinted at his concern.

"Are my customers still out there?" She whispered.

"No, Nikolas closed the shop. It's only us here, now."

She sniffed and opened the door a little bit wider to reveal Horatio, Matteo, and Nikolas crushed together on one side of their booth, looking at her with furrowed brows. Gage was still nowhere in sight. Clay shifted closer and sat cross-legged, with his hands clasped in his lap. "Can you please tell me what happened?"

She chewed on her lip as she tried to figure out where to start and tore a piece of loose skin. The sudden, sharp pain caused the blurriness to vanish and she felt herself coming back into reality. "I went out for a run and was attacked by a vampire."

"Oh shit," she heard Horatio whisper.

"Jesse James saved me." She noticed Clay tense up. "He killed him and threw him into the ocean, then walked me home. I came here and everything felt weird, kind of like I was high, but I didn't take anything. And Jesse James didn't give me anything—he was nothing but a gentleman. I don't know what that was, but it was the most uncomfortable experience of my life."

"It sounds like the attack caused a derealization episode." Everyone turned to look at Matteo, who shrugged. "Psychology was my favorite class in high school. Did you feel like you were in a movie and nothing was real?"

Willow shook her head, glad that there was a term for whatever the hell it was. "Kind of, more like I was playing a video game or on autopilot. I could see myself doing what I needed to do, like making orders, but I wasn't fully in the moment. Then these terrible thoughts started happening. I thought I was going crazy, but I was too afraid to tell you. I'm sorry if I freaked you out."

Rapid knocking on the front door startled her, and Clay put up a hand to signal for her not to be scared. "It's only Gage."

Nikolas left the crowded booth and unlocked the door. Gage pushed past him and she could feel the anger radiating off him. "What the fuck happened?" His eyes landed on her and he stopped, his anger turning into alarm.

A feeling of extreme exhaustion overtook her. He was the last person she wanted to see right now. "I think I want to go home, I'm so tired."

Clay nodded. "I can take you home."

"No, I can drive myself. I want to be alone."

"I would feel better if someone were with you. Gage?" He turned to his son, who shoved his hands in his pockets and shifted uneasily on his feet.

"No, I'll be fine," she answered for him. She stood up, brushing the dust from the storage room off her rear.

"Is anyone going to tell me what happened?" Gage asked in a calmer tone.

"I don't feel like talking to you right now, they can update you." She waved her hand toward the three boys in the booth. She turned back to Clay. "If you really want someone to be with me tonight, I'll call Marla and have her come over. Would that make you feel better?"

He gave Gage a questioning glance before responding. "Yes, that would. I can lock up tonight if you want to head out now."

"Thank you." She stepped over him and grabbed her purse from behind the counter.

"Willow," Gage started, but cut himself off when she glared at him.

"I told you, I don't want to talk to you. So fuck off." She walked past him with her head held high and slammed the door behind her.

Twenty

Gage

"How sick is this hotel room?" Robby swung open the connecting door between his and Gage's rooms and looked around their new environment.

Before leaving for Miami with his cousin, Gage's boys had informed him of the attack on Willow. He could smell a setup a mile away and knew that Waldo had planned it all to try to be her rescuer. It was a repeat of Venice all over again.

He knew leaving Willow with Waldo still in town wasn't the smartest idea, but her blatant rejection of him in front of everyone made it clear she didn't want him around. Explaining to them why he was supposed to fuck off was the most uncomfortable conversation he ever had. Clay had agreed that maybe some time away would be best and Nikolas promised to keep an eye on her. Horatio and Matteo sat there and looked at him like he was the biggest idiot on the planet.

They weren't wrong.

That second time they had sex wasn't supposed to happen. He had it all planned out how he was going to tell her about Venice, his trust issues, and he was even going to take Robby's recommendation and tell her that he was a little scared. Because he was. The feelings he had for her were stronger than he had with Venice, yet he had known Willow for a much shorter time.

That night, it was like his brain had turned to mush when he looked at her and all he wanted was to be inside of her as she clung to him screaming his name. He'd let his primitive part out and took her on that table instead of having the civilized conversation he wanted. Then he ran away scared like a dog with it's tail between his legs. When he got home he'd destroyed his painting of the beach scene out of anger at his stupidity. He'd thought about how she would never talk to him again, and he turned out to be right. To make it worse, it had seemed like Waldo was trying to snake his way in and take his place.

He'd blown his last chance at love. He would be lucky if he could even get her to the point where she would be willing to be civil toward him. So he'd left for Miami to get some information on why Waldo was going north and to try to revert to his old ways to help him move on from Willow.

Robby continued, "We've got front row seats to the ocean, an in-ground pool, room service with a five course meal as an option, and everything looks so clean. I'm used to staying in some sketchy motel on the mainland where you're lucky if you get a working toilet."

"I figured you would pick the cheapest option available, that's why I booked the room."

Gage opened the small fridge that was settled into the TV stand and pulled out a mini bottle of tequila and took a shot. He noticed a small switch on the wall and flicked it, triggering blue LED lights to flash on behind the 52-inch TV. Robby let out an astonished gasp as he turned off the main lights and the entire room glowed blue.

"Dude, imagine taking acid and having sex with these lights on. It would be the most magical time of my life." Robby spun around and let out a small laugh. "Actually, scratch that. I don't think I would be able to get it up since I would be too distracted by the beauty of this room."

"You are so easily amused, it's alarming. Speaking of sex, are you going to be my wingman tonight or what?"

Gage grabbed a pair of cufflinks with fangs engraved on them and attached them to his black dress shirt. It wasn't often he dressed up, but tonight he was hoping putting extra effort into his looks would help this depression over Willow. It hadn't fully settled on him yet, but he knew if he was alone with his thoughts for too long the depression would jump off the sidelines and take over.

Robby stared at him out of the corner of his eye and spoke slowly. "Your wingman for information about Waldo, right? Not sex?"

"Both. Tonight's goals are to find out what we can about Waldo and finding me a pretty girl to fuck."

"Whoa whoa whoa. I may be a whore, but I'm not a *cheating* whore. There's no way I'm going to help you cheat on Willow while we're here. She's way too sweet and deserves better than that."

"Don't worry, we're not together and she completely hates my guts. So I'm in the clear to get with whoever I want." He threw his empty tequila bottle into the trash and headed toward the door. When he noticed that Robby wasn't following him, he turned around a raised an eyebrow. "Are you coming?"

Robby's face scrunched up in confusion. "What happened? I thought you were going to talk to her and apologize for saying sleeping with her was a mistake."

"I tried, but then I fucked it up even more. It's to the point now where she straight up told me she doesn't want to talk to me."

Robby covered his mouth with his hand. "What did you do?"

Gage closed his eyes and groaned. "I chickened out and had sex with her again instead of talking to her."

Robby dropped his hand and screamed, "What do you mean you chickened out and had sex again! How does that even happen? The sex comes *after* you talk it out, not before! What did you say afterward?"

"Nothing. I said absolutely nothing and left. Then she was attacked and saved by Waldo after I acted like a piece of shit, and now not only do I feel like an idiot, but I feel like a *guilty* idiot. Maybe if I wouldn't have been such a fucking pussy, we could've worked things out and she would have never been out alone. But that's not what happened, and now she wants nothing to do with me. I'm going to lose another girl to Waldo." He ripped open the hotel door and his voice came out bitter and sarcastic. "But hey, like I've been saying, I'm not the dating type. I'm just a lowlife scumbag vampire that can't handle a relationship. So, let's go."

To his surprise, Robby kept his mouth shut and did not continue the conversation. To start their night, they ended up at a dive bar next to the hotel. They planned out which clubs would be best for finding those who were a part of Waldo's family and would spill some information about what "north" meant. They would also scope out potential new family members, though Gage was less concerned about that and more concerned about finding a woman he could bury himself in to block out his ever-growing thoughts of Willow.

Gage downed his sixth shot of the night. "How many men does Waldo have in his family?"

"I don't know the exact number, but I know it's a lot. The stupid bastard has adding new members down to a science. I swear he's like a Mormon and goes around knocking on doors asking if people are interested in eternal life."

Gage snorted. "Could you imagine him in a white button down with slicked-back hair and a bowtie? I think I would have to punch him just for looking like a dork."

Robby frowned. "Yeah, well, there's many reasons why I would want to punch him."

Both Robby and his attention were dragged toward the TV above the bar, which stated there was breaking news. Half the crowd in the bar also noticed the alert, so the bartender turned up the volume.

"Another surfer was attacked today, this time near West Palm Beach. This marks the second dolphin attack within the past month, something that is not only confusing, but also unlikely. Dolphins have been known to drag people underwater to cause accidental drowning or have attacked when provoked, but Florida has never encountered dolphins that have purposely attacked humans. Scientists are looking into causes as to why this phenomenon is occurring, but for now the reasoning is unknown. It is advised to stay away from any wild dolphins if you are participating in ocean activities. Stay alert, stay calm, and most importantly stay away. Back to you, Mark."

"Well, there goes my plan to take that surfing class tomorrow." A feminine voice sighed and Gage turned to find a petite blonde perched next to him at the bar.

"Yeah, that's not the best activity to do right now." He responded.

He gave her a once over, noticing that she had the legs of a supermodel, pin-straight hair with platinum highlights, and a rounded face that matched her round, blue eyes. She was wearing a white sundress that accentuated her tanned skin, which smelled like coconuts and water lilies. She looked like the perfect distraction.

"Such a shame I drove all the way down here from Nashville to learn how to surf. Guess I'll be laying around the pool all day instead."

"You're from Tennessee?"

She giggled. "No, Nashville, Georgia. I get that a lot though. I'm down here for my friend's birthday, it's her big three-oh so we decided to plan a girl's trip to Miami. What are you here for?"

"My cousin and I just wanted to take a vacation. We're from up near Daytona, but the clubs are better down here."

"Clubs? Is that what you guys are doing tonight?"

"Yeah. You know, you and your friends are more than welcome to join us. We're probably going to start at Peter's Bay, then go club hopping to whatever seems interesting."

"Oh, that would be so much fun! Let me go ask the girls and see what they say."

Gage watched her ass wiggle as she headed toward a table packed with similar-looking girls. Robby leaned over and whispered, "Why did you have to invite them? She's got like eight other friends with her, none of them male."

"That's eight potential girls to convince that they want to join our families, and one for me to sleep with."

They watched as the girls squealed and clapped at their ring leader's suggestion to join them. "They seem annoying as hell and I know you don't have the patience for them." Robby said.

"What does that matter? I thought we were viewing them more like employees than part of our family. It's not like they'll be living with me."

"For what job would we hire them for, Gage? What job! Also, two of them clearly have fangs and are already probably part of a family. It's a grey area when we start enticing others to leave their current one. You have enough drama happening and don't need to add more by starting stuff with other families."

The boys dropped their conversation as the blonde bounced her way back across the bar. "They said that would be an awesome adventure! My name is Gabby, by the way."

"Mine's Gage, and this idiot is Robby." Gage nodded his head toward his cousin.

The group of girls collectively stood up from their table and made their way over to the bar. He hated to admit that Robby was right. His nerves were put on edge as three of them cackled at some ridiculous joke, two swooned over Robby, and three more flagged down the waiter to order one last drink. Gabby was the only one who seemed somewhat tolerable.

"I'm sorry, my friends can be a little much." Gabby smiled at him.

"It's fine."

"Your face tells me differently, you look so annoyed."

"My face always looks like that, don't take offense to it."

A faint blush crept up her cheeks. "If you don't want to go out with them, I would be fine with staying behind and doing something else. I wouldn't mind getting to know you better and I don't think we'll be able to talk much inside these clubs."

Gage looked over his shoulder at his cousin who was surrounded by a sea of blonde women, suddenly adoring all the attention he was complaining about a few seconds earlier. "I think our party will be just fine without us. Where were you thinking of going?"

She pursed her lips and looked up at him from under her thick eyelashes, cocking a brow. The look reminded him of Willow as she waited for his reaction after naming the drink, The Rich Brat, after him. It took everything in him to keep his focus on the pretty little mouth in front of him and not let the cloud of depression consume him.

"I think your hotel room would be pretty quiet, what do you think?"

"I think it'll be quiet until we get there." He smiled and wrapped his arm around her, guiding her away from the bar and to the hotel next door. On his way out, he noticed Robby look at him with a sad smile.

The two crashed into the room, barely closing the door behind them, their lips entwined together and tongues desperately searching for each other's mouths. No matter how much he tried, his mouth had not found the sweetness he was craving.

Gabby broke the kiss and stepped backward, and he smirked as she began to lower the sleeves of her dress to reveal the white strapless bra she was hiding underneath. As she slowly slid out of her clothing, Gage sauntered over to the switch and flipped on the LEDs, turning her white lingerie an iridescent blue.

She uttered an astonished noise, then watched him as he stepped toward her and wrapped his arms around her to undo the bra. Her pink nipples were hard, begging him to take them between his teeth. She laid down on the bed sensually, never breaking eye contact with him, and let her hair fan out behind her.

He tried to stay in the moment, but his mind was a traitor and kept wandering off. The excitement in him wavered as he imagined a flash of brown hair and recalled Willow's face as she looked up at him so affectionately at Sammy's party. He wanted nothing more than to worship her that night as she spread herself out for him. He knelt before her and tasted her, reveling in the wetness he had caused.

Tonight, he was not kneeling for Gabby.

He pulled her off the bed only to take her place. He slipped her underwear off and placed his hands on her hips to guide her to straddle him. She let out a soft moan as she began to grind on his pelvis. He tried his hardest to focus only on the topless blonde that was pleasuring herself on top of him, but a knife of guilt was beginning to rip into his heart.

"Is something wrong?" She whispered. He knew he was as limp as a dehydrated plant, but instead of being frustrated or embarrassed, he was simply sad.

She tried to thrust her tongue back into his mouth, but found his teeth were blocking her way. He pulled back and looked her in the eyes. "There's nothing wrong, you're...just not *her.*"

"Oh." She stopped her grinding and a look of understanding crossed her face. It seemed like this was not the first time this scenario had happened.

"Yeah. I think I need to go." He gently slid her off and stood up to grab his phone off the counter. "If Robby asks what happened, let him know I went to get some coffee, okay?"

She nodded and began putting her clothes back on. "I hope things work out between you two."

"Me too."

Twenty-One

Willow

"Where did you put the little cheat sheet at?" Marla asked as she danced around Willow behind the counter in The Coffee House Bunny.

It was only her first night working here, but she was picking things up quicky. It helped that Willow had spent a few hours crafting her own little book of recipes for all the popular drinks. If anyone ordered anything rare or off the wall, Willow gave her permission to craft it however she wanted. She wasn't a stickler for things like that.

"It's under the register. I think we should make that it's designated spot so it's easier to find." Willow watched as Marla flipped through the pages to find what she needed, then placed it on top of the counter by the tip jar.

Willow sighed and left it there.

She had asked Marla to work in the coffee house the night she was attacked. There were two reasons she had decided to hire her, one of which was that Marla was tired of her boring retail job, the other being that she felt more comfortable having another person with her in the café at night. After learning about the attack, Marla was quick to agree and started the very next day.

She hadn't told anyone about what Jesse James told her, how Clay may not be the innocent, kind man she had come to assume he was. She was still processing the fact that Clay had killed his best friends and father. True, he was getting revenge for a few human lives lost, but why did he go to such an extreme?

She frowned at herself for being so surprised. She knew better—her ex-boyfriend had shown her on more than one occasion that some people could turn violent very, very quickly for no apparent reason. Still, she felt like she was missing a piece of the puzzle.

"Have a good night." Willow smiled and handed the copper-haired man his drink. She had meant to get his name, but he was already out the door before she could ask. He was definitely a squirrely one.

"I'm surprised you haven't asked about Gage at all," Marla remarked.

"I guess I haven't been thinking about him," she lied.

Marla snapped her head around to give her a dramatic stare. "You know I don't believe that for a second, right? You two had amazing sex, once in this very café, then he runs off to Miami without talking to you? Yeah, no, you've been thinking about him."

Willow regretted telling her about sleeping with Gage. She had finally confided in her friend everything that had happened between them, and how confused and angry he left her feeling. After applauding her for telling him to fuck off, Marla's response was to remind her that men were dumb and to give him time to figure out his feelings.

"Miami? Why would he go there?"

"Matteo said something about trying to find new family members with Robby. I don't understand why he can't turn me and add me to the family." She pouted. "He turned Sammy and she's obnoxious as hell. I would make such a cute little vampire, don't you think?"

Willow didn't answer, not comfortable with the thought that her one and only friend here wanted to turn and join a family she wasn't quite sure she trusted yet.

It didn't bother her finding out about Sammy. She had yet to consider Sammy a friend, agreeing slightly with Marla. Sammy gave off the vibe that she was one of those popular, mean cheerleaders back in high school, and Willow was slightly concerned that someone with that attitude had become a vampire.

"I guess they think Waldo—er, Jesse James, as you call him—is planning to attack us and take over this territory since the family is so small," Marla continued. "Gage probably went down there to find out more information about that too. I'm really glad we have the boys to protect us. I wouldn't want to be caught in the middle of a vampire fight without someone making sure we're safe."

"Who's to say we're on the right side of the fight?"

Marla bent down to put the almond milk back in the fridge, but froze mid-crouch. "Um, I think it's obvious that we're on the right side. We have the hotter men and Waldo's a power-hungry psychopath who enjoys tormenting Gage."

"I don't think he's like that, he was very sweet to me the night he saved me. Maybe we can convince them to combine their families instead of having to fight each other."

Marla snorted and stood up. "I don't think that would happen. I see the way Matteo talks about Waldo and he spits every time he says his name. Did Gage not tell you about what happened with Venice?"

Her voice was more bitter than intended. "Who the hell is Venice?"

"I don't know the details, but Matteo said that Gage used to date this stripper chick named Venice."

Willow rolled her eyes. "Was that her real name, or her stripper name?"

Marla shrugged and continued, "I guess they were really in love. Well, *he* was really in love. Matteo thinks she was only with him for his money and status."

Willow hated that a seed of jealousy was beginning to bloom in her chest. Marla must have been able to tell from the look on her face because she continued, "Don't worry, any leftover love he had for her is dead because the skank cheated on him with Waldo and ran off with him. No one has heard from her since, so who knows what he did to her. You should really talk to Gage about this, maybe that has something to do with why he pushed you away. Or maybe he's already falling in love with you but is scared?" She cooed and brought her hands together over her heart, "Oh how cute is that! Some big, tough vampire is scared of love, but you can change that! Damn, you really are living the dream."

"Yeah, I don't know if I ever want to talk to him again."

"I would bet money that he's going to come back from Miami and you two will work it out. How cool would it be if we both dated vampires from the same family? I think you would get to pull rank though, since you would be with the head of the family. Don't forget to think of us poor peasants that have to date lowly normal members."

"I think you're living in a fantasy world, Marla. When did you and Matteo officially start dating?"

She pouted. "We're not official yet. We hang out a lot, mess around a lot, and that dinner at the Italian restaurant felt date-ish, but he never called it that. He's also never referred to me as his girlfriend, so my status is still a single lady. That's where I get jealous of Sammy. Horatio is so good to her, and basically worships the ground she walks on. I wouldn't be surprised if they get married soon."

"That would be a whirlwind romance. They haven't even been together that long."

"When you know, you know."

Marla greeted the two nurses who had walked in. They both looked like they had been through hell tonight. One had her frizzy blonde hair in a ponytail that was coming undone, with dark blue bags under her eyes. The other had a matching brunette ponytail with light stains over her scrubs, like she had accidentally sprayed herself with bleach.

"Tough night?" Willow asked as she readied the espresso machine.

The blonde one took the double espresso shot from Willow. "Yup, Daytona has been sending their overflow our way. I'm not sure what's going on, but a lot of people have been getting attacked both here and in Daytona. You two girls be careful tonight. It makes me nervous that you're open all night, but I'm very grateful."

Willow scrunched up her face in concern, realizing that she could have been one of their patients the other night. "What's going on with these attacks? I haven't seen anything on the news."

The brunette responded, "And you won't. You must be new to the area. Most stuff like this never gets talked about on the news because they don't want people to panic and kill the tourist income."

"Do we know who's causing all the attacks? It's not the dolphins, is it?" Willow asked.

"No. It's all the damn vampires." The blonde one gave a sad smile and turned to leave, her coworker hurriedly following behind her.

Willow turned and faced Marla. "Was I the only one living here who didn't know about vampires?"

"There are some who genuinely don't know or choose to ignore the signs.That's why the news doesn't usually cover vampire stories, unless it's something sensational like a teen goth who kills people. But even then, they say it's a delusion. I guess it's to keep us all dumb and ignorant about the real world. It makes me wonder what else the government and media is hiding."

"I miss being dumb and ignorant. Those were the good old days when I could have sex and only worry about STDs or pregnancy. Now I have to worry about if I'm going to get my blood sucked too. How awkward would that be if he killed me and the police found my corpse naked and mid-orgasm?"

"Do you think you would be frozen with your O-face if you did die like that?"

"I really hope not. I can't imagine that would be pretty." Willow looked at Marla and the two broke out in laughter.

The heaviness that had been weighing on Willow's chest since the night of her attack began to lift. Laughing about being murdered by a vampire might not be sane, exactly, but it was her form of therapy, and she was glad that she had a friend to share it with.

ꙅꙅꙅꙅ

Willow sent Marla home early since Matteo had come in and invited her to stay the day at his place. Her usefulness dissipated as she began bouncing in place and all common sense left her at the promise of spending time alone with him. Willow only had three hours left of being open and she was feeling confident enough to be able to handle them alone. The sun would be up by the time she left, so she felt safe walking to her car.

She did not have much to do, so she leaned against the counter and researched cookie recipes on her phone. Baking was not her strong suit, but she was eager to add bakery items to her menu. She made a mental note to ask Marla if she was any better in the kitchen.

As she was scrolling, she heard the chimes on her door open. "Hi, welcome to—"

Her voice abruptly quit on her as she made eye contact with brooding green eyes and a mane of shaggy blonde hair.

She put her hand on her hip and narrowed her eyes. "I was wondering when you were going to make an appearance."

"I figured you might need some space." Gage made his way up to the counter carefully, like a man approaching a sleeping lion.

She nodded. "I did."

"How are you doing after the attack?"

"Well, I never want to physically fight a vampire ever again."

He looked around the café and a spark of anger flickered across his face. "Why are you here alone? Nikolas said he would watch over you."

"I don't need a man to watch over me. Marla was here earlier. She actually works here with me now, but I sent her home early to go spend some time with Matteo. I thought you were supposed to be in Miami?"

"I was, but something happened and I needed to see you."

"What happened?"

He hesitated, like he wasn't sure if what he was about to say would make the situation worse or not. "I…I tried to sleep with a girl, but I couldn't get you out of my mind."

The jealousy from earlier came back full force. It ignited her anger, and she could tell it showed from the way he took a step back from the counter. "Oh? And how far did you go with her?"

"Well, my dick wouldn't get hard, so we didn't go far."

She cackled. "Serves you right." She wondered if her mother's spirit was seeking revenge for her in the afterlife and had cursed him with a limp dick.

"I wasn't lying when I told you that you consume my every thought, Willow. I don't get it. I've never met anyone like you who has taken over my mind like this."

"Let me guess, that's a line you used with Venice?" As soon as the question left her mouth, she wanted to take it back. She knew it was a nasty thing to say and could tell by his hurt expression that it was a low blow.

"Who told you about her?"

"Marla. She said you were in love with her, but she ran off with

Jesse James."

"There's more to it than that. Can I sit, or would you rather just chop off my dick and call it a night?"

She motioned toward the stool at the counter. "Have a seat. I have to sharpen my knives first."

"Wouldn't a dull one be more fun?"

She side-eyed him and they both gave each other a small, wary smile. "Tell me about Venice."

"Before I tell you about her, I have to tell you about my father's family. He had a big one, but he knew them all by name. Hell, he even knew their children's names. One thing about my dad that I respect more than anything is how much he can care about the people he's in charge of. The humans in Vista Maria were considered part of his family, even if they didn't know it, and he designed his rules not only to keep them safe but to better their community.

"I wasn't raised by only my mother and father. I considered everyone in his family like an uncle. They would come over for holidays, birthdays, big sporting events, you name it. Our lives were entwined. But then one day that was all destroyed. Miami ran by different rules and would kill innocents in other territories. They chose to kill a group on our beach and my father got justified retribution."

Willow nodded, "I know, Jesse James told me that already and he seemed genuinely remorseful about what he and his friends had done. I don't understand why Clay went to such extreme lengths—surely that's not the first time an innocent has died on your territory."

"Waldo's playing you, that's what sociopaths do. They're expert liars and know how to manipulate emotions." He looked away and clenched his jaw. "My dad lost his cool after the beach incident, because he almost lost me. I was with the group that night and almost died trying to protect them. I can still remember what it felt like as two of Waldo's friends held me up while he repeatedly stabbed me with a knife."

Willow's breath caught in her throat. "Oh, he left that part out."

"I'm sure he did, but I'm surprised he didn't brag about almost killing me. I still don't know why he didn't, unless he kept me alive because he wanted a new toy. He must find some kind of sick joy in messing with my life. My dad had to pull me out of the sand and carry me home after the damage Waldo did, and even with our ability to heal quickly I still was not in the best shape when Gerald came and attacked. Waldo wasn't with his father, so if he said he had nothing to do with their slaughter, he's not technically wrong."

"Slaughter?" She came around the corner and sat next to him.

"My dad's entire family was wiped out in one night. We didn't even see it coming, but Miami stormed our city, killing any humans they could get their hands on, so my dad rounded up his family to stop them. They had it all planned out and lured us to the beach to trap us. They came in on all sides and cornered us against the ocean and started murdering everyone we loved."

His voice cracked and his gaze looked far away like he was reliving the night. "I tried to fight, I really did, but there were too many of them. We had called Daytona, but by the time they arrived, it was over. They walked up to a beach soaked in blood and littered with bodies. We were able to kill a lot of the Miami family, though some ran away probably to tell Waldo the outcome. My dad and Gerald were left, but my dad screamed at me and Uncle Al to stay out of it—he wanted to kill Gerald himself. And he did just that. Ripped his head right off his body and beat his chest in until there was nothing left but bloody pulp. I had never seen my dad cry like that, even at my mother's funeral. He was covered in so much blood his tears looked like they were made of blood themselves. And he was just screaming, and screaming, and nothing we could do would make him stop."

He finally turned and looked at Willow, his eyes glassy. "It was fucking horrible. He stayed in his room for days before he finally came out and told me that he was stepping down and I was to take over the family. I was thrown into a role I wasn't ready for, while also having to start my own family from scratch. Thankfully I had met Nikolas long before this, and he became the first member."

He rubbed his face and sighed. It took everything in her not to reach out and touch him. "I was in a terrible mindset for obvious reasons, so Nikolas took me hunting for this rapist to get my mind off things. We found him in a strip club, which is where I met Venice. We also met Horatio and Matteo there that night, but I was more focused on Venice the Vixen." He rolled his eyes. "That was her stage name, Vixen. Fucking stupid. Anyway, she knew who I was and came over to me. I was in such a vulnerable state, I let her in and like an idiot, I fell in love. We were together for months, but it was the most toxic relationship. I clung to her, though, because she would give me a sliver of happiness and I craved that after all that happened."

Willow nodded, understanding exactly what he meant.

"I never suspected that she was cheating on me, but she had been for weeks with Waldo. The very man who was the reason my dad's family was slaughtered. And she *knew* about that. Then, on the night I was going to propose, she left me a note saying how Waldo treated her better and that she was in love with him, so she was leaving me."

He gave a dry laugh. "I had that whole night planned, but looking back I realize it was stupid. I'd set up an elaborate picnic on the beach during a full moon complete with candles, wine, and rose petals. I'd spent over ten grand on a ring I customized myself, and had it put on top of this molten lava cake. I'd even planned out how to hold the damn dessert just right so the ring would reflect the moonlight."

"I don't think that sounds stupid, it sounds romantic," she whispered.

"Yeah, it was real romantic as I waited there for over three hours. Nikolas was the one to find the note and bring it to me. I already knew something was wrong by the time he showed up, though. To top it off,

I threw the fucking ring into the ocean in my rage and couldn't even get that money back. I hope some fish choked on it."

He looked down and played with some stray coffee grounds that she'd missed in her wipe-down. "Ever since then I've been telling myself I'm not the dating type, because I can't survive another heartbreak like that. It was better to be alone. But then you came along and opened this little café in one of my dad's properties."

She placed her hand under his chin and made him look at her. She meant to say something about how she understood what it was like to prefer being alone to risking pain. That she knew what it was like to get sucked into an abusive relationship, never feeling like you could fully escape the memories. She was even ready to disclose to him what happened the night she left her ex-boyfriend. But looking into his eyes caused all thought to leave her mind except one.

She leaned forward and kissed him.

Twenty-Two

Willow

Willow was sitting on her balcony trying to convince herself not to change her outfit for the fourth time. Her first one had been too frumpy, with a hoodie and leggings. Her second outfit had been too sexy, with a tight red halter top and low-cut, black skinny jeans. Her third outfit was in-between, with an off-the-shoulder lilac sweater and leggings, but she felt the sweater made her look fat.

When she decided to throw on a different shirt, the rumble of a motorcycle filled her parking lot. She abandoned the fourth wardrobe change and dashed out the door and down the steps to her waiting ride. It wasn't until she landed on a sharp rock outside that she realized she'd forgotten her shoes. Gage looked at her behind black-tinted sunglasses and lifted his brow as she balanced on one foot and massaged the other, biting her bottom lip to keep the string of curse words inside.

"Did you forget something?" She couldn't see his eyes, but could feel that taunting laughter that was behind his shades.

"I'll be right back!"

It took her less than a minute, and by the time she was standing next to Gage preparing to throw her leg over the bike, she was breathing hard.

He looked over his shoulder and slowly tilted his head down. "I wouldn't recommend riding a bike with flip-flops on."

"Aw come on, don't make me run up to my apartment again."

"It's your own fault for not putting on real shoes to begin with. I don't want to have to listen to you cry when a rock flies up underneath your toenail."

She grimaced at him, but decided she liked having all her toenails intact. She could hear him chuckling behind her as she once again ran into her building and climbed the stairs, this time much slower.

By the time she returned she felt sweaty and gross, regretting not changing into a short-sleeved shirt when she had the chance. "Does this work?"

He slowly looked her up and down, then sucked his teeth and shook his head. "You're probably going to get cold. The wind off the ocean has been cool lately, on top of the wind from the bike. You should probably run up those stairs one more time to grab a coat."

"You're just messing with me now."

He shrugged. "Suit yourself, but I'm not giving you my jacket when you start complaining."

"I wouldn't wear it anyway." She pouted.

She hesitated and glanced up at her apartment sitting high above her. She never thought she would be the type to think sixty degrees was cold, but here she was. And he was right—the breeze was chilly tonight, and the lack of sun made her shiver. She made one last trip upstairs and changed into the first outfit she'd originally planned.

He was laughing as she came down her steps with sweat starting to line her brow. "You know I was joking, right? I totally would have given you my jacket."

"Why did you let me go back up there, then?" She whined.

"'Cause I like watching you run up stairs."

She rolled her eyes and slid gently onto the back of his bike. She could smell the light scent of leather from his jacket, mixed with his mahogany and black teakwood bodywash. He sat up straighter as she placed her hands on his sides, preparing for the sendoff.

Unlike the previous time they'd ridden together, he was not as kind. He hit the throttle, causing her to jerk backward and dig her nails into his jacket. His cackling could be heard over the roaring of the engine and she slapped him in the side hard enough that her hand stung. She doubted he felt it under the protection of a hoodie and jacket.

His smirk filled the side mirror. "Hit me harder, mommy."

"Oh, you're gross. If I'd known this was the type of mood you would be in, I would've stayed at home where I could be comfortably lounging in my pajamas, not being harassed by a man."

His only response was to laugh again and pat her thigh. Turning her head to hide the blush that climbed up her face, she watched as the world streaked by.

This was their first date after his disclosure. Marla had been right—Venice was the reason he'd pushed her away and seemed so confused about his feelings. But after she leaned forward and kissed him, neither of them were confused anymore. He about took her right there on top of the counter when a customer walked in and she had to go back to being a professional barista.

He had been so easy to forgive. She had never had a man show her such a vulnerable side to himself like he'd done when he'd told her about Clay's former family. Her heart hurt for Clay, given that he'd lost his wife to suicide, which carried its own unique weight, found his son beaten half to death, then lost his entire family. The burden she carried seemed trivial compared to that. She felt more emboldened to tell Gage the truth of why she left Michigan. Maybe tonight would be the night she got that off her chest.

She leaned her cheek against his shoulder and they rode this way for a while. Her plan had been for him to come over to test out a cookie recipe she was experimenting with for the café, but when he'd suggested a motorcycle ride, she eagerly changed her plans. The cookies could wait.

He pulled up to a familiar spot on the beach. It was down a ways from the boardwalk and she held on tight as he guided his bike over the sand. There were a few couples walking along the moonlit shore hand in hand, but they paid them no mind as he parked and helped her off.

"I hope you don't think I'm going to strip naked and wade into the water again. I learned my lesson the first time I did that."

"Damn, I was hoping to get some inspiration for a new painting." He smiled down at her and pulled out a blanket from his saddlebag. They walked closer to the water, the soothing sound of the waves relaxing her, and he spread it out for them to sit on and watch the endless ocean. Off in the distance, she saw two dolphins jump into the night air.

She chuckled. "Leave it to Florida to get man-eating dolphins."

"Yeah…about that. I think Nikolas may have accidentally caused that outbreak. You should totally harass him about that next time he's in the café."

"How did he manage that?" She could tell her question made him uncomfortable as he cleared his throat and thought through his answer.

"So, you know we have to drink blood to survive, and that we don't kill innocent people. But sometimes we kill not-innocent people and have to dispose of the bodies."

He glanced at her quickly to gauge her response, and she shrugged to help put him at ease. "We do the same thing to animals, only we torture them and force them to live in dirty, cramped environments first. At least you kill these people quickly, right?"

"Sometimes. Do you really want me to make a pedophile's death quick and painless, though?"

She didn't even have to think about her response. "Nah, drag it out. How often do you have to kill?"

"About once a week, unless I lose a lot of blood, then I need to refill sooner. We still have to eat food to keep our bodies running, but our bodies can't create new blood, so we have to replenish it. Think of blood like gas in a car, we have to top it off every once in a while. Newer vampires need to drink more often, but the older and stronger you get the less you run through it."

His thumb made mesmerizing small circles in the sensitive space between her thumb and index finger. She watched it as the next question burned at the tip of her tongue. "Have you ever thought about drinking *my* blood?"

He paused and rubbed the back of his neck. "Yeah I have, but I would never hurt you. You smell sweet, that's all. It would be like if you walked past a bakery—wouldn't you think about eating whatever they made?"

Willow scrunched her nose. "I smell like a bakery? That's weird."

"More like vanilla candy. Most people don't smell like that, so you kind of stand out."

"Oh great, that makes me so much more comfortable knowing that I'm a giant, smelly temptation for vampires. Can I ask another question?"

"What, are we playing twenty questions about being a vampire tonight?" He smirked.

"I'm curious, okay? This is all new to me. After Waldo rescued me, he told me a little about why people willingly give blood to vampires. He mentioned that your bite can uh…feel good." Her face burned red.

She had seen this man naked twice now, had his face buried between her legs, but for some reason asking if his bite would make her orgasm was making her feel like a schoolgirl asking a question in sex ed.

He furrowed his brow. "Why did he bring that up?"

"He offered to mark me and explained that a bite mark can keep me safe from rouge vampires."

His face turned pale. "You didn't let him, right?"

"Of course not! But he told me to think about it and I have. If anyone marks me it should be you."

He snorted. "Don't tell me you've developed a weird fantasy of me biting you? Are you going to become like your friend Marla and become obsessed with me like she is with Matteo?"

"Marla isn't obsessed, she's very fond of him."

"They're both weirdly obsessed, but Matteo doesn't want to admit it." He turned and gave her a feline smile, revealing his fangs. "But if you seriously want me to bite you, I'd be more than willing. In fact, I already have a spot picked out. We could do it right here."

"Gage! There are still people on the beach, I don't want them to see that, especially if it makes me…you know."

"But you're hot when you come. Let them watch."

The way he growled the last three words had her underwear instantly soaked. She didn't trust herself not to pounce on him, so she rolled her eyes and stood up. "Come on, you need to take me back to my apartment. I have cookies to bake."

"Is that a euphemism for something?"

"How about you take me back and find out?"

ɔɔɔɔ

Willow hummed to herself as she danced around her kitchen getting all the ingredients together for the cookies. Gage sat on a bar stool, arms crossed and leaning against the counter, watching her through her kitchen's pass-through window. His disappointment was clear when he realized that "cookies" was in fact *not* a euphemism. It brought her joy to slowly torture him like this—he deserved a little bit of payback, even if she did forgive him.

As she opened the fridge she gasped and dug through all the drawers, not finding the sticks of butter she thought would be there. Hoping she had some spare in the freezer, she stood up on her tip toes to dig through an abundance of frozen vegetables, different shaped fries, and bags of dino nuggets.

"There *butter* be some butter in here." She side-eyed Gage to see if he had heard her joke. He stared at her, and her insides twisted with how much she was cringing at herself.

"I'm sorry, that sounded much funnier in my head."

"There *butter* not be any in there with how bad that joke was."

She abruptly turned to face him, her laughter tinkling through the kitchen. She shut the freezer, abandoning the search and turned her full attention to the golden god that was perched on her chair. He looked so at ease in her apartment and stared at her with a gaze that made her want to squirm under its intensity.

Her breath caught in her throat as Gage pushed back his stool and walked around the corner to enter her kitchen. She shuffled backward as he blocked her into the corner of her counter and placed both hands on either side of her, trapping her. His mouth was mere inches away and she could feel his breath whisper across her skin.

"Your heart's racing," he whispered. He traced light line over her chest, dipping down to tickle her cleavage.

A slow, wicked smile crawled across his face and a realization came over her. He was a vampire twice her size, they were alone in her apartment, and he was close enough to rip open her throat in less than a second. But he smelled so good, and felt so *safe*. The paradox made her head spin.

Before she could think about it anymore, his mouth covered hers and she stopped thinking all together. It felt like he pulled all of her fears, sadness, and loneliness out through his kiss as she melted into him and wrapped her arms around his solid torso. Pulling him tighter against her chest, she pushed her tongue against his, wanting to taste him deeply. With her eyes closed and her mind empty, she explored him and tasted every inch that he was willing to give to her.

She jumped slightly when her tongue brushed against his long canines. Her reaction caused him to press against her harder and grab her by the back of the thighs, lifting her up to sit her on the counter. From this height, she was able to embrace his face with her hands and deepen her investigation of his mouth. She licked one sharp incisor gingerly with the tip of her tongue. She appreciated his patience as he allowed her to play her tongue across his teeth until she had her fill. She felt like a virgin again who'd recently learned how to French kiss, and was slightly embarrassed by her behavior.

She pulled away only for him to bend his head and place soft kisses along her neck and down her exposed shoulder. He grabbed her hoodie at her waist and bundled it into his fists as he slowly pulled it up and over. The slow sensation of the fabric gliding across her skin sent shivers down her body, which were only heightened as he continued his onslaught of gentle kisses along her collarbone.

She let out a small sigh and unclasped her bra to expose even more of herself to him. He didn't hesitate, and lowered his kisses along her breasts, circling each nipple with his tongue. She arched her back, allowing him to fully draw her into his mouth. He slipped his hands under the waistband of her leggings, and she lifted herself off the counter so that he could slide them off with ease. She didn't realize he had slipped off her underwear with them until the cool granite teased her hot center.

"I'm surprised you didn't slide off the counter with how wet you are." He chuckled into her ear as he glided one finger along her slit.

He brought his glistening finger to her face and pushed it into her mouth. She obliged and began sucking on it, wishing it was something a little bigger that was forcing its way between her teeth.

"Tell me, Willow," he purred, "do you trust me enough to let me bite you?"

With closed eyes, she continued sucking and nodded her head, more than eager to find out just how good his bite would feel. She opened her eyes halfway and released his finger with a pop. "I trust you not to kill me, but I don't care if you hurt me. It's not like I haven't been hurt before." She wrapped a naked leg around his waist and tried to bring him closer to resume her study of his mouth.

He resisted and stepped back to lower himself to his knees. "You don't deserve to be hurt. You deserve to be adored and worshiped like the goddess that you are."

She clasped her legs shut and frowned down at him. He placed his head on her knees and looked up at her with a sad smile.

"What? Do you not like it when men say nice things to you?"

"I'm not used to it. I guess it just makes me cringe and kind of ruins the moment, you know?"

"No, I don't know. I guess I'll have to train you to accept my compliments." He placed one last, gentle kiss on her thigh before roughly grabbing her knees and jerking her legs apart.

She gasped as he dove his face in between her legs and sucked her clit into his mouth, gently nipping at it with his teeth. His words vibrated against her core. "Now be a good girl and hold your legs apart so I can properly worship you."

Without a word, she did as she was asked and grabbed her legs behind her knees to hold them up. He slipped one finger into her aching center and began massaging her as he kept his mouth around her sensitive nub. He soon added a second finger into the mix, which caused her to dig her nails into her legs to keep from letting go to grab his hair. Something told her that if she disobeyed his one order, he would be sure to punish her.

As tempting as that was, she was enjoying his worship too much to find out what punishment would await her.

She tried her best to stay steady for him, but between the need to grind against his tongue, which was lapping at her, and the intense thrusting of his hand, she was finding it hard to remain balanced on the counter. She whimpered out his name to alert him that she was losing control, but instead of giving her some grace he shoved a third finger inside and stretched her further.

"Fuck, Gage," she moaned, finally relinquishing her death grip on one leg to tangle her fingers through his hair.

He stopped everything, leaving his fingers thrust deep inside her, and sat up to look at her with a dark passion in his eyes. "I didn't tell you to let go of your leg."

She looked down at him with narrowed eyes. "What are you going to do about it?"

A dark smile that matched the passion in his eyes slowly spread across his face.

Instead of responding, he ripped his fingers out of her and landed a sharp slap across her pussy. She held back a yelp as he closed her legs and grabbed her off the counter bridal-style to carry her to her bedroom. He threw her onto her unmade bed and kept the lights off so they were enshrouded in darkness.

"What do you want me to do about it?" He asked.

She heard the whisper of his clothing falling to the ground. It wasn't long before she felt the bed dip down with his weight as he straddled her naked and pulsing core.

"I want you to show me the spot you picked out."

Her breath caught as he grabbed both of her wrists in one hand and pulled them over her head. Her back arched reflexively as he leaned down closer, his face hovering inches above hers. "Are you sure?"

"Yes."

He traced his free hand over her jaw and down her neck. It lingered on the dip at the bottom of her throat before continuing its slow descent down between her breasts. This time, she felt his breath catch as he outlined a triangle on her midriff.

"Here, this is my favorite spot. It's soft and warm and so enticing, much like you are." He flicked his tongue out and licked the center of his triangle. "The dress you wore to the club drove me absolutely mad with that cut out in this exact spot. You were being such a tease and you didn't even know it."

She freed a hand and reached out into the darkness. He found her hand and threaded thier fingers together. He placed a kiss in his spot and she could feel him smile against her skin.

She took a deep breath and waited for the piercing, burning pain of his bite. Instead, she felt him lick the spot one last time and glide his teeth painlessly through her layers of skin.

"Gage! Oh fuck!" She screamed out as an orgasm instantly tore through her body, starting at the spot he was biting instead of her core. The pleasure rolled through her body for as long as he was biting and sucking on his spot. Her fingers grew numb with how tightly she gripped his hand.

She lost track of time until her body began shaking. He broke his suction, licking the line of blood streaming out of the two wounds that would permanently mark her, and quickly shoved his hard cock deep inside of her.

"Fucking hell, Willow," he groaned into her ear as he pounded into her pulsing sex.

Another orgasm was beginning to build within her, each stroke bringing her closer to the edge. She wrapped her legs around his waist and offered herself up to him as much as she could from her position on the bed. Each time he impaled her, it caused sparks of pleasure to explode within her.

His mouth came crashing down onto hers and he encircled her head with his arms as they both came together. This wave of pleasure still made her delirious with passion, but it was nowhere near as concentrated as when he was biting her. Part of her wanted to have him bite her again as she was coming, but she was afraid she wouldn't survive the fervent pleasure. She might combust.

He collapsed on top of her, both of them breathing heavy, his cock still buried inside her. She silently thanked herself for staying on her birth control as she kept her legs wrapped around him as his cock pumped the last of his seed into her. They eventually untangled each other and repositioned themselves under her covers. She grabbed a tissue from her bedside table and blotted the wound on her chest.

"I have a question," she asked.

"I might have an answer."

"Why do your bites make me feel that way? Isn't it weird when you go to kill someone and they have an orgasm before they die?"

His loud, sudden snort of laughter startled her. The vibration of his laughter shook the bed.

"Trust me, if someone pissed me off to the point I wanted to kill them, giving them an orgasm is the last thing I want. Not all bites feel that way, only when I want them to. It has something to do with our saliva, it has an aphrodisiac in it and if we fill the wound with it it'll cause intense orgasms."

"Huh, so you spit in my wound?"

"Way to take the romance out of it. No, I don't spit on you, though that's kind of hot in its own weird way. I *lick* you."

A tingling sensation crawled through her stomach. "Way to put the romance back in."

"Our saliva can also heal wounds if I were to lick it again. But, I don't want this one to heal." He traced it lightly and goosebumps rose on her skin at the ticklish sensation. "Then it won't leave a mark."

She snuggled up against his chest, holding the tissue to her new modification.

"Do you feel safer now?" He murmured as he stroked her hair.

"Yeah, I do." She whispered before falling into a deep, restful sleep.

Twenty-Three

Willow

Willow opened her café the next day with an extra bounce in her step. Marla had requested the day off to attend a concert with Matteo, so Willow was alone. She placed her hand beneath her breasts to remind herself that she was protected. Plus, she was sure the boys would be in soon for their nightly dose of caffeine.

"Hey Willow!" John beamed as he strode into the café with Ryan quietly behind him.

"Long time no see!" She beamed back. It had been a while since the two IT guys had graced her with their pleasant presence.

"Yup, I'm officially married!" John held up his hand to show off the golden band that was glittering in the light. "We were having trouble with both sets of parents trying to plan our wedding for us, so we said screw it and ran off to elope in Vegas. Ryan came with me like the true best friend he is. It was magical."

"Yeah, the Elvis priest was pretty magical." Ryan softly spoke.

"Oh congratulations! I'm so happy for you!" Willow clapped. Her emotions were shifting and instead of finding hurt or jealousy in another's love, she could enjoy it with them. She finally felt that she might know what it was like to be truly loved.

Her face flushed at the thought, so she quickly turned from the two to make their drinks. She listened in on their conversation about some maintenance issue at work silently, not understanding a damn thing they were saying, but appreciating the background noise.

"So, what's been up with you? You always ask us what's going on in our lives, but I don't think we know that much about you. Plus, you seem happier and, dare I say, a little dreamier than usual," John asked after they finished game planning and were handed their coffees. She hadn't realized it until now, but she'd had a grin on her face while stirring the drinks.

Willow shook her head at the money John tried to offer her. "Keep it, this is another one on the house to celebrate your wedding. And thank you for asking, it's rare I have customers that think about me like that. I've been doing really well, actually. I hired a new staff member so you might see her soon. Her name is Marla and she's a close friend of mine. You guys will get along with her, she's very sweet."

"Is she single?" John asked, pointing to Ryan. His friend glared at him but did nothing to retaliate.

"Sadly, I don't think so. I don't know what their official status is, but she only has eyes for Matteo."

The friendly look in John's face died at the mention of his name. "Matteo? Like the guy that occasionally comes in here with the other three?"

"Yup, that's the guy. And don't worry, she knows all about him being a vampire and is safe." Willow winked and began cleaning up.

The friendly look did not return to his face. "So, you know that they're serial killers that feed on people?"

"We know they're *vampires*. They're not the evil jerks you two think they are."

"You seemed smarter than that," John frowned, "You didn't strike me as the type to be so blind. Haven't you been paying attention? More and more people are dying because of their kind. It won't be long before over half of Florida is dead and replaced by these blood-sucking creatures."

"I understand that there are some evil vampires out there. In fact, I was attacked by one of them, but not all of them are like that. I've gotten to know the boys pretty well, and they care a lot about us humans. Clay set up rules for his kind specifically to keep us safe."

"All vampires are evil, Willow. They're here to take over America by taking our jobs, our money, or freedom, and our women until we become a nation full of them. I guess you are one of the women they stole."

"The only good vampire is a dead one," Ryan nodded his agreement.

Her stomach twisted and she tasted bile at the back of her throat. "I'm pretty horrified that this is how you talk about them."

"They need to be hung in the streets for what they do! Their sole purpose is to kill, rape, and destroy." John stood up, leaving his coffee behind, and headed to the door with Ryan close behind. "I guess this is goodbye. I can't support a business that supports *them*."

Her voice shook, tears welling in her eyes. "That's fine. I don't want customers that are close-minded and full of hate."

She wasn't sure if they heard her as they slammed her door closed before she could finish her sentence. She noticed two other customers who had been listening to the argument get up and leave. The rest nodded at her with sad smiles and continued with their personal discussions.

The rest of Willow's night went by with enough customers to keep her distracted from the argument. With only an hour until dawn, her café was empty and she had already restocked her barista cooler and wiped up the milk rings that decorated her counter. She drifted into the back room to grab almond milk and vanilla syrup when she heard the bells on her door chime. When she came back up her stomach dropped.

"Hello." She said.

As promised, Waldo had stopped in to see what she decided. She knew his reaction would not be pleasant when he discovered Gage had been the one to mark her.

"Well hello there Miss Willow, what a surprise to see you here." He sauntered up to the counter and gave her a smooth smile.

"Is it though? I do own the place."

"It was a joke my dear. Are you having a rough night? You seem a little cranky."

She changed her cool expression to her fake customer service smile. "No, my night has been fine. What can I make for you?"

Abandoning her quest in the stockroom, she took her usual spot in front of the espresso machine. She had been tempted to call him Waldo, as the boys still called him, but was afraid of his reaction. She felt safe enough for now, but was wary due to what she'd learned from Gage.

"I think I'll skip the caffeine tonight. It's getting close to my bedtime. That's not why I stopped by, anyway. I was wondering if you'd considered my proposition?"

"I have."

There was a deadly silence that amplified the tension building in the café. Willow knew she had to tell him no, but felt that he was not the type of guy to take rejection well.

"Before you give me your answer, how about I add a little more to it to help you decide? I know you hired a new girl here, which is honestly perfect timing because I wanted to offer a spot down in Miami for you. You seem to be pretty successful here, Miami definitely has a nightlife that could use a midnight coffee house like this, and I have a freshly-vacated building that needs a new business in it ASAP. Not only would you be able to turn your dream café into a chain, but you would be closer to me. It's really a win-win situation. And of course I would give you a discount on the rent."

He smirked in a way that gave her a sneaky suspicion that she would have to offer sexual favors in return for the discount. That made her very, *very* curious as to where Venice was. Surely he didn't think he could start a harem with her and that bitch?

"How did you know I hired someone? I haven't seen you in here recently."

"I have eyes everywhere, my dear. That's part of being a high-ranking, successful leader."

"But this isn't your territory, so I'm confused why you would have eyes here."

She didn't hold back on her attitude, annoyed that he had the audacity to assume she would give up her life here to follow him down to Miami like a lost puppy looking for a home. She was already building her own home here in Vista Maria.

"Did something happen since the last time I saw you? I know you had a pretty traumatizing experience with a vampire, but I thought you figured out that I was one of the good ones? I can't lie, I'm hurt by this defensiveness you have all of a sudden. You're a very attractive woman and very business-savvy on top of it. I'm interested in you as more than a renter. I would like to get to know you personally, too."

"Oh? But I thought you had a girlfriend already? You know, *Venice*." The name felt like venom on her tongue.

The confident appearance he had plastered on his face since he walked in disappeared and his eyes narrowed into a predatory gaze. Just as quickly, his expression returned to normal and a cold smile took over.

"Ah, so you've heard about her? I suppose Gage told you I stole her away. In reality, I saved her from a very abusive relationship."

"Save it Waldo, you're talking to someone who's been in an abusive relationship and I can tell who's bound to become an abuser. It's not Gage. Where is she? Did you do something to her?"

His smile twitched, but she had to give him credit because he was still restraining the rage-filled beast she could sense was smoldering underneath his calm exterior. He didn't seem like he enjoyed being spoken to so directly, let alone by a woman. Her hand was shaking and she clenched it at her side hoping he didn't notice.

"Gage got to you, didn't he?"

She shook her head at the random accusation. "What?"

"I'm offering you a once-in-a-lifetime chance to build up your career and offering you a coveted position as my main girl. I have a waitlist of women who want to date me, yet I've had my eye on you, so I've turned them all down. You're passing up not only wealth—because may I remind you that I am the highest-ranking leader in the state—but also a partner who can satisfy any of your desires and grant you any wish you might command from me. Gage must have brainwashed you into believing I'm a bad guy for you to turn that all down."

"What are you, a genie? I'm not a gold digger and I'm very content with how my life is now. You can't buy me with material things or whatever weird sexual innuendos you are referring to. The answer is no, and it will always be no."

Her brazenness shocked her, she never thought she would be healed enough to stand up for herself. The fire she had in her was coming out, but this time in a controlled way. She knew her mother would be proud of the woman she was turning into.

His voice was cold. "You have not answered my question about Gage."

"And you have not answered my question about Venice."

"Why are you so concerned for her? Are you scared that she'll come back and steal Gage away?"

"I want to know if you hurt her."

"She's fine, living very contently at the bottom of the ocean." His smile finally disappeared. "You'll join her one day, you know. You picked the wrong side to be on, and you will fall with the rest of them. I offered you safety, and you spat in my face. Tell me, where did he mark you? I can smell his scent on you from a mile away."

"That's none of your business." This time there was no hiding her shaking as her voice gave her away. She felt like all her attitude and confidence had been gut-punched out of her at his confession.

She slipped her phone out of her back pocket and prepared to call Gage. "Get out."

"You've made your choice without knowing the full story. Stupid girls like yourself always think they know better. Tell your *man* that there's no point in fighting—my territory is triple the size of his and growing. He can't stop me now, we're past that point." He turned and stuck his hand up in a lazy wave as he left. The tinkling bells on the door offered little solace to her fear.

As soon as he left, she ran to the door and locked it. Everything about Waldo had reminded her of her ex, and she cursed herself for letting the fear win at the end. Mixed among her racing thoughts were flashes of memories that strengthened her dread.

Her ex would use cruel names, but would play them off as jokes. He would break things or hide items of hers, but convince her she was the one who did it. He constantly demanded that she tell him her every move. She couldn't go to the store without his permission, couldn't talk to her friends anymore, couldn't even take a walk around the block without him tagging along. He accused her of not knowing how to handle money, so he eventually took control of her bank account to make sure she was spending it appropriately.

As time went on, he escalated. The verbal abuse grew physical the day she had to stay late at work. She could still feel her clothes being pulled from her body as he stripped her naked to inspect her for any signs of sexual evidence, roughly pulling her arms and legs apart and twisting them in ways that felt torturous. He ended the invasion with a sharp slap across her face that stung her pride more. She was scolded like a child and sent to cry by herself in a scalding hot shower.

He was a toxic poison and had been slowly seeping into every fiber of her being. She'd stayed until she had almost been fully infected by it. He'd made her believe she could never escape him, so there was no point in even trying—he would hunt her down like the prey he turned her into. He'd shaped her world so that she relied on him, from financial control to cutting off the small number of social ties she had, there was no way out.

But he didn't account for the centuries of female rage that were burning in her soul. Her mother raised her to be cunning, to only appear weak but always be ready to run. Her ancestors' stories of being burned, abused, tortured, and raped all at the hands of their husbands helped her see the need to escape.

But it hadn't turned out how she planned. The idiot hadn't kept to his schedule, even though he demanded that of her, so he'd walked into their apartment as she was walking out with her small bag of essentials and cash she had secretly saved gripped tightly to her side.

An argument had ensued and carried out into the hallway as she utilized the power of her personal rage to walk past him. He'd followed her down the corridor, yelling until his face turned red, and into the stairwell. She'd known her neighbors could hear the expletives that were flying out of his mouth and welcomed their ears as it would provide proof of his enraged state. Because when men were angry, sometimes they stopped thinking. And sometimes they made dumb mistakes.

She'd felt her mother's spirit with her as she'd turned to look at him. He had spittle hanging from his bottom lip, his face blotchy from the high blood pressure, and his eyes wide with crazed rage. It would be the last image she would ever have of him alive.

She'd placed her bag down and grabbed him around the waist before throwing them both down the concrete stairs. She made sure to stay on top as best as she could as they tumbled down and crashed into each sharp step. A blur of grey, black, and red flashed around her as they fell, plummeting to his demise. The sound of his bones cracking and flesh smacking into the hard surfaces had fueled her adrenaline. It had felt like an eternity until they'd landed on the final step with him groaning beneath her like a wounded child.

She'd felt no pity and sat up to grab his bloodied head between her palms. She'd slowly bent down to his right ear with an earring ripped out and licked the trail of blood making its way to his collar.

"My mother's waiting for you." She'd whispered before using the last of her strength to smash his head into the edge of the step.

Blood had squirted as his skull had cracked and his eyes had rolled back as his body went into an intense seizure. It had lasted for a minute before he'd went still, but she'd made sure to watch every second of his last moments on her plane of existence.

Once he was dead, she'd played the innocent, small girlfriend who he'd attempted to push down the stairs, but accidentally tripped and caused them both to fall. Her pleas for help had been heard by her neighbors, and they'd rushed to her assistance, soothing her over the heartbreak they assumed would happen once she learned that he did not survive the fall. It was a quick and easy clean up—the police had never questioned her too closely after the reports of the screaming from the neighbors. Soon, she had been free to leave and made her way down to Florida to restart her life.

She sat down in her booth until her heart rate lowered. She knew she should call Gage, but his voice wouldn't be enough. She wanted his arms around her. She sat there for a while, reliving the memories of her ex and contemplating what Waldo meant that his territory was already three times bigger and growing. He must have taken over other territories and was coming for Vista Maria next.

Looking at the sun creeping through the slits in her blinds, she decided to finish closing up and drive over to Gage's home to crawl in his bed. She couldn't picture him complaining about that surprise.

When she arrived at his home, she knocked on the door and waited. The mansion was dark, so she knocked much harder. She was surprised to find a groggy and slightly hesitant Sammy who opened the door.

"Willow?"

"I'm so sorry to bug you, but I need to see Gage. Waldo came into my café last night."

The tiredness instantly left her eyes. "Oh shit, are you okay?"

"Yeah, I am. Is he asleep already?"

"He is and he sleeps like a rock so good luck waking him up." She shuffled to the side to let Willow in. "If you need someone to talk to, we can grab a beer and head down into the basement. I was heading to bed, but a beer always helps me sleep better."

As much as she wanted to curl up with Gage, she also wanted to talk to someone. Plus, she wanted to know Sammy better. "A beer sounds great."

Twenty-Four

Willow

W illow lightly made her way down the plush carpeted steps into the cool, dark basement. Sammy flipped on the lights that were embedded into the ceiling to reveal a basement that was the stark opposite of the upstairs. There were no gothic paintings and intricate décor with dark hues throughout; instead, the color scheme was beige, with more beige furniture and a weight set in the corner. The only thing that stood out was the large TV screen lining the back wall, with theater-style seating in front.

"Is it safe to assume Gage didn't decorate this area?"

Willow walked around the overstuffed couch in the middle of the room. She plopped down into it and shivered at the cold touch of the leather, but was comforted by how she sunk into it.

"Good guess," Sammy chuckled and pulled out two glass bottles from a mini-fridge hidden underneath the staircase. "This is Matteo and Horatio's man-cave, while Nikolas and Gage get the upstairs. I love my boyfriend, but the man has no taste whatsoever. Thank God he found me."

Sammy handed Willow her beer, then twisted off the cap on her own and started chugging as she relaxed into the couch. Willow copied her and finished off the bottle within a minute, followed by a large burp.

Sammy laughed and slapped the cushion. "I think we're going to make great friends. I know you wanted to talk about Waldo—" she rolled her eyes and gagged "—but first, I have to ask about Gage. He came home in such a good mood. I've never seen him like that, and I'm assuming you had something to do with it."

She shrugged like it was no big deal, even though it was monumental to her. "We made up. I guess we're official now." She brushed the mark hiding under her shirt lightly. "He marked me."

"Cute, Horse put his on my hip. I tried to convince him to let me bite him after I turned, but he said that's not how it works. It's always the man who marks the woman, such misogyny."

Willow scrunched her nose. "Having matching marks would be cute, though. If I ever turn, I'm sure Gage would let me. Horse is Horatio's nickname, right? How did he get it?"

"Cause he's hung like a horse."

Willow tried to hide the look of disgust that was creeping onto her face.

"I'm joking! He told me a story once that when him and Matteo were little, Matteo couldn't say Horatio, so he called him Horsey. As they got older it sounded weird, so he shortened it to Horse. He hasn't called him that in years, but once I heard it I thought it was cute and brought it back. No one else is allowed to call him that except me and Matteo, though."

Sammy popped up from the couch and fetched another two beers, both girls sipping on them this time. Willow picked at the label on the bottle, knowing that Sammy was staring at her and waiting for her to bring up Waldo.

Willow took a deep breath, planning where to start. She recounted what had happened when Waldo first entered her shop, how he'd saved her from the rouge vampire, and how he'd been eerily calm and collected during their last encounter. With each disclosure, Sammy's face turned more and more serious until she was almost frowning.

"It sounds like he thought you were dumb enough to join him like Venice. He really said she's at the bottom of the ocean?"

"Yeah, do you think I should tell Gage that part?"

Sammy squinted off into the distance like she was using all of her focus on that question. "Probably. It could be the closure he needs, and then he can be totally committed to you. I'm not saying he's still in love with her or anything, but he's still angry with her. Knowing she's dead could help him let that go."

"Wow, that was pretty wise."

A flash of hurt briefly fluttered across Sammy's face. "Yeah, I'm not a total drunk dumbass. My Granny is pretty wise herself, and I spent a lot of time with her growing up, so I like to think some of that rubbed off on me."

"Where is your family?"

"They're back in Louisiana. I don't really like to talk about them. My childhood wasn't so great."

"Does anyone have a perfect, happy past?"

"Marla seems to," Sammy grumbled under her breath.

"You don't get along well with her, do you? She's one of my best friends and I really wish you would give her a chance to see how sweet she is."

"Trust me, I see enough of her here with Matteo to see how sweet she can be. It's gross, and I'm tired of them groping each other in public all day long. I don't know why they can't go into Matteo's bedroom." She glanced at Willow. "Sorry, I needed to vent for a second."

Willow was growing uncomfortable with where the topic was going. She wanted to stand up for her friend, but didn't want to burn the bridge with Sammy, especially if she had any hope of helping the two get along. "If you're in the mood to talk shit, then let's talk shit about Waldo."

A grin broke across Sammy's face. "Shit talkin' is my specialty. He's a slimy jackass who likes to manipulate people. I've never had the pleasure of talking with him, but the things I hear from Horse and the others are not good."

"I can see why he's not a popular man, there's something off about him."

"I think it's the fake tan. He can't use tanning beds or natural sun so he sprays that orange tanner on himself." Sammy covered her mouth and let out a snort. "He's such a douche."

Willow pulled her knees up to her chest and wrapped her arms around them. "He's a douche, but he's also unpredictable and that's terrifying to me. I want to know what he meant that his territory is three times the size of ours. That makes me so nervous."

"I overheard Gage tell Horatio that him and Robby met some girls down in Miami who were living in some vampire-only area in Georgia. The girls didn't bring up Waldo's name, though, so they weren't sure if it was connected to him."

"What, like a whole village of only vampires?"

"More like a trailer park of vampires." She shuddered dramatically. "That sounds like my worst nightmare. I may have grown up poor in a rough neighborhood, but I never had to live in a trailer."

"What's wrong with that?"

"Trailer trash, especially the kind that live in Louisiana, are a different breed. I can only imagine *vampire* trailer trash."

"Sammy, I was raised in a RV. Calling people trailer trash is actually pretty offensive. Trailers are just another type of home, it's no better or worse than a house."

"Oh, well, RVs are way different from trailers." She toyed awkwardly with the label on her beer bottle. "I guess this is why I can't make friends, I'm a judgmental bitch. Thank God Horse likes that. He enjoys putting me in my place." She laughed and chugged the rest of her beer.

Willow pitied her, remembering what it was like to face the world alone. "You have lots of friends. You had a whole house full when you threw that party."

"Those weren't my friends, they were here for the free alcohol. Hey, want to see something cool?" Sammy stood up and motioned for her to follow.

The two walked through a doorway into a large room that housed what appeared to be dusty slot machines, old posters that advertised past events at Clay's casino, a broken-down miniature carousel, and boxes upon boxes of various decorations. It looked more like an antique store in Vegas than a vampire's basement. In the very back, Sammy located a large plastic container and drug it back into the main room. She dug around it and pulled out a velvet maroon photo album that she handed to Willow.

"I found this when I was looking for decorations for that party. I think Clay hid this back here with this surplus storage because it's too painful to look at. It's got some cool pictures, though."

Willow took the album and returned to her spot on the couch as Sammy retrieved their third beer. On the first page was a black-and-white photograph of Clay and a man who she assumed was his brother, Al. The two had their arms over each other's shoulder and were standing in front of a small, abandoned building. Their outfits looked like styles from the 1920's, but Clay looked the same as he did currently.

"Clay's style clearly hasn't changed much. The poor guy still rocks that slicked-back hairstyle, but I guess if you find something that works you keep it. It accentuates his chiseled jawline," Sammy giggled.

"Don't tell Horse that, I don't need him getting all weird that I have a slight crush on Clay. He gives off daddy vibes I can't ignore."

Willow eyed her. "Don't worry, your weird secret is safe with me. What's this building they're standing in front of?"

"I think Horse said that was where they were making moonshine during Prohibition. This photo is super old. Fun fact, that little building eventually turned into the casino! They tore down all but one room and built around it, but the manager's office in the center of the casino is the original room! How cool is that?"

"That's actually really cool. Who are all these random men?" Willow flipped through the first few pages but didn't recognize anyone.

"Those were Clay's family members."

Silence filled the room as they both looked at the faces of all the men who were destined to die in a brutal fight. More sadness enveloped Willow when she turned the page to show a color portrait of a beautiful women with blue eyes and long, teased blonde hair that hung past her shoulders. Between the big hair and shoulder pads, it was clearly from the 1980's. She was wearing a green shirt that stood out against her milky-white skin and had red lips that were split into a loving smile. Willow wondered if she was looking at Clay while the photo was being taken.

"That's Gage's mother, isn't it? She looks just like him." Willow traced the outline of her face before flipping the page to show another portrait of her, this time with a small, blond baby swaddled in her arms.

"Aw!" The two shrieked in unison.

"She was beautiful. I don't know how she died, Clay doesn't ever talk about her and Horse doesn't want to ask." Sammy said.

"Suicide."

Sammy gasped but made no comment. Willow flipped through the pages and watched Gage grow up right before her eyes. He was a very small child with a smile permanently plastered on his face that matched Clay's. She never saw a father look so openly happy and loving in pictures, but there were multiple ones of Clay kissing Gage on the cheek. Her feelings about Clay being an amazing dad doubled as she looked upon pictures of stereotypical family outings and how happy he appeared to be spending time with his wife and child. He was always holding his wife's hand or touching her shoulder, his eyes locked onto either her or Gage, never distracted by the things around him. It was obvious his whole world was made up of them. Her heart broke at how in love he looked, only to have it end.

As the pictures got newer and Gage grew older, his mother's smile began to disappear until only the corner of her lips were curved upward but no joy reached her eyes. Nearing the end of the album, Gage had his growth spurt and was rocking a blond mullet. Willow made a mental note to harass him later about it.

She turned the last page and her breath caught in her throat. The final picture was of his mother's gravestone covered in a blanket of red roses.

Willow closed the album and finished off her beer. The alcohol had made her feel warm and the depressing final photo had her ready to curl up in bed.

"Thanks for showing me this, it's always fascinating to see photos from the past. It's interesting to see Clay with his former family. It makes me ten times angrier with Waldo for destroying that. I know he technically wasn't there to kill them, but he put everything in motion by killing innocents on the beach. So screw him."

"Oh, I like this spicey version of you. Angry Willow is kind of badass."

"Sometimes. Sometimes she can be dangerous, too." She stood up and stretched her arms above her head.

"I think the beers have done me in, I'm ready for bed. Goodnight,

Sammy."

"Sweet dreams, Willow. Thanks for hanging out with me." She whispered her last sentence and Willow almost didn't catch it as she trudged her way upstairs.

Gage
Sometime in the Middle of the Day

Gage woke up to a warm lump pressed into his back. For a split second, he assumed it was Buffy until he realized the lump was six times bigger than his beloved cat. Buffy was also not the type to snuggle against him—she would rather smother his face.

Curiosity overrode his panic and he cautiously rolled over without disturbing the sleeping creature that had taken over his bed. To his surprise, Buffy was there, but she was not alone. Curled up underneath the purring, white ball of fur was Willow. She looked blissfully unaware that she was about to suffocate underneath the feline.

"Where the hell did she come from?" He whispered to his cat.

Buffy gave him a slow blink, then tucked her pink nose into the fluff of her tail.

Sleep was still lingering and he tried his best to rub it from his eyes to check the time on the grandfather clock looming in the corner of his bedroom. It told him it was only three p.m. There was no way he was getting up this early.

He slowly slid his arm underneath her pillow and wrapped his other arm over her waist. He was careful not to disrupt Buffy as he molded the bend of his arm around her. A tranquil feeling overcame him as both Buffy and Willow seemed to sigh in unison and melt into him. It wasn't long before he fell back into a peaceful sleep.

Twenty-Five

Willow

Willow felt a whispery tickle on her face. She cracked open her eyes ever so slowly to find a furry face staring back at her.

"Good morning, Buffy." She wrinkled her nose as the cat yawned, releasing the stench of warm tuna.

She gently pushed the cat off her chest and onto the floor so she could stretch her arms up over her head. That was when she realized that Gage's arm was heavily draped over her torso.

His voice was a deep purr. "It was nice waking up next to a pretty girl, but rather risky of you to fall asleep next to a vampire. I could've had my way with you while you were asleep."

"Maybe that was what I was hoping for." Willow grinned and rolled her head to the side to look at him.

His hair was messy with strands falling in his face and he looked comfortably sunken into his pillow with the blanket pulled halfway down, revealing his bare chest. She took a closer look at his rosary tattoo and used her finger to trace it. She started at his collarbone and followed the black beads of ink around his neck, following the curves that made it look as if he'd quickly tossed it on, down to the cross that was resting on his left pectoral. It was intricately drawn, with red vines wrapped around a black iron cross, and shading to give it a three-dimensional look.

She could feel his breath catch as she outlined the cross and was curious about what else she could do to him.

She continued her tracing, leaving the tattoo to slide her hand down lower on his chest, tracing small circles as she made her way down his abdomen. She noticed small goosebumps as she lightly dragged her nails over his abs, which were still surprisingly defined in his relaxed state. Her hand took on a mind of its own as she reached the top of his grey boxer briefs and slid her finger down the gap that was halfway open due to his erection. Using her nails again, she inserted her pointer finger underneath the fabric and traced a delicate line down his hardening cock. This time, his breath caught audibly as he gasped at the sensation.

She felt her confidence rise as he rolled over so he was flat on his back to allow her complete access to his body. Following his cue, she stuck her hand into his underwear and gripped his length softly as her other hand removed the rest of the covers. She began stroking him, her underwear almost soaked through at the feeling of his length. Her insides tingled as she imagined herself climbing on top of him and inserting that monstrous member into her tightness, but she wasn't ready to give up her torment just yet.

She sat up and pulled his cock out of his underwear to take in its full extent. She bent down to bring it closer to her face and slowly brushed his tip against her lips, savoring the frustrated sigh that escaped him.

"Do you want me to suck it?" She asked, making sure that she was close enough to him that her breath could be felt on his throbbing head.

He ran a hand through her hair and looked at her in a way that would have made her knees weak if she were standing. "I would love nothing more than to watch your pretty little mouth wrap around me."

A smile curved that pretty mouth, and she moved her hand to his base. She slowly inserted his tip between her lips, caressing it with her tongue as it sunk further into her mouth. His size almost choked and she felt her saliva begin to seep out of the corners of her mouth as she tasted and sucked on him like he was the greatest lollipop that was ever created. The sounds of her slurping and sucking filled the room and only managed to make her wetter. The size of him filled not only her mouth, but also her mind as she only focused on his taste, her sounds, and the feeling of his hand tangled in and pulling on her hair.

His hips thrusted up and he pushed deeper into her mouth, hitting the back of her throat. She removed her hand from his base and allowed him to thrust all the way in, surprising herself at her ability to fully take him. She couldn't breathe, and involuntary tears were welling at the corner of her eyes, but she loved it. She loved the feeling of him filling her mouth, but the emptiness of her center began to creep into her thoughts. She wanted him to fill her down there too.

She quit her sucking and released his cock with a pop, swiping her tongue around her mouth like she had ate a decadent meal. His groan made her want to continue, but she wasn't ready for him to come yet. She wanted him inside of her while he climaxed and was growing bold from the control she had over his orgasm.

"I don't want you coming too soon before I get a chance to ride you." She pouted and caressed his face before taking off her shirt.

She took her time taking off her clothing, enjoying the look of impatience that was growing stronger on his face. Once she was naked, she slipped his boxer briefs down over his thighs leisurely and pulled them all the way off, trailing her nails over his skin again as she dragged her hand down his legs chasing after the underwear. She straddled him and looked over his beautiful form.

"You're being so patient, I'm impressed," she whispered.

"I'm only patient for things that are worth it."

He ran a hand up her thigh and along her side, stopping underneath her breast. He traced a circle around her nipple before gliding his hand to the spot where his bite mark rested.

"Do you want me to bite you again?" He asked as he traced his mark.

"As amazing as that felt, I'm afraid it will override the feeling of you inside me. I don't want to miss that." She lifted her hips and brought him to her opening, relishing the feeling of him stretching her as she slowly sat all the way down on it.

"Oh fuck." She tilted her head back and moaned.

Her body felt like it was picking up every sensation and amplifying it by ten, from her hair tickling her bare back, to his hand, which had moved from touching her mark to squeezing her hip. She felt every inch of him in her and whimpered as she sat up again, almost releasing him from her wet embrace, to slide back down on his length. It didn't take her long for the beginnings of an orgasm to build as she continued her slow glides.

His breathing grew heavy and with both hands he grabbed hers and entwined their fingers. She picked up her pace and began slamming her hips down onto his shaft. Her clit smashed against his pelvis and it wasn't long before her orgasm peaked and she screamed out his name while tightening her grip on his fingers to the point it would have been painful if he was a normal man.

She ended with one final slam against him, only to find herself thrown onto her back and him over her, continuing his pounding thrusts. As she lifted her leg to allow him deeper access, his head bent down to her collarbone and she felt his teeth pierce her.

Another, more intense orgasm coursed through her body. She forgot how to breathe, how to think, how to behave. An animalistic scream left her throat as one hand sunk her nails into his back and another grabbed his hair and pulled.

"Fuck," he growled from below her, thrusting harshly against her before his warm seed filled her as her warm blood filled him. In the moment she felt connected to him in a way she had never felt with another person, and grew mournful when it came to an end.

She could have lived in that pleasurable chaos forever.

He licked the new mark, sealing up and healing the puncture holes, but stayed inside of her as he laid on top and buried his face into her neck. She wrapped her arms and legs around him and did the same.

It was a few minutes before either of them moved, Willow being the one who untucked her head to breathe the cool, fresh air. He finally slid out of her to roll onto his side, and her insides felt like they were missing a very important piece.

"That was…phenomenal." She sighed but kept her eyes on the ceiling. She was afraid if she looked at him, it would start all over again. Her shaking body needed a few minutes to recover first.

"I didn't know you could make noises like that. I think the sound of you coming alone was what pushed me over the edge."

A blush swept over her face. "Do you think anyone heard us?"

"Oh, they definitely heard that last scream of yours." He wrapped his arm around her and pulled her against him. She melted into his side like she belonged there.

She was starting to doze off again, falling into that in-between state where she wasn't fully conscious but not fully asleep, when a soft knock sounded from the door.

"Hi Willow, I know you're in there because I heard you moaning. It sounds like you two are done messing around, so I was wondering if you would like to come out and join us for breakfast?"

"Marla?" Willow shot up and looked at the door. "Did you spend the night too?"

She paused before responding. Willow could tell she had a huge announcement to make, and wondered if telling her with a door between them made it easier for her to confess.

"I meant to tell you this once it was more official. I'm kind of in the process of moving in. Not fully yet, since my lease isn't up at my apartment, but I don't plan on renewing it and most of my stuff is here in Matteo's room. Is it safe to open the door?"

"No," both Willow and Gage shouted in unison.

"Okay, well Horatio is making chocolate chip pancakes if you want some! I'll see you in a bit."

"Wait, Marla! What do you mean you're living here now?" Willow listened to the sound of Marla's footsteps retreating down the hall as a response and turned to Gage with her mouth hung open. "How long has she been living here? I never knew they were officially dating, let alone slowly moving in."

"To be honest I didn't realize she was even here, which is surprising because I thought she would have been super annoying to live with."

"Marla isn't annoying, she's sweet and a little weird, which makes her cool in my opinion. She's also a really good friend, which is why I'm concerned that things are moving so quickly between her and Matteo."

"I trust Matteo not to break her heart. Like Marla, he is also a little weird but a very good friend. Once he gets to know someone and get comfortable with them, he develops a rock-solid loyalty to them."

With that, he rolled out of bed and headed toward a closet door she had never noticed before. Her mouth dropped open yet again when he opened it to reveal a closet the size of her bedroom.

"That's the closet of my dreams. How do you even have enough clothes to fill that?"

He shrugged. "I'm obsessed with hoodies and they take up a lot of space, so I renovated the bathroom into a closet."

"So you're handsome, can give head like a god, a great artist, and now you're also a contractor? Is there anything you can't do?"

He thought for a moment.

"I can't sing," he said as he disappeared into the closet.

After they both were dressed and Willow tamed her massive cloud of hair, they walked into the kitchen together to have five pairs of eyes on them. All five zoned in on their hands interlocked together.

"Glad you two decided to join us," Horatio said as he flipped a perfectly round pancake onto a plate.

Sammy was sitting on a bar stool next to him at the stove, cheeks puffed out from the large bite she had shoved into her mouth. Marla and Matteo were sitting together at the marble island, both huddled over their stack of pancakes and whispering unintelligibly to each other while glancing back and forth between Willow and Gage. Nikolas was on the opposite end of the island smirking at Gage.

Willow wanted to curl up right there and die. It was clear they all had heard their morning antics.

"Yeah, we uh…had a late start to the night." Gage responded.

Willow could tell he was trying to be casual, but his uncomfortable energy was giving him away.

"Oh, that's a good idea!" Marla excitedly cooed as she broke away from her and Matteo's private conversation to look at Willow. "Matteo reminded me that the haunted house at Floral Farms opened this past weekend. It is officially spooky season and we should all celebrate it by going tonight! What do you two lovebirds think?"

"I don't think they can stop humping each other long enough to enjoy a haunted house," Matteo suggested.

"Don't be gross." Willow squinted her eyes at the grinning boy. "And it's you and Marla I'm more concerned about. I would bet money that you two can't make it through the house without finding a dark corner to get freaky in."

"Nuh uh, we totally can," Marla scoffed. "I can resist this sexy beast for at least an hour. It shouldn't take longer than that to get through the house, right?"

"Please don't call him a sexy beast," Horatio whispered as he stared into the freshly poured pancake, like he was imagining himself anywhere but there.

"How much do you want to bet?" Willow purred and joined her friend at the island. She gave Gage a small smile as he placed a plated pancake in front of her before getting his own.

"Twenty dollars," Marla suggested.

"That's it? No, let's bet at least one hundred. I'm trying to make some money here."

"Fine, you'll owe me one hundred dollars once we get through the house without a single kiss. Easy money." Marla sealed the deal by wrapping her arm through Matteo's and popping a loose chocolate chip into her mouth.

Willow turned to Nikolas, who was sitting quietly, minding his own business and picking at his stack of pancakes. "Are you going to bring a date?"

"No, I don't do dates and I don't do haunted houses. I've seen enough horrors in my life, so I would rather not pay to have to see more."

Willow nodded. "Fair enough. Well, if you ever do decide you want to go on a date, there's some girls in my yoga class I used to attend that would probably love to go out with you. I need to start going again, anyway. If you're into dudes, I can't help you there. The only other guy I know is Waldo, and I have a feeling you two won't get along."

Nikolas shrugged. "No, I'm not looking to date dudes or women. I just want to exist by myself right now."

Willow shoved a forkful of pancake into her mouth. "Nothing wrong with that."

Twenty-Six

Willow

Willow's heart raced as she watched a man dressed in a torn tuxedo with white and green zombie face paint chase after a group of teenage girls. Their shrieks sent a chill down her spine and she wrapped her arms tightly around herself. Gage walked closer to her and wrapped his arm around her waist as the group made their way through the apple orchard, sparsely decorated with wooden signs signaling the way to the haunted house. The night had brought in a cool breeze that caused Willow to shiver.

"You know, if this is too much, we can go back home. I'm kind of an idiot and didn't even think about how this place is probably triggering after your attack."

"No, I'm fine," she assured him.

"You look terrified. My bed is a much safer place, and I wouldn't mind staying in it all night if I had you to keep me company."

"It's a haunted house, Gage, I'm supposed to look scared. As tempting as your bed sounds, I'm trying to make some money here. Speaking of which," she leaned closer so no one would hear, "do *not* let Matteo out of your sight. I've got my eyes on Marla and between the two of us we should be able to catch them making out at some point tonight. I can already tell they're going to try to be tricky about it, but I know Marla and she is obsessed with Matteo. Add in the fact that she's going to be scared and want to feel protected by him, so they're bound to find a hidden corner to get freaky in. The only thing I'm worried about is how I'm going to spend that hundred dollars."

"You could take me on a date. A nice steak dinner sounds like the perfect end to this evening."

"Hmm, yes, that does sound good, but so does getting a mani-pedi."

Marla whipped her head around and glared at the couple. "I know you two are whispering about us! Cut it out, you're not going to win the bet."

"Yeah!" Matteo followed suit with a sarcastic gleam in his eyes. He swung his hand down and smacked Marla on the ass.

"I should have bet more." Willow frowned.

She stopped in her tracks as a different zombie jumped out from behind a cluster of trees and screamed at them. Sammy's scream was louder and Horatio burst out laughing as he watched his girlfriend run off, the zombie man hot on her heels.

"Are you not going to go save her?" Willow hiked up her eyebrow, waiting for Horatio to attend to his screaming beauty.

"Nah, I guarantee she is scarier than a fake zombie. I once woke her up trying to get my phone charger untangled from underneath her and she literally bit me, like it was my fault she fell asleep on top of it."

"I guarantee she is about to be downright terrifying once she comes back and discovers you didn't try to save her," Marla said.

Horatio shrugged at her response, but held back a smirk like he was anticipating that moment. The group entered the open field that revealed a few booths selling oddities from taxidermy to custom wands, a cart selling caramel apples and fudge, a shack decorated like the witch's house from a fairytale, and a long line that started from a large, decaying barn and snaked around the field.

"I take it we're going to be in line all night?" Willow sighed.

"Yeah, but at least we have good company to entertain ourselves with." Matteo pulled Marla closer and nuzzled his face into her neck.

Before Willow could make a comment, Gage pulled her toward the shack as the others marked their place at the end of the line. She followed willingly, intrigued by the unusual building.

"What's in there?" She asked.

"It's a small bar and they serve the best drink you will ever have."

They entered the building and she was overcome with the sweet scent of freshly pressed apples, autumn spices, and wood. The dark floor beneath them creaked with every step and a small cast-iron stove crackled to her left. In the middle of the large, open room stood a bar littered with customers, all holding the same drink.

"I'm pretty sure their Poison Apple drink is the only thing they serve here," he responded after seeing her curious glance at the matching golden liquid.

"Hi Gage!" The perky, cute blonde behind the bar noticed him instantly, and Willow felt a small fire of jealousy start in her gut. She noticed Gage side-eye her with a smirk.

"Hi Melissa, Dad told me you put in for some vacation time at the casino to work here, though he wasn't very pleased about it."

As quickly as her fire began, it extinguished once she realized the girl was one of Clay's employees. She was slightly embarrassed with how quickly she'd let herself grow jealous, and hoped it didn't show on her face.

Melissa scoffed. "Oh, he'll get over it soon enough. It's hard to pass this gig up when I make double what I would at the casino's bar. Plus, it's easier, since people only ever order the Poison Apple. Speaking of which, should I make you two?"

He nodded and Melissa made their drinks, adding a double shot of caramel vodka to some cider. Willow was positive most people only received one shot, but having connections to the head of the Vista Maria family seemed to have its benefits. Melissa graciously took the one hundred-dollar bill Gage handed her. When he shook his head at the change, her smile grew even wider.

"You two have fun tonight!" She called as they turned to leave.

Gage lifted his hand in a lazy goodbye before heading out the door with Willow. She took a sip of the drink and her eyes grew wide.

"You were right, this is the best drink ever."

"Told you."

"Hey, looks like Sammy came back in one piece. I wonder if she ripped Horatio a new one for not running after her." She quickly made her way back over to their friends, and noticed that they had not moved up very far in line.

"Ooh, is that their famous Poison Apple drink?" Sammy's eyes grew wide and she sniffed the cup in Willow's hand. "Horse, you owe me. Please go get us one!"

"You too!" Marla nudged Matteo toward his brother. The twins rolled their eyes in unison, but were obedient to their girls.

Willow smiled at the cute scene, but felt Gage tense up next to her. When she looked over to him, he was as still as a statue and glaring toward a small group of couples that were a few people ahead of them in line.

"Are you okay?"

"Yeah, I'm fine." He pulled out his phone and sent a text to someone. Willow had to fight her urge to peer at his phone to see who he was messaging.

"You don't seem too fine."

Instead of a reply, he quickly took a photo of the group and frowned at the even quicker response from the other person.

"Stay close to me for the night, okay? And you two," he nodded toward Marla and Sammy, "stay close to Horatio and Matteo. There are some people here from Waldo's family, and I'm not sure if it's a coincidence, or if they're planning something. I highly doubt they would come all the way up here from Miami just for a haunted house, though."

Another text lit up Gage's phone and he sighed as he read the message. "Also, Robby has decided to join us tonight with some of his boys."

"Was that who you were texting?" Willow finished her drink and looked up at him with what she hoped were round, curious eyes, and not a suspicious glare.

"Yeah, I had to make sure they were from Miami before I got paranoid. Robby has a better memory for faces than me."

They fell into an uncomfortable silence before Gage kicked her foot playfully. "What's up with you tonight? You seem really on edge and more jealous than normal."

"I'm not jealous." She shot down the rest of her drink, handed him her empty cup, then chewed on the side of her cheek as she mulled over what she was feeling. "I just feel…off. My mom, she was always intuitive, taught me how to listen to my gut. Most people ignore that sixth sense, but not us. It has come in handy too many times.

"I still remember the day I discovered how powerful that sense was. I was about sixteen years old, and we had been at a grocery store. These two men had been following us, but I had been completely unaware and absorbed in some stupid teen magazine I picked up. My mom, on the other hand, had been aware of how they had always been in the same isle as us, but never picked up items to buy. She had known they were planning something, so she turned around and started yelling at them to leave us alone. Of course, they had played it off like they were minding their own business, but she had shoved the cart at one of them and hit him with it. She'd chased after them, continuing to curse them and call them horribly offensive names until they left the store and drove off in their van. I was so mortified, I seriously thought about opening one of the freezer doors and crawling in there to die a slow, cold death. She had walked back into the store with everyone staring, but continued shopping like nothing happened. When we got back to our RV I had cried so hard from shame and embarrassment, but she'd stood her ground and said it was her duty as a loudmouthed Irish woman to chase off the demons that prey on women."

She continued, noticing that Marla and Sammy were both enthralled with her story. "It's funny now picturing this tiny woman that weighed no more than a hundred pounds soaking wet chase off these two men simply by shouting Celtic curses at them in a thick Irish accent. It turned out she was right to do that, though. A few days later on the news, we saw those same two men get arrested for kidnapping and murdering a nineteen-year-old girl. They had kidnapped her from a busy mall, raped her in their van, then bashed her head in with hammers before dumping her in a truck stop dumpster. That could have been me."

They were quiet as they processed her story. Sammy was the first to speak. "That's one perk about being a vampire, I feel so much safer. Yes, terrible things can still happen to me, but I know I can hold my own against human men. Hearing stories like that makes me want to hunt down those disgusting pigs and rip their throats out. That's how I can justify killing to stay alive—trash like that dies while we live and continue to rid the Earth of horrible creatures."

"Yeah, but how do you know if someone is terrible like that?" Marla asked.

Gage replied, "It's easy, you hunt them. My favorite place to start is the sex offender's registry. From there, you stalk them until you catch them doing what put them on the list in the first place."

He turned and his eyes darkened in concern as he looked down at her. "So, what is your gut telling you tonight, Willow?"

Her stomach flipped at the way her name rolled off his tongue, and for a second she lost touch with the warning that was building as a tingling began between her legs. She cleared her throat and focused again on the sixth sense she'd inherited.

"I'm not a fortune teller, so I can't exactly say what is going to happen, but tonight does feel off. And I think seeing the Miami vampires further proves my point. Since this line hasn't moved in a few minutes, how about we come back another night?"

Marla frowned at the suggestion. "But how do you know something bad is going to happen here? What if it happens because we left? Wouldn't we be safer to be out in public like this? I really wanted to go through this haunted house with Matteo, please don't make us leave."

"Marla, those two men tried to kidnap me in a grocery store. Just because we're in public doesn't mean we are safe." Willow watched as the twins returned and handed the girls their drinks. "But, it would be much easier for me to ignore that nagging sensation if I had another drink to numb my thoughts."

"Fine, here." Marla took a quick sip to taste it before handing it over to Willow. "I want to be fully present for this experience, anyway. It won't be as scary if I'm tipsy, and Matteo is paying good money for me to be scared." She giggled and looped her arm around his neck to pull him into a kiss.

Gage coughed and Willow raised an eyebrow.

"Are you willing to lose the bet already?" Willow asked.

Marla quickly dropped her arm.

Gage kept the Miami group in his sight until they disappeared into the haunted house. The line moved slowly, and it took over an hour before they were finally at the entrance. Once there, the worker held up his hand and closed the door.

"Once this group goes through, you'll be the next batch," he said.

Marla began bouncing in her spot and turned her attention to Gage. "Where's Robby at? I thought you said he would be joining us?"

"He should have been here by now, I'll text him."

Five minutes passed before Gage started to tense up. "I think you were right, something is wrong."

Willow looked up to him as a cold chill swept through her body. "What do you mean? Can't you get in contact with Robby? Maybe he's driving and can't text."

"No, that's not like him. The man will text, eat, and put on eyeliner all while driving. Something's up, I'm going to call."

His sentence was cut short as his phone lit up, with Robby's name displayed. Gage swiftly put the phone to his ear, but before he could say a word his face turned grim. Willow could briefly hear Robby's hurried voice on the other end as he shouted something through the phone. Time seemed to move in slow motion as Gage hung up his phone, ordered Horatio to contact Nikolas and tell him to meet them at Clay's house, then grabbed Willow roughly by the arm and began dragging her toward the exit with Matteo also dragging Marla.

"What happened?" Willow tried to remain calm, but the panic in her chest was making her voice shrill.

"They attacked Robby and killed three of the men he was out with. We need to get you and Marla to Clay's house. I don't know what Waldo is planning, but I want you safe."

"I have to go home and get Snickers!"

"There's no time, Robby is on his way to Clay's house right now and I told him I would meet him there."

"But what if Waldo goes there to hurt me and kills him? Or burns down my apartment complex? He knows where I live, he walked me home after my attack!" A negative storm of thoughts began swirling around in her mind at the potential loss of her pet. "Please let me go get him, Snickers is more than a rabbit to me, he is the only family that I have."

Gage paused and looked at her before sighing and looking over to Matteo. "Tell Robby and Clay we're on our way. We have to make a quick pit stop to pick up this fucking carrot eater."

Matteo frowned. "Are you sure that's a good idea? You said that they killed three of Robby's men right in front of him. That's more than a warning, this is the start of something bigger."

Guilt washed over Willow. "I think he's mad because I turned him down. I haven't had a chance to tell you yet, but he came into my café last night and I rejected his offer to move to Miami with him. I'm so sorry Gage, that should've been the first thing I told you this morning."

Gage's jaw clenched. "Did he hurt you?"

"No, but he told me I would fall with the rest of you. He also told me something else." She paused and made eye contact with Sammy, who nodded her head. "He admitted to killing Venice."

To her surprise, Gage didn't even flinch at the news. Instead, he looked at her with a face full of concern, like he was worried she would be next. "I'm not surprised. He's a psychopath that enjoys torturing people for no fucking reason. Let's go get your rabbit, you'll be staying with me until we kill the bastard. There's no way I'm letting you out of my sight."

The group split up, with Willow and Gage in his truck and everyone else in Matteo's BMW. Gage trailed behind the car, his eyes constantly shifting from the road in front of them to the review mirror.

"What are we going to do once we get to Clay's house?" Willow asked to break the tension.

"I need to consult with Robby about what happened and go from there. If he knows specifically who targeted him, we'll go after them first, before trying to locate Waldo. If he initiated this attack, we have the right to attack him back. There's only one problem with that."

"What's the problem?"

"If we attack and are successful, then I'll have to go—"

His sentence was cut short by Willow's scream as she watched the BMW explode from the impact of a semitruck that appeared out of nowhere. Gage hit the brakes and whipped his truck around to follow the semi as it continued at full speed, dragging the small car with it for almost a half mile before coming to a screeching halt down the road. He had not put the truck in park yet as Willow ripped off her seatbelt and launched herself from her seat to run toward the car, which was imbedded into the front grill of the semi. She could faintly hear Gage calling her name behind her as she raced over and began pulling on bent door handles, desperate to get her friends out of the metal chaos that had flames beginning to rise from it.

"You have to get them out! You have to get them out!" She screamed as Gage ripped her away and forced her back to his truck.

The door to the semi opened up and three men hopped out of it, snarling and laughing. The biggest of the three took a few steps forward and grinned at Gage. "Jesse James sends his regards."

Twenty-Seven

Willow

"How could you!" Willow shouted as she slammed both palms into Gage's shoulder. He had somehow managed to wrangle her back into his truck and was speeding toward her apartment. "You left your friends to die!"

"Enough, Willow." His voice came out rough but quiet. He kept one hand on the steering wheel as he grabbed both of her hands when she tried to hit him again.

"That was a car full of vampires, they may end up bruised up a bit, but they will survive the impact. I had to get you out of there, you're the one who could get hurt."

"But what about Marla?"

Gage's face turned tight as he dropped her hands lightly and returned his full attention to the road. "When we get to your apartment, you have exactly two minutes to grab that stupid rabbit and whatever clothes you might need for a few days."

She clenched her jaw and stared at him before responding. "Don't ignore me. What about Marla?"

"I don't know, okay? Matteo is with her. I trust him to make the right judgement on what to do with her."

"What the hell does that mean?"

Gage sighed, his jaw clenching and unclenching.

"What does that mean?" She asked again, her voice breaking.

"You and I both know no human would survive that crash. He has the two options of letting her die or turning her if there's time. If she died on impact, then there's no way of saving her." His voice grew quieter. "I'm sorry Willow. I'm so fucking sorry."

She wiped the tears that were rolling down her face. She wanted to stomp her feet like a child and scream at the unfairness of it all. She'd finally found a place she could settle down, finally found friends and a community that treated her well, finally was able to live a life she was comfortable with, but it was all being taken away from her. Marla deserved so much better than to die in a horrible, intentional car crash.

Willow could still smell the burnt smell of rubber and gasoline and feel the cold metal of the door handle that wouldn't budge in her hand. She started to picture Marla all twisted and bloodied, crumpled up in her seat like a broken little doll forgotten by her child master. Her heart began to race and her hands went numb.

"You're going to kill him, right?" She mumbled out in between her deep breaths.

"I won't stop until I have his blood splattered all around me."

"Can I watch?"

"Would it help?"

"More than you know."

They rode the rest of the way in silence, Gage sailing through red lights whenever it was safe to do so and Willow focusing her full attention on slowing down her heart rate. When he pulled into her parking lot, he hesitated before unlocking the door.

"Maybe it would be better if I went up and left you in here. You can keep the doors locked and drive away if anything happens."

She shook her head. "It would be quicker if I went up there, Snickers doesn't let anyone except me hold him. I'll only be two minutes, keep the truck running."

"Two minutes. That's all you get before I come busting the door down, okay? I'm setting the timer now."

Willow opened her door, but turned back to place a quick kiss on his lips. He ended up grabbing her by the hair as she tried to pull away and forced her mouth back onto his, deepening the kiss to something much more passionate.

"Two. Minutes," he growled between her lips before letting her go.

She ran up to her front door and unlocked it with more grace than she thought she had. Her panic had subsided and was replaced with a chilling calmness and intense focus. She already had everything mapped out in her head: she would start in her bedroom and grab her duffle bag, a handful of underwear, whatever clothing items were within reach, then scoop up her toothbrush on her way back to the living room to grab the pet carrier that was stored near the rabbit food, ending with shoving her confused rabbit into the carrier before making a beeline back to the truck.

She made it three steps into her apartment before her gut instinct was acting up again, urging her to leave. But her love for her rabbit overrode it and she continued back to her bedroom. Her focus gave her blinders and she saw nothing except the plan in her head.

Her duffle bag was stuffed and thrown across her shoulder in a matter of seconds and she whipped around the corner into her bathroom. She shoved her deodorant and hairbrush into a pocket, not looking up as she hurried into her living room.

"Hello Willow," a deep voice called to her.

She snapped her head up. There on her couch was Waldo's bulky figure, stroking the rabbit that was frozen still in his arms.

After taking a moment to process, she managed to squeeze out a whispered sentence. "Gage is downstairs."

"I know, I saw his truck idling out there. How long do you think he will wait before he comes looking for you?"

"Two minutes."

Something within her snapped. All the unfairness and loss she felt turned into blind rage.

Deep down she knew she couldn't kill him by herself, but she was damn sure she could fend him off for the last minute until Gage came up and finished the job. She dropped her duffle bag to the floor and ran into her kitchen, tearing open a drawer to pull out her serrated bread knife. Part of her wanted to go for the more intimidating chef's knife, but another dark, and more twisted, part of her wanted to feel the resistance of the blade as she sawed it into his arm.

Her voice came out strong and unwavering. "You don't scare me, Waldo. Quite frankly, you pissed me off to the point that I want to see what your blood looks like as it pools onto my carpet."

He responded to her bravery with a bored lilt to his voice. "Sounds like that would be a bitch to clean. Also, the name is Jesse James. Don't start acting like your little troupe of vermin and call me that stupid name. You're better than that. I don't see why you continue to associate with them."

"Would you rather have me associate with *you*? A man who enjoys killing innocent people and bullying other territories? What has Gage ever done to you that you keep harassing him and trying to destroy his home?"

"The only thing Gage has done is be weaker than me. Stealing Venice and killing humans both here and in Daytona has just been for fun. There's nothing better than rubbing salt in someone's wound."

He smiled with a dead look in his eyes. "Life is all about survival of the fittest, Willow. The people we kill are not innocent—there is not one single person on this planet who is fully sin-free. We simply kill strangers as a means to survive. We need their blood, and if we catch them, that just means it was their destiny to die by my hands."

His smile fell and he put his hand around Snicker's neck, squeezing it hard enough that the rabbit began to buck in his arms.

"Let go of him!" She screeched, and ran at him with the knife held high over her head.

Waldo instantly dropped the rabbit, who was gone within an instant back into his cage, and wrapped his hand around her wrist. The two froze as they heard Gage's truck door slam shut and angry footsteps run up the stairs.

"You're about to get fucked up," she snarled into his face.

"That's what you think. He couldn't beat me last time and he sure as hell won't beat me now."

He ripped the knife out of her hand, then picked her up and threw her over his shoulder like she weighed nothing. Almost in unison, as Gage threw open the front door, Waldo ripped open the patio door and jumped from the balcony, landing on the ground with a heavy thud. He did not even wince before running off toward a black SUV that was idling in an alleyway nearby.

"Gage!" Willow screamed with all of her might, but was shoved into the SUV before she could hear him call her name back.

Two men were sitting up front and the one behind the wheel hit the gas before Waldo had fully shut the door. Willow was left watching Gage lean over the balcony railing, watching her as she disappeared into the night.

"Let me go!" Willow screamed into Waldo's face. She began beating her fists against his arms as he tried to tie her up.

"Oh, we have a feisty one, boys. I hope you like a challenge." He grinned to the two up front.

The driver, a lanky man with short, dark hair and a full beard, peered at her from the rearview mirror and smirked while the other one—who was built identical to him except with copper hair and no beard—seemed to ignore her and cracked open his window to light a cigarette. He had a smattering of light freckles that coated his face and arms, and his hair was gelled back so that no strand was out of place.

Willow paused her struggle and gaped at the freckled man. "I've seen you before, you've been in my coffee shop." She turned her attention to the driver. "And you, you look familiar, too. Have you both been in my shop?"

The bearded one shook his head. "No darling, you shook your ass next to me on the dance floor of the Pink Flamingo Club. And what a fine ass that was. I can't want to get it underneath me later." His dark laugh came out as a growl, and the hair on her arms stood on end. "How do you think Jesse James found out Gage was into you? He had us spying on you this whole time."

Waldo took advantage of her pause to grab both of her wrists and tie them behind her back. She tried to ram her shoulder into Waldo's neck, but he wrapped his hand into her hair and slammed her head down against the center console. She whimpered as her eyes began to water from the impact, and felt the start of a bruise on her right cheekbone, which had taken most of the hit.

This wasn't the first time a man had bruised her, though. The abuse she lived through taught her how to be strong. She would be damned before giving him a sense of her fear.

"Stop fighting me and I won't have to destroy that pretty face of yours. Although I might still do that anyway, just so Gage can never look at you again. Who could love a girl missing a nose and a bashed in skull?"

Willow glared and resisted the urge to spit in his face. "He's going to kill you when he finds me."

"I'm sure he will try, but the thing is, he's not going to find us. Your boys like to think they're sneaky and have their shit together, but they really don't. I knew damn well him and his ass-fucking cousin were in Miami trying to discover my secret. It's a shame those dumb bitches they ran into at the bar told them about the compound, but at least they didn't tell them where exactly it's located." He smiled. "They paid their price for betraying their savior, though. I made sure to make an example out of them, and beheaded them before they went back home. And I guess I did you a favor, too, because I killed the little slut Gage was trying to sleep with. You're welcome."

"I never would have wanted that!"

He continued, completely ignoring her. "But don't you worry your cute little face off." She jerked away as he pinched her cheek. "You'll get to see my masterpiece that's taken me years to build, because that's where we're going. You should feel special because my own father never even got to see it. I made sure to keep it hidden from him. It was pretty easy, he wasn't the brightest man. Do you know how easy it was to set up his death?"

He stared at her like he was waiting for an actual response. She didn't give in and sat in silence.

"I'll give you a hint: it was easier than making chocolate milk. All I had to do was get some associates killed, fake cry about my dead friends, then I knew he would get revenge. I was kind of worried that Clay wouldn't have the balls to kill him, he always likes to play pacifist, but I knew he had the physical strength. That's one thing I'll admit to, Clay can fucking fight. Too bad his son didn't inherit any of that grit."

The car sped up as they merged onto an expressway. Waldo watched a road sign fly by and nodded to himself. "Speaking of my compound, I don't want you knowing how to get there. One can never be too careful. Please don't mind as I make sure you're incapacitated."

Before she could even blink, he used his full force to knock her head against the console again. A swift darkness fell over her, and she crumpled into his lap.

ɔɔɔɔ

She dreamed of nothing but empty darkness. It felt like she was trapped underground, being held down by ice-cold chains which refused to let her move an inch. Gage's voice was calling for her, the sound getting closer and closer, but when she attempted to scream she found she couldn't open her mouth. His voice sailed over her, but she couldn't see him and he couldn't see her. She wanted to weep as his voice started to sound distant again.

She was brought out of her nightmare with the feeling of being thrown down. Once she fully regained consciousness, she found herself laying on a small, stiff cot and staring up at an off-white paneled ceiling that reminded her of the one in her dentist's office. For a second she thought she was actually there, with her head fuzzy and tight feeling like she had just woken up from anesthesia and her jaw hurting like a tooth had recently been pulled.

She sat up and saw the dark wood paneling around her. She remembered she was at some compound, possibly in the middle of nowhere, with no one knowing where she was located.

She quickly checked her pockets for her phone, but was unsurprised to find that Waldo had taken it. She scanned her surroundings to find anything to use as a weapon, but there was nothing in the room except the cot, a white plastic folding table, and a matching chair. She debated about pulling a wrestling stunt and hitting whoever walked into the room with the chair, but realized the flimsy plastic would easily break over a vampire's head. Plus, there was the slight inconvenience of the handcuff that was currently keeping her left arm stuck to the cot.

She squeezed her eyes shut and tried to imagine what advice her mother would give in this situation. Unfortunately, due to either the pounding headache that was forming or the pure terror she was trying to ignore, her mother felt very far away and her voice never formed in Willow's mind.

With her free hand, she rubbed circles on her temple and focused on her breathing. Deep down she knew Gage would save her, because that was how all stories ended. The villain would capture the girl, the hero would break in and kick ass, the girl would be whisked away by the handsome, blond hero, only to be fucked into a blissful oblivion. And to top it off, the girl's best friend would have survived the car accident and everything would go back to normal with them making coffee together at their coffee house.

Tears streamed down her face as she dreamed the fantasy. She kept repeating in her mind that everything would be okay. Her inner mantra picked up pace as the door to her room unlocked and a tall, burly woman walked in, her frizzy, red hair pulled back into a ponytail. She looked as if she could have been a linebacker, but the scowl on her face made it seem like wrestling was more her style.

"Jesse James is asking for you," she grunted. She pulled out a set of keys from her jeans pockets.

"What does he want?" Willow whispered in a tone that countered the woman's rich baritone.

She smirked, but the smile did not meet her eyes. Willow saw a flash of a pointed white tooth gleaming behind her thick, pink lips. "You'll see."

Willow's headache turned into a full-blown migraine as she was yanked off the cot by her arm. She could tell this was not the woman's first time using handcuffs as she swiftly unlocked them and twisted Willow's arms behind her back to re-cuff them together in one fluid movement.

The two walked in silence down a narrow hallway and through

a large room that was as empty as the previous one. It wasn't until they were outside that Willow realized she was being held in a trailer that looked like it was from the 1990's. Rust and decay ate away the skirt around the base, revealing cracked cinderblocks holding up the structure, and most of the windows were busted out and replaced with plywood.

"Man, they really spared no expense for my holding cell, huh?" Willow mumbled under her breath.

The linebacker ignored her and continued pulling her through the compound. Similar trailers were set up in rows around hers, but most of them still held actual windows and decks with outdoor furniture. There were some that even had small gardens in front. Two kids on bikes rolled past them and they turned to look, mouths gaping open, with glistening fangs catching the moonlight.

Willow swallowed back the sadness that was blossoming at the idea of children so young being converted into vampires. Never being able to grow up. Never being able to be true adults.

"What is this place?" She asked.

Yet again, the woman ignored her. The further they walked through the compound, the more the trailers began to change. They went from rickety metal boxes to more sturdy double-wides, and eventually modular ranch-style homes complete with white picket fences and golden retrievers panting at her through the slats. They finally stopped in front of a Tudor-style house that stood out against the manufactured homes. Instead of taking her up the cement stairs to the front door, the woman pulled her to the attached garage and punched in a code that caused the door to lift slowly. The loud groaning noise caused Willow's heart to start racing, and her body went cold.

Eventually the door fully opened to reveal Waldo, reclining in the middle of a plush leather couch, with the two men from the SUV sitting on the ground in front of him. The freckled man was smoking another cigarette and the bearded man was hunched over with his head propped in his hand and his arm on his knee. A bored look was across both of their faces, like they had been waiting for a while.

A serpentine smile broke out across Waldo's face. "Oh good, you're up. I was worried we would have to wait until tomorrow, because I wouldn't want you to miss this. Go ahead and chain her up over there."

Waldo nodded to a water heater that was in the corner of the garage, and the woman once again swiftly unlocked the cuffs to attach her to the metal pipe running up the side of it. As soon as she secured the cuffs, she left the garage without even glancing at Willow.

"So how do you like my masterpiece? It's taken me years to develop a vampire-only community. It's still a work in progress, but it's the biggest community in the United States. I was influenced by Russia—they have communities much like this only on a grander scale, whole towns only consisting of vampires. It sounded like a paradise. No more hiding what we are or having to deal with hate and prejudice. So, I decided to create my own community. In exchange for protection and a slice of paradise, all my members must do is devote themselves to me."

"It sounds like a cult." She said.

"Call it what you will, but many call it a home."

Willow was angled so that she could still see the two men sitting at the foot of what appeared to be their master. Waldo leaned forward and propped his arms on his knees. The men sat up straight, eagerness replacing the bearded one's bored expression. The freckled man's expression did not change, but he did quickly inhale the rest of his cigarette, crushing it out into the cement next to him. A slow trail of smoke escaped his lips as his eyes became fixated on a golden flask that Waldo retrieved from next to him on the couch.

"As you may or may not know, each vampire family has a unique container for the head vampire's blood. This flask was handed down from my great-great-grandfather and has eventually made its way to me—" his tone shifted to a sarcastic one "—thanks to the passing of my dear old dad."

He held up the flask and let the light reflect off its iridescent golden exterior. Even from the distance Willow was at, she could see intricate script carved into it.

"My blood allows me to become a god, and with it I shall grant you both eternal life for your commitment to me. Much like His son, you will take communion and drink of my blood to be welcomed into my holy gates."

Willow's mouth went dry and she tried to stop from shaking so that her cuff did not rattle against the pipe. She watched as Waldo tipped the flask into each man's mouth to release a small trickle of red liquid.

"Welcome to eternity," he whispered.

Both men crumpled to the ground and began screaming and thrashing as if Waldo had doused them in gasoline and dropped a match.

Twenty-Eight

Willow

Willow didn't pry her eyes from the two men convulsing on the floor, even as Waldo stood up and walked toward the door. It was then she realized how they were able to sneak into her café and stalk her in the club without being suspect.

They were seen as inconspicuous, innocent humans.

But as red foam began dripping down their mouths and their canine teeth elongated, they were becoming monsters. For a split second, the image of Marla going through a similar process flashed into her mind.

"Well, my dear, it's been fun. I must get going before the sun comes up. I would wish you well, but I know better. As soon as these two finish their transformation, you'll be ripped to shreds. What lucky bastards to have a girl who smells as sweet as you as their first meal. My first meal was some homeless hag who cried the whole time. How annoying." He rolled his eyes like he was joking with a friend.

Willow did not have to debate what to say—her pride wouldn't let her beg and her rage began to consume her. "Fuck. You."

Waldo laughed and waved goodbye before flipping off the light switch and turning his back to her. He hit a button that shut the garage door slowly. Willow watched his feet walk away until the door had shut completely, and she was left alone in the dark with the two men who had quit their convulsions and were eerily motionless on the cement floor. The only thing she could hear was her own steady breath.

It felt like hours, but finally her eyes adjusted to the dark and she saw the dark-haired one's hand twitch. It twitched again, and his fingers curled inward. A soft moaning sound escaped his lips as he sat up in a smooth, fluid movement, with his eyes still shut and his head hanging down. The other one remained on the floor, but he had opened his eyes and he was staring off into the corner of the room.

Willow grabbed the pipe she was chained to and tested its sturdiness. To her astonishment, it wobbled and creaked like it was coming loose. Water trickled out of the top of the pipe, confirming that it was not secured to the valve.

Her attention snapped back to the dark-haired man as he slowly lifted his head from his chest.

"You…smell so…divine."

His eyes popped open in a crazed manner and he crawled over to her, his long legs moving in a spider-like way as he attempted to stand up but failed. His new body seemed to be failing him, and he was not sure how to use his immortal muscles, which gave Willow a spark of hope.

"Come here, fucker," she whispered under her breath.

She positioned both hands to get the best grip on the pipe and scooted so that her feet were placed strategically against the heater. She thought of all the things that had gone wrong for her in life, from her mother's cancer, to her abusive ex, to growing up without a permanent home, to her current home being taken away. She funneled that rage and adrenaline and used her entire body to pull the pipe off the heater, freeing herself and giving her a weapon to fight with.

Kill him, mo stóirín.

At the sound of her mother's voice returning, Willow raised the pipe and slammed it down on the man's head with a sickening thud. He hissed and fell over, but reached out to grab her ankle. She angled the pipe vertically and slammed it down again, this time impaling the man's hand. She twisted the pipe before ripping it out.

"Stupid bitch!" He screamed, spittle dripping onto his beard.

Her only response was to smile as blood oozed out of the hole she had made. He lunged for her again, but was met with a kick in his face, her shoe creating a satisfying crunch against his nose.

She developed tunnel vision as she focused on the beast withering on the floor beneath her. Everything around her blacked out, until it was like a spotlight had landed on him. His blood was a glittering, blackish-red, and his skin was as white as moonlight in the dark.

She kicked him in the face again, not giving him another chance to reach for her, and slammed the pipe down on his spine. He sprawled out on the floor, flipping over onto his back and covering his broken face with his bleeding hand. His other hand was in the air, blindly swiping around for the pipe. But she was quicker and moved to his legs, bringing the pipe down onto his knees repeatedly until she heard them pop. He tried to roll over, but she swiftly straddled his chest and grabbed his arms to trap them against his side with her legs. He tried to wiggle out from under her, but he was losing too much blood and was exhausted from his transition.

"Stupid bitch," he whimpered.

She slapped him across the face and crushed the pipe against his throat. "Didn't your mother ever teach you not to call a woman that?"

He couldn't respond with her full weight pressed against the pipe. His bloodied face began to turn a matching crimson, but she released the pressure as soon as his lips began to turn blue. She toyed with the idea of suffocating him, but decided on a more primal method.

She took her pipe and lifted it high above her head, feeling the whisper of her mother's hands on hers as she brought it down and straight through his rib cage, piercing his heart. She felt as the dull pipe tore through the layers of muscle and sinew and felt the vibration of his heart attempting to pump a few final times before it settled and he went limp.

She wasn't sure how long she sat on top of him, her hands wrapped around the pipe and her knees soaking up the blood pooling around them. The sound of someone slowly clapping pulled her back into full awareness. Her breathing began to slow, her arms trembled, and her body began to ache at the exertion.

"Bravo, that was quite the fight. I am honestly shocked at how quickly you took him down."

Willow looked up to see the copper-haired man relaxing on the couch in front of her, with his disinterested expression back in place. With her focus so intent on the one beneath her, she had forgotten about him. She attempted to pull the pipe out, but her hands were slippery and all her strength dispersed.

"Do not worry about that, I will not hurt you. I have come to like you, actually. Your café is so inviting. My original plan was to leave as soon as I turned, leaving Waldo and this stupid compound behind. All I wanted was to become a vampire, not join a cult. I wished I would have met Gage first instead of Waldo. I feel like he would have turned me without any commitment, but alas that is not what happened." He pulled a pack of cigarettes out from between the couch cushions and lit one. "I am truly sorry for bringing you out here. It was the last thing I had to do before he would turn me. I had no idea he wanted us to feed off you."

Willow stared at him. Her instincts were quiet, and she decided to take a chance. "If you help me get home, I'll make sure Gage lets you live."

He took a puff as he mulled over her statement. "Deal."

He stood up and walked over to her, being sure to avoid any blood, and held out his hand. She took it and was startled to find how coordinated he was compared to the other man as he pulled her up and helped her stand. It was like he was meant to be a vampire. He patted down her hair and wiped some blood that had splattered her cheek.

"The name is Alistair, by the way. First things first, I need blood and you look exhausted. There is a motel not too far from here we can probably walk to before the sun comes up if we are quick." He checked the gold watch on his wrist. "Most of the others are in their homes by now, it should be easy to sneak out of here without being caught. We only have twenty minutes before the sunrise, though."

"Can we steal a car instead of walk?"

"Are you alright with that?"

"I killed a man, Alistair. I don't really give a shit about stealing a car."

"Technically you killed a vampire, and some people find that heroic. Me, on the other hand? I have always been a piece of shit, so we should steal an expensive sports car."

Willow stared at the bloody mess of a corpse next to them, and something about the situation made her want to confess all her sins. "No, I've killed a human man before."

"Listen, I may be a piece of shit, but I am not a priest. We have to go, we are running out of nighttime."

He gently took her wrist and pulled her toward a door that led out into the backyard, and helped her creep through the darkness until they came across a black Mercedes-Benz. It was sitting in front of a modular with a window that had been left wide open.

"Well, it is not the sports car of my dreams, but it will do. Wait here while I look for the key."

He left her leaning against the trunk as he quietly removed the screen from the window and slipped inside. It took him less than a minute to slip back out with the keys dangling from his long fingers. For the first time since she met him, he smiled.

"The guy who lives here is named James, and I completely loathe everything about him. He is a pompous ass and a narcissist. I wish I could see his face when he wakes up and finds his precious car gone from his driveway."

A small smile spread across Willow's face, but it did not match her feelings of fatigue. All she wanted was to lie down in a bed and disappear forever. Twice now, she had been attacked by a vampire, and she was tired.

She was barely aware of the drive to the motel, or walking herself into the room he rented. She hardly acknowledged him as he said goodnight and left her alone to go hunt down his first prey.

She stripped off her clothes and took a scalding-hot shower that turned her skin bright pink. She scrubbed her skin dry with the sandpaper motel towel, and fell into bed naked, still feeling the thick blood covering her skin. She fell asleep to the image of the red liquid pooling around her knees.

She dreamed again of being underground, held down by chains that wrapped around her wrists and ankles. The darkness consumed her and became her.

Gage's voice called her name, this time close to her, and his desperate tone was replaced with a whispering love. She felt a caress on her forehead and the darkness that had nestled into her mind began to stir. A soft kiss followed the caress, and the chains disintegrated so that she was able to move.

"Willow, baby, wake up."

The moment she realized his voice was real, the darkness completely fled her body. She flung her eyes open and saw his green ones crinkle with the smile that spread across his face.

"Gage!" She sat up and wrapped her arms around his neck, pulling him tight against her.

He pulled the fallen bedsheet back into place, covering her exposed breasts from the three other men that were standing behind him, pretending to look anywhere but at the naked girl that had a death grip on their leader.

"Hey guys, will you give us a minute?" Gage asked.

Horatio raised an eyebrow. "Is that all it's going to take you?"

Nikolas shook his head and started to herd the twins out, but he stopped and turned back around.

"I'm glad you're safe, Willow. We were all worried about you."

Once the boys had shut the door, she cupped Gage's face with her hands and pulled him toward her for a kiss. She was hesitant to let him go, but her curiosity had her pulling away.

"How did you end up finding me? Where's Alistair? You didn't hurt him, did you?"

"No, I didn't hurt Alistair."

He placed a kiss on her forehead and stood up from the bed to grab a new set of clothes that were sitting on the dresser. He helped her into her shirt and pants, trailing his fingers down her sides as he slid the fabric over her skin. The blood she thought had been a permanent feeling was removed with his gentle touch.

"He was the one who called me to tell me that you two were in a motel in Georgia. Not going to lie, I was about to head out in the sunlight to strangle the prick who was sharing a room with my girl, but lucky for him he was able to convince me that he wasn't here for sexual reasons. It was merely a pit stop to recover."

His face shifted and he looked like he was on the verge of tears. "I should have never let you go up to your apartment alone. Waldo can't handle rejection, so I should have known he would be up there ready to hurt you. I'm so sorry, Willow. I'm so sorry I messed up and you were attacked again. Though Alistair *did* say you did an impressive job with him."

"Please don't feel guilty, it's my own fault for telling you to stay in the truck. Neither of us were thinking straight after watching our friends get hit." Marla's crumpled body flashed through her mind. "I saw Horatio and Matteo were okay, what about Marla?"

He gave her a gentle smile and she prepared herself for the worst: funerals, and crying, and never ending grief.

"Marla is making sure Snickers is getting fat on carrots and hay back at the mansion."

"So she's okay!" She quickly pulled him back onto the bed and hugged him, but he was still tense. She pulled away and looked him in the eyes. "She's okay, right?"

"Yes, she's okay, but Matteo had to make a tough decision when they were hit. She had severe injuries and a broken back, and was seconds away from dying." He hesitated. "He had to turn her."

"Is she okay with that decision he made for her?"

"To be honest, I don't know. I haven't had the chance to see her, because as soon as I got the call from Alistair, I was more focused on getting you back. I'm going to assume that with her obsessive love for Matteo, she's probably okay with it."

"That's still a huge life change that she had no say in, though. I know if you ever did that to me, I would be livid."

"Even if it meant saving your life?"

Willow chewed the side of her lip. "I mean, I would be grateful to be alive, but I would also make sure that you made amends for taking that decision away from me."

His voice deepened and he leaned forward, touching her nose with his. "Oh? And how would I have to make amends?"

"Well, you could start by buying me whatever I wanted."

"Mhm." His hand trailed over her stomach, then traced an invisible line up and down her thigh.

"And then by giving me unlimited rides on your motorcycle."

"That's too easy." His hand inched closer to her inner thigh.

She let out a small sigh and let one leg drop open, giving him easy access to what she really wanted him to caress.

"Oh, and then every night you would have to get on your knees at the end of the bed and put your head between my legs until I moan your name in ecstasy."

His chuckle rumbled through her. He sat up and pulled her so that she was laying down, legs splayed open. He started to undo the pants she'd struggled into earlier when there was a knock on the door.

"Put some clothes on, you two horny youngsters, Alistair is back with a plan!" Horatio called from the other side.

She looked at him with a gleam of hope in her eyes. "So not only did you not kill him, but you already put him to work?"

"Don't get me wrong, I'm not pleased with him by any means, but he can help us. He's currently in the process of setting up a meeting with Waldo."

"I know he helped Waldo kidnap me, and he didn't save me from the other guy, but he had a change of heart and helped me escape the compound. All he wanted was to be a vampire, but Waldo made him jump through hoops before he would turn him. What if—and stop me if this is stupid—but what if you offered him a spot in your f—"

"Stop."

"Gage! I'm serious, he's a new vampire and he might need help, plus I also have seen how you run things with the others. You pretty much give them the freedom to do whatever they want within reason. And I highly doubt he would want to live with you, so you don't even have to offer that. I feel bad using him to get to Waldo, then throwing him to the wild. Something tells me he has potential to be either really good or really bad, and right now he's choosing to be good. But if he's left on his own with no support, who knows what will happen."

"So I'm hearing that there's potential for him to be bad, and we should kill him after he helps us."

Willow punched him lightly on the shoulder. "That is not at all what I am saying."

Gage rolled his eyes and helped Willow off the bed, readjusting her pants and placing one last kiss on top of her head. "I'll think about it. Let's go get some revenge babe, I'll make amends to you later."

Twenty-Nine

Gage

Horatio, Matteo, Nikolas, and Alistair were huddled in a half circle around Gage's black truck, and he noticed Willow repressed a smile at how easily Alistair fit in with them. She held his hand as they approached the group, and he wondered if it was her near-death experience or Alistair calling him during her time of need that caused her to want the red-haired snake to stay around.

"Were you able to get a hold of Waldo?" Gage asked Alistair, refusing to make eye contact with him.

"Yes, as of right now he believes Willow is dead and you have tracked me down."

An image of his love being at the bottom of the ocean next to Venice flashed in his mind and he tensed, but Willow squeezed his hand to remind him she was still here. He knew that if Waldo thought she was still alive, he would try to kill her himself. As much as he was impressed that she had been able to kill the new vampire, she was still repairing from yesterday and did not have it in her to take on an older, stronger one. He would do anything to keep her safe, even if it meant pretending that she was dead.

He turned to Nikolas. "Is there a way we can get him back to Florida? It would be easier to lure him back down to our territory where we have backup. There is no way Robby would be willing to leave his family to come up here after three of his men were just killed."

Alistair continued before Nikolas could respond. "Here is the problem. He is also under the impression that I currently have you tied up in this motel room."

Gage laughed. "*You* have *me* tied up? As a brand-new vampire? And just how did you explain that so he believed it?"

"I said that you came up here alone, were very distraught at the death of the love of your life, and were making some stupid decisions—such as being drunk—that made it easy to overcome you and tie you up. He did not question it, so I am assuming he thinks you were pretty weak to begin with."

The last comment caused Gage to lock eyes with him. "I am not weak."

The bored expression, which seemed to be a permanent feature of Alistair's, didn't faulter as Gage's glare burned into him. "I never said I thought that, but Waldo clearly does. Prove him wrong."

"Don't tell me what to do."

Nikolas rolled his eyes. "What time is Waldo getting here?"

"He said within the hour, so we better set this up quickly," Alistair responded.

"I am not letting you guys tie me up. That's the dumbest shit, and this whole plan sounds like it came out of an 80's action movie."

Alistair leaned over to Matteo and whispered loud enough that everyone could hear. "Is he always this difficult to work with?"

Matteo smirked. "He's stubborn, but you get used to it. You basically have to use reverse psychology and get him to believe the idea was his."

Gage shifted his sizzling glare to Matteo. "I can hear you."

"Good. Now stop being a stubborn ass and let me tie you up like a good little boy." Matteo grabbed a bundle of rope from the back of the truck and slapped it against his palm.

Horatio cackled and headed off with Nikolas to hide their motorcycles in the nearby woods. Willow let go of Gage's hand and pushed him toward the leering Matteo.

"I changed my mind, if you ever had to make amends I would want to watch you get tied up every night instead." She smiled.

"You're not staying around to watch that happen—in fact, I want you to leave now, since Waldo could be on his way here. The compound is not that far away. I'll have Matteo take you back home. Sammy and Marla are waiting for you."

"There is no way in hell I'm leaving you after all that happened."

"Please, I don't want you to get hurt." He turned to Matteo. "Promise me you'll get her out of here and back to safety."

"You got it, boss."

Willow crossed her arms. "Excuse me, do I not get a say in this?"

"Not this time." Gage tried to kiss her, but she dodged him and went over to Matteo and grabbed the rope from him.

"If you're making me leave, can I at least tie you up?" She asked.

Gage released an exhausted sigh. He was on edge with not knowing how close Waldo was to their motel, and felt that every second standing outside was putting her in more danger. "Fine, but be quick, and make sure it's not too tight so I can get out of it when he gets here."

Matteo turned to Alistair as Willow and Gage began walking back to the motel room. "To add on to what we were saying earlier, we can use either reverse psychology or Willow to get him to do what we want."

"I can still hear you!" Gage shouted over his shoulder before slamming the door shut.

Once the two were alone, Willow wrapped her arms around him and squeezed him tightly. He took a deep breath before returning her embrace and rested his head upon hers, completely melting into her.

"You're making this very difficult. I would give anything to be the one tying you up," he said.

"Well, once you're done with Waldo, I can make sure that happens," she purred.

She tilted her head up to nip at his lip with her teeth. He placed his hands around her face and deepened the kiss, only to push her away and point to the rope.

"Let's get this over with so we can get to the good part."

"Can I hog-tie you?"

"Absolutely not."

"How about if you lay down on your back and spread your legs, then I'll wrap the rope around your thighs and tie it around your neck?"

He stared at her, holding back his laugh at the eagerness in her expression. "Just tie me to the damn chair you freak."

She rolled her eyes and huffed, pulling out the rickety wooden chair from the small desk tucked into the corner of the room. They were both silent as her hands fluttered around him, gliding the rope around his torso to tie a bow in the back with a strand that reached discreetly to his hand. One quick tug and he knew he would be able to free himself. She gave a sad smile at her handiwork and gave him one more passionate kiss.

"Please listen to Matteo and stay safe. I'll see you in a little bit," he murmured.

He was not religious, but silently prayed to whatever deity was listening that she would leave in time, and that everything would go smoothly.

He watched her walk to the door, both of them freezing when the handle moved. Alistair's unintelligible voice could be heard on the other side, with a nervous twinge to it. Before Gage could tell her what to do, she ran around him to the bathroom and quietly locked the door just as Waldo walked in.

"Well holy shit, I'm kind of disappointed. I was prepared to walk into a trap and thought I would get a satisfying fight. I even told my men to stay behind because I wanted a little bit of a challenge tonight. I didn't believe it when Alistair said he managed to contain you. I barely believed that he was able to kill that stupid girl of yours, but I guess he is full of surprises. I think he might have earned a spot as my second-in-command."

Rage ran through him as he watched the smirk broaden into a full-blown smile, but he was able to contain it knowing Willow was still in the motel room. He couldn't risk losing control of the situation.

"He said her blood was as sweet as candy. Tell me, did you used to drink from her while you fucked? Did her pussy taste just as sweet?"

"I'm not talking about her with *you*," Gage hissed through gritted teeth.

"I liked the way she whimpered when I left her alone in that garage with them. My only regret was that I didn't stay to watch them tear her apart and fuck her corpse after. How much money do you think I could have made selling that snuff film on the dark web? There are some sick people out there who would have absolutely loved to watch my dick spread her asshole open."

Gage took in a deep breath and released it slowly, counting to ten. Nikolas had always talked about meditating to control his anger, and now seemed about as good of a time as any to try it. He figured out what Waldo was doing and was not going to play his game.

"Stop baiting me. Are you here to kill me or not?"

"Where would the fun be in that? I thought we could have a good old-fashioned brawl out in the parking lot, and whoever loses has to buy the other one dinner." He chuckled. "Just kidding."

A sharp pain blossomed from Gage's right shoulder. It had happened so quickly that he didn't notice that Waldo had pulled out a small knife and thrown it at him, embedding it into the soft flesh above his armpit.

"I'm not going to kill you right away. I would rather torture you and slowly chop you to pieces to send to Clay in packages. I have a few extra Amazon boxes I could use. Imagine his surprise when he thought the newest tool he ordered came, in but in reality, it's his beloved son's ear! Or I could send him your fingers. I heard you were into painting, so it's only fitting that I take away the tool you need to create your masterpieces."

"He won't let you get away with that. He'll have both my family and the Daytona family coming after you."

Another knife landed in his left leg and he bit his lip to keep from groaning. Even with his high pain tolerance, the strength behind Waldo's throw caused the knives to sink deep into his muscles resulting in a painful throbbing.

"Don't worry about that, I've been having my men kill off your cousin's family in Daytona. Actually, they were able to kill three of them recently. They decapitated them and fed the remains to the dolphins; I heard those creatures have developed a strange taste for flesh."

A third knife came flying through the air and stuck in his right kneecap. He covered his grunt of pain with a growl. "Goddammit, what is it with you and knives? Enough!"

"Aw, what's the matter? Are you not having fun? That's okay, because I'm out of knives anyway."

Waldo took a few steps forward to retrieve the knives, and Gage took advantage of this opportunity. As he pulled the rope to untie himself, he lunged to grab Waldo around the neck and shoved him backward into the wall. Waldo let out a surprised grunt, but quickly slammed his hand into the knife that was protruding out of Gage's shoulder, causing it to slide all the way through and out the other side. It fell to the carpeted floor with a thud, and blood began pouring out of the gaping wound.

Gage let him go and bent over to rip the remaining two knives out of his legs, only to quickly stand back up and stab them into Waldo's own shoulders. The knives only seemed to ignite his fury, and he came toward Gage with an insane glimmer in his eyes.

"Never mind, I've decided I'm going to fucking kill you and get this over with." Waldo snarled.

Waldo lunged toward him like the knives were not even there, and the two locked arms as they both tried to push each other. Gage's legs gave out and he landed on his knees, the impact causing him to groan silently. He worried that if he was too loud, Willow would try to intervene to help him. He let go of Waldo's arms to try to push the knives further into him, but Waldo landed a punch to his face before he could.

Gage knew that somehow, he had to get Waldo out of the room and into the parking lot to not only get him further away from Willow, but so that the others could join the fight. He stood up and tried to push him toward the door, only for Waldo to pull a knife out of himself and try to slice him across the face.

"Dammit," Gaged huffed as he ducked away from the blades.

Waldo continued to slice through the air furiously, causing Gage to take a few steps back to avoid them. This was going the opposite way he wanted, and his frustration was muddling up his logic.

He decided to rush toward Waldo to try to knock him off balance, but instead took the impact of a knife into his shoulder right above where it previously had been. By now his adrenaline had muted his pain, and he pushed through to grab Waldo's other wrist and bent it back far enough that he dropped the other knife.

Both men had knives sticking out of them as they wrestled each other, Gage pushing Waldo to the front door and Waldo trying his best to push Gage backward. The two continued to push and punch, neither making much movement toward their goals. Waldo finally kicked Gage in the knee that had been stabbed, and he fell to the ground again.

With the thought of Willow scared and hiding in the dark bathroom behind him, he finally let go of the rage he was trying to tame. He used all his strength to grab Waldo around the legs and threw him over his shoulder so that he crashed hard into the wall behind him. Gage spun around and landed on top of him, throwing punch after punch into Waldo's face. His knuckles started to bleed as Waldo's teeth ripped his skin, but he didn't stop.

Waldo was able to find the strength to push Gage off himself enough that he was able to get to his knees and pulled the knife out of his shoulder to throw. Gage ducked and the knife soared over his head and lodged into the bathroom door.

"Well, it seems you've been practicing since the last time we fought. Do you remember the sound of those humans as I slaughtered them? It was like music to my ears." He chuckled. "Venice's scream as I tore a hole into her throat? Now that was a beautiful melody. I wonder what Willow's screams sounded like when Alistair tore her apart?"

Gage gave a guttural roar as he came toward Waldo again. This time, the man was prepared for the attack and stopped him from landing another punch. He used his massive, stocky body to push into Gage again. The force was strong enough that Gage flew backwards, crashing into the bathroom door and ripping it off its hinges. He didn't look for Willow—his only thought was to keep his eyes on Waldo and prevent him from getting into the bathroom any further.

"I'm going to rip *your* throat out," Gage yelled as he pushed himself off the ground.

He noticed Waldo's eyes shift slightly to the left.

"That fucking liar," Waldo scoffed and braced himself. "You're still alive!"

A white porcelain soap dish came flying through the air and over Gage's shoulder, making an impact in the middle of Waldo's face. A slight surge of pride went through him knowing that she was ready to defend herself, even if her choice of weapon wasn't the most destructive.

"How does it feel to know that one of your own hates you enough that he's willing to stab you in the back and join our family?" Willow asked.

"Shame on me, I should have known better than to trust that sniveling little rat. Next time when I need someone killed, I'll be sure to do it myself."

Waldo lunged forward, but side-stepped Gage and went straight into the bathroom. Within a second, he had grabbed Willow around the neck and lifted her off the ground, her feet kicking wildly in the air. Waldo's fangs extended and he was mere inches away from biting into her neck.

Willow's eyes widened and she stopped her struggle to look at Gage. The look she gave him was one of trust, like she knew he wouldn't let this happen.

Gage thought the rage and adrenaline had already surged through him earlier, but a new wave tinted with fear flooded his system. He had failed the humans and let them be murdered by Waldo and his friends. He had failed his father and let his family be slaughtered at Gerald's hands. He had even failed himself by letting Venice into his life.

He would not fail Willow.

It happened in slow motion. He didn't hear the primal noises that came out of him as he reached his hands out and dug his nails into

Waldo's round head, pulling it back quick and sharp enough that the skin of his neck stretched and began to tear. Gage lifted his bloodied leg and planted his foot at the base of Waldo's spine, yanking his head from side-to-side, relishing in the sound of his vertebrae cracking. It took all of five seconds, but it felt like an eternity before Waldo's neck finally snapped and Gage was able to rip his head off in one smooth movement.

Waldo's headless body stood up for a second before collapsing on top of Willow. She didn't scream as she patiently waited for him to come back to his senses, drop the dripping head, and move the corpse off her.

They were soaked in blood as he helped her up onto her feet and held her in a tight embrace.

Thirty

Willow

A plate of chicken and dumplings was placed in front of Willow and she looked over the five boys sitting around her at the table. Before making the drive home to Vista Maria, Willow had requested they stop for a rest at a nearby diner after changing out of their bloodied clothing. Gage had an extra work t-shirt in his truck, and she was covertly enjoying finally having a piece of his clothing she could add to her wardrobe.

Even though everything had turned out okay and Waldo was dead and burned to a crisp in the woods behind the motel, she was not sure if she was ready to be alone with her thoughts during the long car ride home. She needed time to sit with people she cared for and clear her mind.

She thought she had lost the twins. Their nightly appearance in her café brought her more joy than she realized. They would always tell her the most interesting things, from the current wild anime Matteo was watching, to Horatio's oddly-specific facts about dinosaurs. The two were nerds in their own unique way. The car crash had almost taken them away forever.

From across the table, she watched as they eagerly retold the story of Waldo's demise to their girlfriends over the phone. The two had called them together, putting Matteo's phone on speaker, and were talking over and interrupting each other so frequently Willow wondered if Marla and Sammy understood anything that was being said.

Nikolas was quietly eating his waffles, seemingly entertained by the twins. He was the quiet, wise one of the group, and even though she didn't come close to losing him, she still cherished him just as deeply. When he would come into her café, he always asked about her day—and listened. Asking how she was wasn't an automatic saying for him, he actually cared. But even underneath all that wisdom and caring, there was a sadness to him she couldn't figure out. Anytime she would ask, he became an expert at deflecting.

On either side of her sat Gage and Alistair, and she could feel the tension between the two. Even Nikolas had noticed when they first sat down, and pointed out that it was like watching two feral cats try to get along.

She made it her mission to convince Alistair to join Gage's family. *Her* family. She owed him the safety for helping her, and she knew it would only benefit them. She had a feeling that things were not quite over with the Miami family, and that they had a long road ahead of them trying to figure out what to do with the compound.

She felt Gage's hand rub against her thigh. He had not spoken much since killing Waldo, and didn't order anything to eat or drink.

"Are you okay?" She whispered low enough that no one but him heard.

"Yeah, I'm just ready to get home. Clay's been texting me constantly asking if you're okay. I'm not sure what you did, but you seem to have him wrapped around your finger. He's more concerned with your safety than my own."

Willow smiled and rested her head against his shoulder. "I pay my rent on time. I'm a source of reliable income for him."

"I think you have every guy at this table wrapped around your finger. Even that one." He side-eyed Alistair. "If you wanted to join us, I don't think there would be anyone against it."

She froze at his sentence. That was a commitment that would affect her for eternity. Joining them would mean giving up her mortality and turning. As much as she was coming to love Gage, she wasn't sure she was ready for that next step. Yet.

"That's something I'm going to have to think about."

"I know, but the offer is there whenever you're ready."

She wrapped her arms around Gage and pulled him close. She gave him a light kiss on the cheek, but he wasn't content enough with that. He placed a hand to her face and held her in place as he traced his tongue along her lips, begging her to open. She smiled and complied.

"Gross," Matteo muttered in the background.

"Now you know how it feels to be around you and Marla all the time," his brother responded.

"Oh are they kissing?" Marla squealed from the phone. "They are the cutest couple ever! Well, next to me and Matteo. This is perfect timing, too, with Sammy and Horatio's wedding coming up. I can't wait to see you two all dressed up—"

Before she could finish her sentence, Horatio hung up and stared awkwardly at the table, avoiding all eye contact.

"What wedding?" Matteo whispered.

Horatio looked into his matching dark brown eyes. "Listen, it happened real quick and I didn't even get her a ring yet. And before you get all sad on me, I was going to tell you once we got home and ask you to go with me to pick out the ring. That car accident really freaked us both out, especially after hearing you scream for Marla and seeing her crumpled body."

Matteo drew in a sharp breath and winced. A shadow crossed over both their faces as they relived what was probably the worst night of either of their lives.

"Emotions were high, and we never wanted to lose each other like that. I know marriage won't prevent that—if it's our time, it's our time. But I wanted to be attached to her in some way. I wanted her to be my wife. I knew I loved her, but I never realized how much I loved her until that night. So, while you were helping Marla turn, I asked her unofficially. I was waiting until I got that ring to officially ask her."

"I guess I can forgive you for keeping me out of the loop if you promise to make me your best man," Matteo said.

"Well of course, there's no one else I would rather ask." Horatio looked around at the others. "I mean, I would want you guys, too, but it's only fair Matteo is the best man. We shared the same womb and room our whole childhood. You all get to be groomsmen, though."

Alistair's bored expression cracked slightly, and he raised his brow. "Surely you are not including me in that sentence."

"I surely am. You helped Willow out and I feel like you could make a good addition to our family. It would be weird if you weren't included."

"Oh, I was not sticking around. I am going to continue with my plan of traveling. I heard the Midwest is nice."

Willow scoffed. "I've lived in the Midwest. It's cold and boring, plus there's tornados. I know I'm not an official member yet, but I would be honored to have you join us. I'm worried for you being out there all alone as a new vampire. Life is hard enough as it is without having to figure out how to live in the dark and get blood without being caught. Plus, Horatio is right, I think you would make a great addition."

Matteo nodded his agreement. "I vote yay, we need a bigger family anyway. And we have a lot of spare rooms back at the mansion if you need a place to crash. You don't want to be homeless, new, and lonely."

"I agree," Nikolas joined in, "but it's ultimately up to Gage."

Willow turned her whole body around to face him. She watched as he chewed on the side of his mouth, locking eyes with Nikolas in such a way that it seemed they were having a silent conversation with each other. She must have looked extra pathetic, because when he shifted to look at her, he rolled his eyes.

"Fine, welcome to the family. We're going to need help with the compound, and you're the only one here that knows the most about it. How do you feel about overseeing it until we figure out what to do with everyone living there?" Gage asked Alistair.

Alistair nodded slowly as he mulled over the question. "I think that could work. I do not feel comfortable moving to Florida and taking up space in your home. I already have a house being built at the compound, plus the people there know and trust me. If you wish, I can help relocate them to families that will fit their personalities and try to find any who were die-hard Waldo followers that want revenge. I do not think there will be many, though."

"Why's that? I thought this was a brainwashed cult he was running?" Gage asked.

"Not anymore. There have been a few attacks where families were murdered in horrific ways. We do not know who is attacking, but the community refers to him as the 'rogue vampire'. Waldo was not concerned about their safety and did little to help, so many hated him and will be glad to see him gone. Especially if there is a stronger, more caring leader to take his place. In fact, many of them might stay and join that leader's family if he proves to put their safety first."

Willow looked over to Gage, who was staring into her chicken and dumplings, lost in thought. "What are the dumplings telling you?"

His gaze snapped up to her and she bit back a smile. She continued, "You know you can do this, right? You're the empathetic, responsible leader they need. You still have Clay around to help, a family that respects you, and I'll be here for support."

His eyes sparkled at her last point. "This is a lot we'll be taking on. I'm going to have to go to Miami and find a suitable leader for that family since Waldo didn't have any children. We can't have just anyone taking his spot, or else we'll end up with another Waldo."

"How long will that take?" She asked. The idea of him leaving for longer than a minute made her feel sick.

"Probably a while, because I'll also have to deal with anyone who wants revenge. The compound may have hated him, but he spoiled his family members in Miami with free drugs and money to buy their loyalty. Plus, they'll have to adjust to the new rules of not killing innocents. I know there will be a few that have a tough time with that change."

An idea popped into her mind. "You know I'm going to go with you to Miami, but I'll need something to keep me busy down there. I'm a workaholic and couldn't sit around for a month while you do all this. Waldo offered me a building there to start a second Coffee House Bunny. With Marla here to run the one in Vista Maria, I could start a second location there, get it staffed, then turn it into a chain! Do you think Clay would be willing to teach me how to run multiple businesses?"

Gage nodded. "He would adore being able to turn you into a miniature, female version of himself. I already told him I didn't want to inherit his rental empire, so now he'll have someone to leave it to."

"If you're both going to go to Miami, who will be here to set up your motorcycle shop?" Horatio asked with a deep, worried crease etched into his brow. Out of everyone at the table, he seemed the least thrilled at their plan.

Gage sighed, leaned back in his chair, and closed his eyes. "There goes my dream. I knew something was going to mess with that."

It was the first time Willow had ever seen him look so exhausted, with sunken cheeks and dark bags underneath his eyes. A spark of worry sprung up, but it was quickly crushed when he opened his eyes halfway and smiled at her.

"All I know right now is that I'm tired and ready to go home to fall into bed with you. Oh, and a quick refill on the way home wouldn't be half bad either."

"Should we stop at the bridge on Towline?" Horatio asked.

Alistair looked confused. "What is that?"

"It's a huge bridge that's notorious for housing homeless pedos who have recently been released from jail. We sometimes refer to it as our favorite fast-food restaurant." Matteo giggled and rubbed his hands together.

"That's one thing you have to know if you do join us. When we hunt, we leave the innocents alone. If you want to visit Florida for a few days, we can show you some of our favorite spots to hunt, and you can meet Clay," Gage informed him with a yawn.

Willow had to hold back her matching yawn. It was time to go home. She stood up and dug Gage's truck keys out of his pants pocket. She heard him chuckle as she felt around for the cool metal.

"Be careful what you stir up down there," he purred into her ear.

She felt a hot flush through her body, but repressed it in order to solidify the plan. "Ok, so we'll be in his truck with me driving because he looks way too tired to drive. Alistair can follow me in his stolen car, which we will probably have to figure out what to do with once we're back in Florida. The rest of you are on the bikes and leading because I have no idea where this bridge is. Sound good?"

"Yes ma'am," Nikolas said with a smirk and stood up to follow her orders.

"I guess I am going to Florida," Alistair muttered under his breath.

Horatio also stood. "Would you look at that, you two start dating and suddenly she's bossing us around like she's the true leader of this family."

"Oh, shut up, he needs a break after getting stabbed in the kneecap and ripping Waldo's head off." She looked down at him and they both shared a smile before heading out the door and back to the place she could finally call home.

Thirty-One

Willow

“Take your pants off.”

“Huh?” Willow looked at Gage with a frazzled expression. They had both walked into her apartment after a three-hour drive from Georgia and a pit stop at the Towline Bridge, where she sat in the car waiting for the boy's feast to be over. The sun was beginning to make its appearance on the horizon and she was working on wading through glass to shut the blinds to prevent him from burning to a crisp. He had warned her on the drive back that she would need a new patio door, and he was not wrong. Apparently in his distress at losing her, he had slammed it a little *too* hard.

“I didn't think I stuttered. Take off your pants.” He made a brisk walk over to her and grabbed her by the waist, pulling her tight against him.

“Jesus, Gage, we just got home.”

“And I slept on the whole way here.” He grinned and began placing ticklish kisses on her neck. She tried to bat him away, but he only tried to bite her hand, and continued his pecking down her neck and onto her shoulder.

"Do you know how hot it was to watch you stand your ground against Waldo?" He mumbled between kisses.

"I'm guessing it was extremely hot if your erection is any indication."

He chuckled and began slipping his hands underneath her t-shirt. "I would have taken you right there on the bed for him to watch if I didn't think he would have interrupted to kill us."

"Thank you for not trying that. Now if you don't mind, I want to brush my teeth, throw on some pajamas, and go to bed. I take it you're spending the night?"

"Am I allowed to?"

"Where else would you go? It's almost sunrise." She paused and pulled his hands off her abdomen, entwining her fingers with his. "Plus, I don't think I want to be alone."

The mood changed at her confession and he placed a gentle kiss on her forehead. "I won't leave you, Willow."

She leaned into him and dropped his hands to wrap her arms around his waist. "Take a shower with me?"

His eyes darkened and he gave her a sly smile before pulling her toward the bathroom. Once inside, he shut the door and began slowly taking off her clothes.

So painstakingly slowly.

Once her shirt was completely off, he paused and frowned. "Where did these bruises come from?"

She looked down at herself and also frowned. "I don't know. I guess they happened when I was fighting that vampire."

A guilty look washed over him. "I should have never let that happen. How am I supposed to be a leader like my dad when I can't even keep my own girlfriends safe?"

She noticed the plural and placed her hand on his face, using her thumb to rub small circles on his cheek. "I know you think it's your fault Venice died, but she made her choice and you have to accept that. Even if you would have tried to go to Miami to bring her back, she would have fought you or Waldo would have killed you there. It's okay to be sad that she's gone, I'm not mad at you for that, but don't beat yourself up over something that was out of your control."

"I never wanted her back, but I felt like I had unfinished business because she was still out there. I'm not sad she's dead—I'm kind of relieved, in a weird way. Is that wrong?"

"No." She sat down on the toilet and wrapped her arms around herself. "I get that. You know, that vampire wasn't the first person I killed."

He raised his eyebrow and a small smile danced on his lips. "Oh? Did I get myself involved with a serial killer? I guess we have more in common than I thought."

"Remember how I told you that my ex wouldn't be following me down here? Well, it's because I...killed him."

The smile disappeared, but there was still intrigue sparkling in his eyes. He sat down on the ground in front of her like a child waiting for a storybook to be read.

She continued, "There were times where I wished for death instead of having to put up with him screaming at me, shoving me into walls, punching me for telling him how I was feeling. One time he even held my face over a stove burner and threatened to scar me so that I could never leave him, because who would love a burned woman?

"Then one day I decided to leave. But he came home unexpectedly and caught me. He chased me out of our apartment screaming at me, and I snapped. I couldn't take it anymore and I wanted out, but there was only one way out I could see. I grabbed him and threw myself down the stairs. I was honestly hoping I would die with him."

Gage's lips thinned and rage filled his eyes. He didn't speak, though, and let her continue.

"Somehow I managed to survive and made sure he didn't. I killed him by smashing his skull against a step. So please, don't worry about me being traumatized by having to kill that vampire—it wasn't my first rodeo."

He placed his head in her lap and looked up at her, his green eyes glittering with love. "You're going to make a great vampire one day. Just think of all the abusive assholes we can take out together. Think of all the women you can save from a relationship like you had."

"My mother always told me to find meaning in life, and I think I found it. I'm glad I found it with you."

She unwrapped herself and slid her arms around his neck. Their lips came together and a small moan escaped her as his tongue explored her mouth. He pulled her toward him and onto his lap, and she straddled him, fitting his hard length between her legs. She clawed off his shirt and dug her nails into his back as he flipped them over.

A small hiss escaped her as her back met the cold porcelain floor. She watched as he undid her pants and pulled them off, her underwear quickly disappearing next. To her frustration, he kept his pants on and came back to devour her mouth. She ground against the rough fabric of his jeans, wishing he would undo them and pierce her waiting entrance. She tried to wiggle her hand in between them to accomplish that, but he grabbed her by the wrist and pinned both arms against her side as he made his descent down her body.

"Please fuck me," she gasped as his tongue circled her navel and trailed down. "I don't want to think about anything else except how you feel inside me."

"Patience," he growled as he nipped at the sensitive skin near her hip. The awareness of his teeth reminded her of how intense and glorious his bite could be.

"Bite me."

Her command caused him to pause for the briefest of seconds, but his chuckle vibrated against her skin. She shivered from the ticklish sensation.

He rose back up to his favorite spot beneath her breasts, where he had marked her. Another shiver ran through her from the way he brushed his hand over the two small holes that marred her tender flesh. His fangs followed after and she felt them slip through her skin as a wave of pleasure swallowed her whole. She shut her eyes, spread her legs wide, and arched her back against his strong body. He took advantage of her position and quickly freed his cock to sheathe himself inside of her.

The pleasure didn't stop flowing around her once he ended the bite, but a smaller, more intimate feeling took over as he slipped into her. She moaned out his name and wrapped her legs around him, trying to take him deeper. She used her heels to try to finish taking off his pants so she could have full skin-to-skin contact. He quit his thrusting long enough to help her with her task, both giving off a breathy laugh at the awkwardness of the removal but neither of them ready to untangle themselves to make it easy.

With a few thrusts, Gage was able to get back into a rhythm that made her want to throw her head back and scream. She could feel every inch of him penetrating her, her nerves still highly sensitive and on edge from the orgasm that had previously devoured her. His thrusts grew quicker, and she matched his pace by grinding her hips against him. They climaxed together, both wrapping their hands in each other's hair and crushing their lips together. She felt like she was free-falling through space from the pleasure.

"Fuck," he groaned into her mouth before breaking their kiss.

He collapsed on top of her, the pressure reconnecting her to her body and reminding her they were laying in the middle of her bathroom floor next to the toilet.

"That was amazing, but I really do want to take a shower now." She patted him on the back and began to sit up. He followed her into the tub like a puppy waiting for more attention.

His face scrunched up as he read the multiple bottles that lined her bathtub while she adjusted the water to get the perfect, scorching-hot temperature.

"Are my only options for body wash pomegranate or spring floral scent?"

She smiled up at him shyly as she prepared a loofah with the aforementioned pomegranate soap. "Sorry, I don't have more manly-scented soaps. I've been single for a while."

He took the loofah from her and lathered up her front, paying special attention to her breasts. "I don't mind smelling like you." They continued in silence until his next question echoed against the shower walls. "When we get back from Miami, will you move in with me?"

"Do you think you can handle living with Marla, Sammy, and me? That's a lot of female energy under one roof."

"You'll be a nice buffer between Marla and Sammy, they don't seem to get along well."

She frowned and wondered if they would ever get along. He spun her around and watched as the water washed away the white suds from her silken skin. She looked up to him and her frown instantly turned back into a gentle smile.

"Yes, I'll move in with you."

They took turns washing and caressing each other, eventually ending up in bed where they made love once again. This time it was slower and more romantic, but the climax was just as sweet. Willow fell asleep in his arms, content knowing that he would be the man she would spend all of eternity with.

cccc

Willow flopped down on the couch feeling overwhelmed with all the papers, booklets, and two tablets displaying pictures of different wedding venues. She looked over to Sammy, her dark curls reflecting her stress by sticking up every which way. Her new ring was shining brightly on her left hand, a beautiful princess-cut diamond placed on a silver band embedded with small emeralds, which stood out on her brown skin. Willow wondered how long it took both Horatio and Matteo to pick it out, but was impressed they were able to find one that matched Sammy's style so well.

She had moved Snickers into the mansion so that Marla and Sammy could watch him while she was away in Miami. Gage had decided not to leave until after the wedding, as it seemed like no one was in a hurry to take over Waldo's position. Until then, she would be staying here and slowly moving her things over, much like Marla had done.

The sound of a spoon hitting glass alerted her that Marla was in the kitchen preparing mimosas for the three of them as they began the wedding planning. They had the mansion to themselves, as the five boys and Clay were out trying on tuxedos. Clay had connections with the owner of a tuxedo shop, who had no issues staying open extra late to fit them while the sun was down.

Sammy whined and collapsed on the couch next to Willow. "I love Horatio, I really do, but I'm regretting accepting his proposal because of how awful this is. Why do I have to make so many choices? Why can't I purchase a package deal and have someone else do all of this for me?"

"You can do that—it's called hiring a wedding planner." Marla frowned as she carried in a tray.

"But where's the fun in that?" Willow asked.

She noticed that Marla had three tall glasses filled with a bright orange liquid and a pitcher filled to the brim with a matching substance.

Willow bit back a smile. "Do you think we're going to drink all of that?"

"We'll need all of that if we're going to make a dent in any of this planning garbage," Sammy answered, immediately reaching for one of the glasses. "So far, the only thing we have picked out is the cake. We went with red velvet, obviously because it's the color of blood, and a traditional white frosting. Horse said he wanted them to drip red food coloring around it to make it look like it's dripping with blood, but I told him absolutely not. I want us to be a little bit classy for our wedding."

"How about we start with picking out the colors?" Marla asked and took a seat next to Willow.

Sammy groaned and shut her eyes like she was remembering a recent argument. "He originally said he wanted black and red with a Victorian theme, but I want green and orange with a tropical theme. But then Nikolas brought up the great idea of doing blue and white with a nautical theme since we met at the marina, and now Horse won't let that idea go."

"How did you two meet?" Marla asked.

"Oh, that's a story for another time." She pulled over some booklets and flipped through them. Marla frowned again and shifted uncomfortably on the couch.

"Well, I'm glad I met both of you. You two have given me the friendship I've always longed for. I finally feel like I belong somewhere." Willow knew her eyes were getting glassy with emotion and tried to blink away the tears.

"Stop." Sammy pushed the booklets away. "If you start crying then I'm going to cry, then Marla will cry, and our boys will come back from suit shopping to a giant tear fest."

Willow giggled and raised her glass. "Okay then—no crying, only drinking and deciding which venue to get you hitched at."

The other two girls lifted their glasses and clinked them together in a toast. Willow didn't think her heart could get much fuller than it was in this moment.

She was ready to start her new life with the rich brat she had come to love.

Beth Page is one of those childless cat (& one dog) ladies men warned you about. She has two careers: one as a therapist helping children heal from trauma and the other one creating cute vampire romances for other childless cat ladies. In her free time she can be found crafting, exploring the world with her pup, lifting heavy shit for fun, or watching the Golden Girls.

Follow her on Facebook @Author Beth Page, Instagram @authorbethpage, or Tiktok @authorbethpage for updates on her books (& all her critters).

Keep an eye out for Sammy and Horatio's story. Coming Summer of 2025

You can connect with me on:
https://bethpagenovels.wordpress.com